A Cry of Players

A Cry of Players

Jonathan Hales

CABLE PUBLISHING

Brule, Wisconsin

A CRY OF PLAYERS

First Edition

Published by:
    Cable Publishing
    14090 E Keinenen Rd
    Brule, WI 54820

    Website: www.cablepublishing.com
    E-mail: nan@cablepublishing.com

Hardcover: 978-0-9566795-3-6
Soft cover: 978-0-9566795-4-3

Library of Congress Control Number: 2012953426

Cover design by Norm Dodge, www.normdodge.com

 Printed in the United States of America

for Sarah, of course

As *Plautus* and *Seneca* are accounted the best for Comedy and Tragedy among the Latines, so *Shakespeare* among the English is the most excellent in both kinds for the stage. For Comedy, witnes his *Gentlemen of Verona*, his *Errors*, his *Loue Labors Lost*, his *Loue Labors Wonne*, his *Midsummer Night Dreame*, & his *Merchant of Venice*: for Tragedy his *Richard the 2, Richard the 3, Henry the 4, King Iohn, Titus Andronicus* and his *Romeo and Iuliet*.

Francis Meres
Palladis Tamia:Wits Treasury, 1598

 ONE

MISS BROWNLOW SMILED. "FRANCE, most likely. There's a group of us going to explore the Loire. Like, you know - the chateaux and stuff."

She slid the pages of her essay into a transparent folder and put it down by her feet: twin clumps in green plastic sandals. She leaned back in the broken armchair, exposing a strip of tanned midriff above the low-slung frayed jeans. A paler patch of left knee showed through the thread-bare denim lower down.

"We're going to get bikes and just follow the river. See where it takes us and stop off where we feel like it. No real plans. You know - just let it happen. Anyway, that's the idea."

"Sounds wonderful," Adam said.

Miss Brownlow pursed her mouth, crinkling the skin around her lips, making her seem for a moment quite old. Was that how she would look in thirty years' time?

"But if it doesn't work out I'll probably go up to Scotland for a few weeks. I've got a sister who lives there in Edinburgh. She's a nurse and a bit boring - no, that's not true, she's *amazingly* boring - but hey, what's it matter? It's somewhere to stay and it's free." She laughed, looking young again. "How about you, Doctor Searle? Anything exciting planned for the summer?"

"Not really. I imagine I'll be mainly at home."

"Where's that?" She looked surprised.

"Devon. A little village on the edge of Dartmoor. Quite pretty. Fairly remote."

"Is that where you grew up?" Miss Brownlow cocked her head to one side, looking along her nose and frowning slightly, as if trying to picture him as a little boy and finding it hard. Yes, that was definitely how she would look when she was old.

"It's not as boring as it sounds. I'll walk on Dartmoor. Maybe see some old friends. Do some fishing."

"Fishing? What – in the sea?"

"No, in the rivers. Well, that sounds a bit grand. They're more like streams, mostly."

"Is that fun?" Miss Brownlow looked doubtful.

"I think so. Then, too, I hope to start some work."

"A new book? Hey, cool. What's it going to be about?"

He looked at her eager face. If you ignored the casual scruffiness she was really quite pretty. "Oh. I think it's a bit early to say."

Feet sounded on the staircase outside his rooms. Male voices called loudly. Another voice responded from the foot of the stairs. He was bored, he realised, and slightly irritated. The feet clattered past and down. He glanced at his watch.

"Sorry. I'm keeping you," Miss Brownlow said.

"Not really." He made himself smile. "Well."

She leaned forward, picked up her essay and the orange backpack lying beside it and stood up from the battered armchair. An inch of dark knickers showed above the line of her jeans.

"Is it all right if I say how much I've enjoyed this term?"

"Of course it is. And – ah - thank you." He looked down at the carpet and frowned at its worn pattern. Why did he always feel awkward when someone paid him a compliment? Say something nice to her. "It has been for me, too. I mean – a pleasure."

Miss Brownlow fumbled in her backpack. "And can I ask…?You know.

Would you mind…?" She held out his book.

"Not at all." He went to the desk and took out his pen. He opened the book at the title page. "It's Joanne, isn't it?"

Miss Brownlow's neck turned a delicate pink. "Actually, Jo would be like, amazing," she said.

He wrote, *To Jo, with all good wishes* and signed his name. Then underneath, *A fellow student.*

"Wow, cool. Thank you." She stuffed the book into the little backpack and hoisted it onto her shoulder. "See you next term, then."

"I look forward to it."

"Unless…" She stopped, halfway to the door. "Some of us are getting together this evening, in Third Court. It's not a party or anything, although there's going to be like, drinks and stuff. And if you don't have anything else on, we'd be really pleased if…"

"I'd love to. I really would. But it's the Feast of Benefactors."

"Oh shit, so it is. How stupid can you get? *Duh.*" Miss Brownlow made two fingers into a pistol and pointed them at her forehead. "*Feast.* It sounds fantastic. Is it?"

"I've no idea. This will be my first."

"Well, have an amazing time. And see you next term."

"Have a good summer," Adam said.

Half an hour later he closed the outer door to his rooms ("sporting your oak" was what it used to be called but no one used the term now) and went down the two flights of stairs to Second Court. Outside, it was brilliant and he stopped for a moment to give his eyes time to adjust to the glare. May had been glorious and now in early June it was at least as good, if anything better. Heat rose in waves from the wide, pitted flagstones. If it went on like this they were going to have an exceptional summer.

Five students, three boys and two girls, walked past him giggling. They had towels around their necks and looked flushed with the sun. Back from the river? Or on their way to the baths in Fourth Court? For a unisex shower? They did sometimes, he knew. Or at least, that was the rumour. One of the girls punched one of the boys on the shoulder and they burst out laughing, pushing and shoving one another as they disappeared round the corner of the Fellows' Building. *When the sun shines, let foolish gnats make sport.* He followed the flagged path with its border of ancient cobbles to the low doorway leading to the screens passage and ducked his way inside.

Both sets of double doors to Hall were wedged open, allowing a stream of college servants to pass back and forth to the buttery and kitchens beyond. They carried wicker baskets of silverware, plates, glasses and cutlery of various kinds and the noise inside Hall was considerable. Clearly, preparations for the Feast were well in hand. He hung back for a moment, judging his time, before taking advantage of a gap in the traffic to nip through to the far doorway and arrive in First Court, where he stepped onto the lawn and headed for the Gatehouse at the other side.

Beneath his feet the turf was immaculate, razor-cut smooth and sprung like a dance floor. It had been – how long? Not quite a year since his Fellowship allowed him the privilege of walking on College lawns. He still got a thrill from it. Would he always? Probably not. A pity. The thought that it might one day become something unremarkable, barely noticed even, made him feel suddenly sad. Which was stupid, wasn't it? Stupid and adolescent. Stop being an idiot, Searle. Grow up. He arrived at the Gatehouse and went into the Porters' Lodge.

There was a fat pile of mail in his pigeon hole. Most of it the usual junk. He picked out the three or four envelopes that looked personal and stuffed them into his jacket pocket. The rest he dumped into the big wire-mesh basket that stood in the corner below the framed photograph of the Gatehouse taken in Queen Victoria's time. Seven burly porters, stolid and unsmiling, stood in line outside it. Six of them wore splendid moustaches.

The seventh, clearly the head porter, was magnificently bearded. He wore a silk hat and frock coat with an imposing double-Albert watch chain spread across his belly. The photograph was sepia-tinted now and slightly foxed in the upper left-hand corner, but the Gatehouse looked unchanged. *Spite of cormorant devouring Time.*

"Everything all right, Doctor Searle?"

Crompton, the current head porter, emerged from the inner office. He took down his bowler from its peg and set it foursquare on his head, level as a die, the curled brim strictly parallel to the thick line of his eyebrows.

"Yes, thank you, Crompton."

"Anything I can do for you, sir?"

"No, thank you."

They stood facing each other in silence for a moment. Crompton gave a brief nod.

"Very good, sir."

He took off the bowler, replaced it on its peg and returned to the inner room. Adam sighed. Crompton was a decent-enough type. Fine College servant, salt-of-the-earth, last-of-a-kind, don't-make-them-like-that-anymore sort of guy. But why did he have to be so – what was it? – so bloody *punctilious*? Politeness was one thing. Wasn't it supposed to ease social intercourse? Not with Crompton it didn't. In Crompton's hands, politeness was more like a weapon. *I know my place. Make sure you know yours – and keep to it.* Was that why the man always made him slightly uneasy? Or was it that being sirred and deferred to by a man old enough to be his father was simply embarrassing?

Behind him across First Court the Chapel clock struck the three-quarter hour. What was there still to do? Pick up his dinner jacket from the cleaners, that was the main thing. With maybe a quick stroll down to the river first. The Feast of Benefactors was at eight; before that the Thanksgiving Service in Chapel was at seven. And – yes – before that there was sherry with the Dean at six. Bugger. Oh well, if he was a bit late for the Dean it wouldn't matter. No one would notice. He walked out of the

Gatehouse, passing under the enormous heraldic beasts supporting the brightly gilded College crest, and entered the busy Cambridge Street.

Out here, away from the seclusion of College walls and engulfed by jostling traffic, it seemed even hotter. Nearly everyone else – mostly tourists and foreign language-students from the look of them - was dressed in T-shirts and shorts. The younger ones were virtually half-naked.

He took off his tie, rolled it up and put it in his pocket. He wished he had left his jacket back in his rooms. Should he carry it? Better not. All the same, the worn tweed felt heavy on his shoulders and already his armpits were starting to feel sticky. Maybe he should buy one of those smart linen jackets on display in the window of Varsity Outfitters. He had noted them several times, on the last occasion stopping and hesitating for almost a minute, wondering whether or not to go in. Maybe he should have. Except it wouldn't necessarily be an improvement, would it? Truth to tell, it might even be worse. That was the trouble with linen: it looked great until you actually put it on. Ten minutes later it would be tramlined with creases and you were walking around in a used dishrag. Oh, well.

He walked through the Market Place past Great St. Mary's and turned into Trinity Street. Up ahead on the right was Heffer's bookshop. He could see its jutting-out sign. Should he cross over like the Pharisee and pass by on the other side? Don't be silly. Keep going. And whatever you do, try not to look in the window as you walk past.

He wasn't completely successful. Not one hundred percent. He couldn't help it, couldn't stop himself seeing out of the corner of one eye the neat pyramid of brightly jacketed books. Not, he was relieved to see, in the very centre of the window anymore; and they had taken down – at last! – the photograph that made him look like a resentful schoolboy. But even where the stack was now, on the side near the doorway where you couldn't help but notice it as you went in, it was prominent enough.

This Wooden O: Shakespeare and his Company. It was in its second printing already and well on the way to its third. His publishers were delighted. He'd received another cheque from them only yesterday. The paperback was due out in the autumn and they said he was in line for at least one literary prize. They had set their sights on the Duff Cooper and were already lobbying hard. Apparently, that was what you had to do if you wanted to win prizes. There was a fair amount of networking involved, a lot of back-scratching. The London literary world was a deeply incestuous setup, they said.

Fine. Let them get on with it. It was their business after all, and he had to admit they seemed to know what they were doing. The German and French translation deals had already been done and now they were in negotiation, they said, for the Japanese rights. *Japanese!* There was something unreal about it all, something he still couldn't wholly believe. Part of him was sure it wasn't true. And even if it was, it was an unearned benediction because he owed it all to Farlow, didn't he? Or most of it, anyway.

It was Farlow who had first encouraged him; told him it was a topic worth pursuing; directed the work on his doctorate; spurred him on when he thought it was going nowhere; told him not to be a bloody fool when he thought of giving up. It was Farlow who got him the research grant; Farlow who said he thought it might make a book and put him in touch with his own publishers; Farlow who proposed him for the Junior Fellowship, piloted his candidacy through the treacherous shoals of College politics and saw him safely home.

And it was Farlow, his friend and mentor, who at the beginning of last year was diagnosed with cancer of the colon and, before anyone was properly aware of it, was dead inside a month. George Wentworth Farlow, Regius Professor, R.I.P. He owed him everything, even the splendid set of rooms he occupied in Second Court. Those had been Farlow's. He had got them almost by default, to the fury, he knew, of several of the older, more senior dons. Did that account for the nagging feeling that he, Adam, wasn't properly entitled? That in truth he was here under false pretences?

From somewhere close by, a bell started to chime. Then another joined in, then another and another. Suddenly, Cambridge was a city of bells. What next? Oh, yes - pick up his DJ from the cleaners. The river would have to wait. The Dean's for drinks. He was definitely going to be on the late side but he'd slip in at the back, mingle a bit and no one would know. All the same, better get a move on. He stepped out more briskly, quickening his stride.

 **TWO**

THE DEAN'S HOUSE WAS in the road that ran along the back of College. If you were in a hurry you could get to it through an iron gate from Fourth Court and go in through the Dean's garden, but in spite of the time – he was at least twenty minutes late - he chose the long way round, going back out of the Gatehouse and following the curving road to the right.

The Dean's green-painted front door stood half-open. He went through into the hallway, stopping for a moment by the mirror above the umbrella stand to stare at himself and adjust his black tie. There was a half-collapsed baby buggy next to the umbrella stand, and several brightly coloured plastic toys lay scattered on the hall carpet. How many kids did the Dean have? Five, was it? Six? He didn't remember. As far as he could tell, the Dean kept his wife in a state of almost permanent pregnancy.

He frowned. His tie looked uneven and drooped on one side. He gave it a couple of tugs and a straightening twist that was only partly successful. Should he re-tie it? No, there wasn't time. He turned from the mirror and made for the stairs. Then he stopped, listening. Something was seriously wrong. Why was the house so quiet? Why couldn't he hear the hum and chatter of drinks guests from the big reception room upstairs? Had he made a mistake, got the time wrong? Or else – Jesus! – he wasn't the only one to have been invited, was he? Please God, *no!*

"There you are at last, Adam." The Dean's wife was on the landing above. She smiled down at him hatefully. "We'd quite given you up."

"I'm so sorry."

How to deal with it? Male idiocy, that was the answer. He started up the stairs, grinning foolishly.

"The fact is, I lost my tie. Couldn't find it anywhere. And when I did, I couldn't – ah – couldn't tie it. Couldn't for the life of me remember how it went. Would you believe it? So in the end I had to ..." He trod heavily on a stuffed blue hippopotamus lying across the next step, said *Christ!* and nearly fell. He clutched at the banister and hung on. The Dean's wife showed her teeth nastily.

"Well, at least you're here now," she said. "You might as well come in." She turned away from him, side-on, displaying her swollen belly. Yes, the Dean had rung the bell again. "Darling – he's arrived."

Inside the big room, the Dean rose from his chair. "My dear chap." He held out a dry hand. "Merry Christmas."

Adam flinched inwardly. Why did the man do it? Who did he think he was kidding? What was the point? God knows, there were enough genuine eccentrics, real nutters, at the University. Every College had its share. Some of them were truly scary and if you were wise you kept your distance, but at least you knew they were the real thing. The phonies you could spot a mile away. Like the Dean, for example. The Dean was a phony of the first-class.

Perhaps it was the *naevus*, the mottled purple blemish that covered the left side of his face. It would explain his self-consciousness, the habit of keeping his face always half-turned from you, causing him to look at you sideways most of the time. Growing up with that must have been difficult. Kids are cruel. You could understand and sympathise. But it didn't excuse the posturing, the silly outfits: the deerstalker hat and swirling brown cape, the ivory-handled ebony stick. Even the Dean's dinner jacket was a peculiar shade of turd-green - teal, was it? - with black velvet piping on the cuffs and lapels. And why go around saying Merry Christmas to everybody? It wasn't even funny the first time. After a while it was obscene.

He took a glass of sherry from the Dean's wife and mumbled some more apologies. The Dean waved them away. "Sit yourself down." He indicated a rush-seated, uncomfortable-looking chair. Adam sat. The Dean's wife sat opposite him, her eyes bright with dislike.

"Well now, how has your first year been?" said the Dean. "What do you think of us? Do we pass muster?" He laughed mirthlessly.

"Oh, it's..." Adam took a sip of sherry. "Everyone has been..." He cleared his throat. "Although I don't know if I've..."

"Students all right?" said the Dean. "Get on with them, do you?"

"I think so. That is, I hope so. They seem a pretty decent bunch."

"Any high-flyers? Ones to watch?"

"I don't think so. They're bright enough. One or two of them are going to do pretty well, I should say. But no one outstanding. Not yet, anyway."

The Dean looked pleased. "Do they bring you their problems? Love affairs – sex – things like that?"

"Not so far, no."

"They don't?" The Dean lifted a thin, disappointed eyebrow. "I'm surprised. I should have thought, you being as young as you are, they'd confide in you. Think of you as one of their own."

"How old are you?" the Dean's wife said. "Thirty? Thirty-one?"

"He's twenty-eight," the Dean said.

"Twenty-eight? Goodness." The Dean's wife showed her teeth once again. There were little gaps between them. "You must be exceedingly bright." She made it sound like an affliction.

"Maybe they don't have any problems," Adam said. "That is, ones they can't handle themselves."

The silence was broken by a faint thumping on the ceiling above. It seemed to come from a spot directly above his head. He forced himself not to look upwards. He sat back and crossed his legs. There was a sharp creak and the rush seat shifted under him. He uncrossed his legs and sat up straight.

"How's your book selling?" said the Dean.

"Very well, thank you."

The thumping above his head grew louder. He looked down at his glass.

"We saw you on television the other night," the Dean's wife said. She beamed bitterly. "You're not going to become one of those awful TV dons, are you?"

He had appeared on television twice. The first time was on BBC2, when he was interviewed about his book by an intense young woman with a flat chest, round glasses and an unpleasant voice. The second was an arts review programme on BBC4, when he was part of a panel to discuss a film, a play and a recent novel. Both programmes went out just before midnight and he was surprised to learn that anyone had actually watched them.

"I shouldn't think so," he said. "I certainly don't plan to be."

"That's a relief," the Dean's wife said.

There was an outbreak of thumping, violent this time, on the ceiling and a sudden shattering cry. A second voice joined in and then a third. The ceiling vibrated. The Dean's wife sighed. "Excuse me."

She got up, went to the door and stood holding it half-open. "What's going on up there? Whatever it is, stop it at once!" She waited a moment. The shrieks rose in volume. "Annelise – make them be quiet!" It had no effect.

"Honestly." The Dean's wife went out. The Dean gave a dry chuckle. It rattled in the base of his throat.

"Children," he said. "Au pairs." He peered at Adam sideways, shielding the mottled side of his face from the window's evening light. "Something for you to look forward to, eh?"

Nearby, the Chapel clock struck. "Good Lord," Adam said. "Is that the time?" He put down his glass. "Thank you for the sherry, Dean."

"Dear old chap, you are more than welcome." The Dean waved his hand. "It's never less than a pleasure when…"

The noise upstairs erupted again. Adam thought he could hear the Dean's wife's voice screaming loudest of all. He stood up.

"I'll see you in a while, then."

The Dean rose and held out his hand. "Happy New Year!" he said.

The Chapel bell was tolling in a regular, unhurried way as he turned the corner and approached the Gatehouse. By the Porters' Lodge the ramrod figure of Crompton, a kind of domestic Cerberus, watched him enter and then halt as he heard his name called from outside. He turned to see Ivor Williams on the pavement across the street and waited by the notice boards for him to arrive. Across First Court, groups of slow-paced, dinner-jacketed dons were making their way from the Senior Combination Room, to be joined in Chapel by the thirty or so undergraduate Scholars who made up the official body of College.

"Hey, dude, how's it going?"

Ivor held up his hand and gave him a resounding high-five. Adam laughed. A chemist, apparently a pretty good one, Ivor was the nearest thing to a friend he had had since Farlow died. There was something about the Welshman's dark features – the beaky nose, slashed mouth, jutting overbite – that made him smile. And it always amused him to hear American slang delivered in a thick Welsh accent. Plus, Ivor was fun. They'd had some lively evenings together. And he looked good, too. His dinner jacket was immaculate, the bow tie perfect beneath the old-fashioned wing collar. No doubt about it, Ivor had style.

"Evening, Crompton." Ivor acknowledged the head porter's greeting with a snappy American-style military salute. Crompton nodded briefly and looked away.

Ivor grinned. "Let us join our esteemed colleagues in reverent thanksgiving for the life of this ancient seat of learning, baby," he said. He slipped his arm through Adam's and they stepped out across the lawn. "And by the way, what's this I hear about you from the guys at White City?"

"About me? I've no idea."

Adam was startled. Ivor had good contacts at the BBC. He had recently fronted a series of popular science programmes that had been rather successful. If he heard something, it was likely to be true.

"Word is you're the next TV star."

"Don't be ridiculous."

"That's what they tell me. You're hot stuff, kid. The thinking woman's crumpet."

For some reason he felt scared. "Pull the other one."

"No shit, man. You'll be hearing from them. Trust me, dude."

The bell ceased tolling. "And speaking of crumpet..." Ivor nodded towards the Chapel door where a woman in a long dress beckoned them impatiently.

"Hallo, Jill," Adam said.

She frowned. "Hurry up, the pair of you."

Ivor laughed and made a kissing sound. "Honey, you look *edible*," he said.

"Piss off, Ivor." She took Adam's hand. "Now be quick or they'll have started."

His heart sank, and they went inside. She was nearly right. The organ had just started to sound as they made their way across the chequered marble floor of the outer lobby and entered the main Chapel, where they filed into one of the raised pews that ran along the back of each side. They found their places and sat down. Jill leaned forward and closed her eyes. Adam looked round. The place was nearly full.

College Chapel wasn't imposing, nothing like the perpendicular glory of King's or the heavy grandeur of Trinity or St. John's. It dated mainly from the early seventeenth century, when an earlier, medieval Chapel had been torn down - whether from reasons of safety, taste or change of doctrine, he didn't know. It was simple, almost austere, with lots of dark wood, occasional gilding and some nice Jacobean plasterwork. To the left of the altar was an elaborate monument to a seventeenth-century divine, a former Master who these days was entirely forgotten. There were hardly any other memorials.

He liked the plainness, the simplicity of the place, and its Anglican beeswaxy smell. The only stained glass was in the window above the altar and depicted the foundress in nun's habit with a couple of red-robed cardinals holding a little model of College. The foundress – or rather re-foundress; a College had existed here long before she got her hands on it – was the much-married sister of a Plantagenet king, whose life had been a series of lurid murders and betrayals before she got religion in her old age and set about saving her soul. Good luck to you, dear, Adam thought. I hope it worked.

The Chaplain began to intone the opening prayers. Most of the congregation leaned forward or looked down. Adam sat still, relieved to have his hand back. On his other side, Ivor nudged him and winked. Jill knelt, hands together, eyes closed. She looked quite attractive this evening. Not exactly edible, as Ivor had suggested, but not bad. Her dress was a sort of deep fuchsia, scooped low at the front with a frill of black edging. She wore a chain of heavy gold links round her neck and a black stole – pashmina, was it? Or were they out of date now? – draped around her shoulders. Her hair was dark and thick and as far as he could tell was naturally wavy. It shone in the soft light. Yes, she looked good.

Jill Hardwick was in her mid thirties, a classicist who had published a book about Roman domestic customs. He had enjoyed it, although the main thing he remembered was the chapter on sanitary habits, in which she had said that a visit to the Roman baths was a dodgy business at best, since the waters were likely to be seething with bacteria and you were virtually guaranteed to come down with something disgusting as a result. (A bit like the pool at the Golf & Country Club at home, he thought, which was known locally as the sewer.) She was a good-hearted person who took her work seriously and was an excellent teacher. Her students liked and trusted her, he knew. All things being equal, she might be a good colleague and friend.

The trouble was, all things weren't equal. It was his fault. Last term, just before Easter, he had taken her out to dinner and drunk too much — no, to be fair it wasn't just him. They both had. (She had insisted on lots of champagne to celebrate the success of his book.) Afterwards, he had gone back to her rooms for coffee and an Armagnac she said he must try. And once inside, she had grabbed hold of him and kissed him and rubbed herself up against him, and he had responded — sort of — in a fumbling, drunken kind of way before the alcohol got the better of him and he had torn himself free and lurched his way back to the Fellows' Building, where he had thrown up in his wash basin before collapsing into bed.

Thank God it hadn't gone any further. His last memory had been of her on her hands and knees, groping to pick up her blouse from the floor as he staggered to the staircase. But afterwards she had been pretty decent about it. No recriminations or hurt looks or sullen silences. No suggestion he had insulted her or been less than a man. Except that now she seemed to think they had some sort of special relationship. What did she call it? A loving friendship. Something like that. *Most friendship is feigning, most loving mere folly.*

The organ rang out. Prayers were over. They sang a hymn, then the Master rose from his canopied stall to make the Benefactors' Address, celebrating not just the foundress but also the worthies who had endowed College plenteously over the years. It was quite a long list. Beside him, Jill put a hand on his knee. She leaned gently against him and he caught a whiff of her perfume. It smelt of lemons and was rather nice. He looked down into her cleavage. Her dress really was a bit low. On his other side Ivor cleared his throat and nudged him again. Adam closed his eyes.

The Master ended his peroration. The Chaplain intoned a few more prayers. The organ burst into a Voluntary and they rose and went out into the soft evening, crossing the immaculate lawn in easy, unhurried clusters, making their way towards Hall at the other side of the Court.

Inside, it was magical. The Feast of Benefactors was the one time of year when Hall was lit solely by candles. The long, polished tables shone with candelabra and glittering plate: goblets, ewers, salt-cellars, gold, silver and silver-gilt, brought out from the Treasury for this special occasion. By good fortune, College was particularly rich in plate, due to its somewhat questionable behaviour during the Civil War. Where other Colleges had submitted to the needs of King or Parliament, whichever had the upper hand at the moment, and handed over their treasure to be melted down to furnish the sinews of war, College's Master and Fellows of the time had met in secret conclave before creeping out one night and burying all its plate in the garden, to be retrieved much later, after the Restoration of 1660. Result: a Treasury unmatched by any other foundation in the University. Did they act from prudence, greed or plain cussedness, those long-gone old men? What did it matter anyway, after all this time, when the result was so glorious?

The seating plan directed him to a place on the left, on one of the long benches just below high table. Ivor Williams was a couple of places down from him in animated conversation with one of the Scholars, a pretty little blonde in a green silk dress. Jill Hardwick, he saw, was placed somewhere on the other side of Hall. Was it shitty of him to feel relieved? Yes, undoubtedly. He ought to be ashamed. He couldn't help it, though.

He sat with his back to the linenfold panelling and surveyed the great room. Former members of College, some famous, some infamous, all celebrated in one way or another, stared down at him from the walls, their painted features nearly mobile in the flickering light. Above, the carved hammer-beam roof glowed with heraldic colours: *gules, argent, sable, azure, vair*. At a signal from the Dean, everyone rose and the Master appeared with the guest of honour, a minor royal.

A sudden silence, and the Chaplain spoke the grace:

> *Exhilerator omnium Christe, sine quo nihil suave*
> *nihil jucundum est...*

The doors below the minstrels' gallery were thrown open, white-jacketed servants appeared carrying great dishes of steaming food, wine was poured, glasses raised and the Feast had begun.

Thinking about it later, he was bound to say the food itself wasn't all that fantastic. College wasn't known for the excellence of its kitchens and nothing he tasted persuaded him to think otherwise. True, it was pretty exotic-sounding stuff: jugged hare, baked carp, venison, roast swan (thanks to some ancient statute, the Crown was obliged to provide an annual gift of "twelve silver swannes"), but otherwise it wasn't much to write home about. You couldn't say that about the wine, though. If there was one thing College was famous for it was its cellar. The wines were superb. He chatted to the young man on his left: one of the Organ Scholars, it appeared. And to the grey-haired woman opposite: a fiercely intelligent mathematician who had read his book and said several nice things about it. He caught Ivor Williams' eye as he poured more wine for the pretty little blonde and winked at him. He sat back and relaxed. He smiled. He felt *good*.

The Master rose to propose the health of the visitors. He spoke briefly and well. The Master was a former diplomat of considerable experience and charm. They drank the toast. The minor royal replied. Twenty-odd years ago he had been briefly an undergraduate (he never took a degree), spending a few terms largely as companion to a much grander royal at one of the much grander Colleges. He spoke badly but no one minded, or if they did they were too polite or too tipsy by now to let on. He told a rambling story about founding a society called the Cambridge University Naval Training Scheme and most people laughed, although Adam thought he heard Ivor whisper *What an asshole*, and the grey-haired mathematician opposite rolled her eyes. But then it was over, they drank the toast, the minor royal sat down and it was time for the loving-cup.

The great two-handled vessel, beautiful Tudor gilt filled with steaming mulled wine, was passed around the room. The ritual was, Ivor explained to the little blonde in green silk, that when you drank, the person each side of you stood up to protect you, because you had to hold the cup with both hands and so couldn't draw your sword if attacked. So when it got to the person on your right you stood up and he bowed to you and said *In piam memoriam fundatricis nostrae* and drank. Then he handed the cup to you and you bowed to him and to the person on your left who had got up to protect you, and you said *In piam memoriam fundatricis nostrae* and you drank. Then you handed it on and kept standing till the person on your left had drunk and handed it on, and that was it. Got it, sweetheart?

The little blonde said of course she did, did he think she was stupid? and soon after the loving-cup arrived, and when it came to his turn Ivor said *In piam memoriam fundatricis nostrae, dude,* causing the little blonde to explode into giggles and the grey-haired mathematician to roll her eyes again.

Then it was time for port and coffee and brandy, and then high table chairs were pushed back and people rose slowly, and the minor royal was escorted to the Gatehouse where his enormous car was waiting, and figures drifted away into the June night and the Feast was done.

He lingered for a moment in the doorway (it was only fair), looking to where Jill sat with a group of three or four others in what seemed a lively discussion. Or were they arguing? It was hard to tell. One of them – a bearded natural scientist, wasn't he? - had built a pyramid of sugar lumps and was trying to balance a coffee spoon on top of it; another was talking rapidly and pointing to the ceiling. Jill was nodding. The spoon fell off the pyramid and everyone laughed except the natural scientist, if that's what he was. Jill leaned across and patted his arm. She looked up and saw Adam in the doorway. She smiled and gave him a little goodnight wave.

Outside, Second Court was brilliant with moonlight. He couldn't remember it ever being so bright. He could see his shadow keeping pace as he strolled the curve of ancient flagstones and he grinned at it, hands deep in his jacket pockets, content and slightly foolish from all the lovely wine he had drunk. Ahead, the Fellows' Building was made of pure silver. Incredible. He stopped, open-mouthed.

Maybe it really had been designed by Inigo Jones, as some people claimed. God knows, it was impressive enough in the daytime. Seen like this, etched in moonlight, it was something the great artist might have conjured up in the Jacobean theatre. A transformation scene that would appear as if by magic to take your breath away - sheer enchantment! - before it would fade and dissolve. *And leave not a rack behind.* Yes! That was it! His next book. *Gorgeous palaces*: *Shakespeare and the Masque.*

He had sketched out a few ideas already. Why does Shakespeare feature the masque so often in the late plays? First, because it was increasingly popular at James's court - so wouldn't public taste be bound to follow suit? (Of course it would. People would want to see this new form of entertainment. And a canny playwright would cater to that taste.) Then, since 1608, there was the company's new theatre at Blackfriars and the enhanced technical possibilities it offered: smaller, more intimate – indoors – lit by candlelight – increased use of scenery – greater visual effects - music and dance – *Pericles, Cymbeline, The Winter's Tale, The Tempest, The Two Noble Kinsmen.*

He felt the inward pressure of a growing excitement. He would start preliminary work next week, as soon as he got home. He could hardly wait.

THREE

HE STOOD BY THE half-open window, looking out over the garden, where a huge copper beech was in glorious leaf. In the lower right-hand corner of the bottom windowpane someone had scratched their initials: *RJW* and, underneath, the number *36*. The date, he assumed. It didn't say which century. Most likely the twentieth, but it could well have been the nineteenth or even the eighteenth. The rippled glass was hand-made and might easily be that old.

Below, a gardener, one of the five or six permanently employed by College, crossed the lawn past the great tree, glancing up at it as he went by. He wore a wide-brimmed straw hat and was carrying an edging tool and a flat basket with a pair of shears lying across it. *Superfluous branches We lop away, that bearing boughs may live.* The garden looked so immaculate it was difficult to imagine anything could be done that might improve it.

He felt a faint stir of unease. He should telephone his father. Everything else had been taken care of: bags packed, battels paid, tips distributed at the Porters' Lodge – a highly embarrassing couple of minutes this, but it had to be done. (He had waited until he knew Crompton was off-duty before sneaking in and leaving the cash with one of the under-porters.) And Mrs. R's tip was ready in the envelope lying prominently in the centre of his desk, where she would find it when she came in tomorrow morning.

Mrs. R was his bedder and a College fixture. Older by far than all the other bedders, she outdated even Crompton, having worked here longer than most people could remember. She was a "character", self-created, playing the sort of role that used to feature in drawing-room comedies: the lovable daily or all-purpose "treasure". It was the kind of part elderly actresses killed for, because audiences who didn't know any better adored you and you stole every scene. Mrs. R had been performing it for so long she didn't have to act anymore; it was second nature. Personally, Adam found it deeply embarrassing and wished to heaven she would drop it, but it was much too late now. Her little ways were set in stone.

She could remember men's fathers as undergraduates and bitterly lamented the day women were admitted to the place. Before that it was *College*; afterwards it was – well, *what it is now, dear*. (The woefulness of her tone only hinted at how calamitous the change had been – a second expulsion from Eden, at least.) Still, there was no getting rid of her. She would die in harness, no doubt about it. One morning they'd find her on the staircase, slumped over her brush and dustpan, yellow cloth drooping from her apron pocket, and that would be that. Slow curtain. Hushed applause. The passing of an age.

In truth, she wasn't a very good bedder, but she moved the dust around, didn't actually break anything and made sure his sheets were changed once a week. Given the chance, she would talk for hours in her flat, East Anglian voice with its odd fenland vowels (she said *foo* for *few*). He tried not to be there when she came in to clean. Something about her made him nervous. He had dreamt about her once or twice: not nightmares exactly, but strange, troubled dreams in which she had been a dominant presence and from which he had woken feeling vaguely upset. Maybe she was a witch. It wouldn't surprise him. But Farlow had liked her, he knew; and for her part she had adored Farlow. It broke her heart, it really and truly did, she said, when the Professor died.

Another stir of unease, stronger this time. He turned from the window, frowning. Once he had seen this American woman there was nothing to keep him. He would get the early afternoon train to Liverpool Street, take the tube to Paddington and with luck he'd be home well before ten. Yes, it was time to call Dad.

He listened to the regular pulsing at the other end of the line. It would take his father a while to get to the telephone. If he was in the bathroom it would take ages. No hurry. At the first ring the dogs would have lifted their heads, waiting motionless for as long as a minute before settling down on the worn carpet again.

He could see the hallway where they were lying just inside the front door; the rickety hat stand; the shabby outdoor jackets on the row of pegs next to the barometer; the collection of walking sticks and fishing rods in the corner opposite; the motes of dust in the sunlight above where the telephone stood. There was no danger of an answering machine cutting in because the old man had said they were stupid and unnecessary things and refused to have one. And when told that BT had a service that did it for you and was free had said nonsense, he didn't want to hear another word about it.

"Yes?" It was his father at last.

"Dad? It's me."

"Oh, yes."

"How are you?"

"In the pink." It was what he always said – and presumably always would say, even when he was plucking the sheet. "Are you in Exeter?"

"No, still in Cambridge."

"Where?"

"Cambridge. But I'll be on my way soon. Is there anything you need?"

"Anything I need?" His father sounded puzzled. "Like what?"

"I don't know. Food?"

"Food? What sort of food?"

"You know. Milk. Bread. Stuff like that. I could get some on my way."

"Why should you do that?"

"In case you need some. Groceries."

His father made a rude, snorting sound. "There's more than enough here for an army."

"Right. Fine."

"Did I tell you about the tomatoes?"

"Tomatoes? No. Do you need some?"

"Need tomatoes? Whatever for?"

"I thought —"

"The tomatoes are going to be splendid. Absolutely splendid. Just you wait till you see them. Going to be a record year."

"That's great, Dad. I'm looking forward to it. So what I'll do is —"

"Angela Ladbroke came by yesterday. What do you think she wanted?"

"No idea, Dad. You tell me."

"Asked me to join the PCC."

"What did you say?"

"I said I didn't think it was a good idea."

"Maybe you should reconsider."

"I should what?"

"Reconsider. Maybe it's something you'd like to do."

"But I wouldn't. I've just told you."

"Fair enough. Listen, Dad, I've got someone to see in a minute, but once that's over, I'm on my way. What I'll do is, give you a call when I get to Paddington, okay?"

"Where?"

"*Paddington*."

"Proper job," his father said.

"Right. Speak to you later, then."

"Did I tell you about the tomatoes?"

"Yes, you did."

"They're magnificent."

"Yes."

"Going to be a record year, you'll see."

"That's great, Dad. Bye, now."

"Goodbye, son. Watch out for tigers."

It was an old family joke. His father was still chuckling as he put down the phone. Was he getting worse or just deafer? (He had vetoed a hearing aid.) Adam pictured him on his slow trek down the hallway, through the kitchen and out into the untidy vegetable garden, followed by the two rheumaticky dogs. Three mouth-breathing old males moving stiffly together amongst the weeds. It was nice of Angela Ladbroke to drop by — but then she was the vicar's wife and social calls were part of her thing, weren't they? He pictured her bright, conscientious little face, heard her perky, insistent little voice, and guessed how irritating she must have been. Maybe the old man was right and it wasn't a good idea for him to join the parochial church council. Maybe he was starting to lose it in a serious way. He would know once he was home. He sat down at his desk and picked up the letter.

Actually, there were two letters, but it was the first one, the one that had arrived a week ago, that he re-read now. Thick, creamy paper, elegant letterhead. *The Blankenship Foundation. From the desk of Willard Blankenship.* He knew who he was, of course. Anyone interested in Shakespeare did. Four years ago Willard Blankenship had bought the most recent First Folio to come on the market, beating off the competition with a series of bids so swift and so outrageous they had caused hardened auctioneers to blink and the room itself to burst several times into spontaneous applause.

Until last week that was pretty much the sum of what he knew about the man, but after receiving the letter he had googled him. What came up on the screen was extraordinary. He was impressed. How could he not be? The Blankenship Foundation was part — a tiny part, it seemed — of The Blankenship Corporation, a multi-tentacled enterprise that appeared to be involved in everything from open-cast mining to laser technology. The list of companies it controlled went on for at least half a page, double columns, single-spaced. Beyond that, there were very few details, mainly because they weren't available. Nor, it seemed, were they likely to be. The Blankenship Corporation had never gone public. It was a strictly private affair, belonging exclusively to Willard Blankenship plus whatever partners he might or might not have. No wonder he had been able to outbid his competitors. Even well-heeled ones like the University of Texas had been blown away.

My personal representative, Ms. S. Kamali, will call on you to discuss a matter of considerable interest.

Of considerable interest. What could that be? He looked at the second letter. It was much shorter and told him even less, saying merely that Ms. Kamali would be in Cambridge on the 12th and would call on him at 10 a.m. If this was not convenient, would he be kind enough to reply by telephone or email suggesting an alternative day and time? *Of considerable interest.* Well, he would know soon enough. Like now, actually. His telephone was ringing.

"Your guest is here, Doctor Searle."

"Thank you, Crompton."

There was a brief pause. "Will you come down, sir, or shall I escort the lady to your staircase?"

He frowned. Crompton really was a creep. Was it because he had over-tipped him? Or — worse — hadn't tipped him enough and the man was being sarcastic? Whichever it was, he wasn't having any. It was time to put him in his place.

"Don't be ridiculous, Crompton. Just send her along."

A slightly longer pause. Then, "Very good, Doctor Searle."

He put down the phone, refolded the letters and stuffed them into his pocket; then he took them out again and put them into the desk middle drawer. He got up, went to the shelves between the windows and rearranged some books, sliding them in place, patting them carefully into line. He was meticulous with his books. (Too meticulous? Did it matter if some of them stuck out a bit? Why should it upset him if they did? Was he, as he sometimes suspected - and Ivor Williams had actually said - becoming a pernickety old woman?) He walked the length of the room and back again. He stopped, looked at his empty waste-paper basket and kicked it. Bugger Crompton. The man was a menace. Next term he'd have it out with him, no question. Put the guy straight. What was all the fuss about, anyway? There was a knock at the door and when he opened it he understood instantly.

She was very attractive. No, that was wrong. She was beautiful.

"Doctor Searle?" She held out her hand. "Soraya Kamali."

"How do you do?" Why had his throat suddenly seized up? "Do – um – do come in."

She walked – no, *flowed* – into the room and stopped, looking round. "This is so *charming*."

"Oh – ah – thank you."

She had shoulder-length hair, dark, thick and shining, and wore a smoke-grey tailored suit – Chanel, Dior or somesuch, it had to be – with a narrow gold chain at her throat. Her face was oval, her mouth wide and full. Her skin was a sort of caramel colour. He wanted to lick it.

"Won't you sit down, Ms…ah…?"

"Thank you."

She sank into the bashed-up armchair his students used. There was a silk-sounding whisper. He forced himself not to look at her legs.

"Can I – um – get you anything? Some tea? Or – ah – coffee?"

"No, thank you."

Her eyes – startlingly – were blue. An electric, lapis lazuli blue. (He wondered later if they were coloured contact lenses but found out later still they weren't.)

"May I say something, Doctor Searle?" Her voice, with its nasal trans-Atlantic tones, was low and slightly husky.

"Please do."

She smiled. Her *teeth*. "You're much younger than I expected."

"And you're…" He almost said "much more beautiful," but stopped himself just in time. "…Not the first person to say that." What a dickhead! He felt his neck swell with shame.

"I'm sorry. I didn't mean – that is, I hope you're not offended."

"Not at all. Why should I be?" She smiled again.

She was carrying a thin, black leather briefcase which she put down beside the armchair. Then she sat up again, her back very straight, hands folded in her lap and closed her eyes for a second, a little frown wrinkling the space between her eyebrows, as if calling up something she was about to recite. She opened her eyes and smiled.

"Now, sir. The reason I'm here." He leaned forward and made himself concentrate. "You know of Mister Blankenship, of course. Who he is. What he is."

"Yes, indeed. That is, I think so."

"And the Blankenship Foundation?"

"Not – um – not entirely."

The perfect crescent of one dark brow lifted slightly. Could he have offended her? Should he apologise? It appeared not. Ms. Kamali was nodding understandingly.

"The Blankenship Foundation is an educational institution with a partic-ular emphasis on the humanities. As part of its mission, Mister Blankenship has created – is creating – an archive for the use of bona fide students who are interested in pursuing avenues of original research." Ms. Kamali paused for a second as if checking that she had got her words right, gave herself a little nod of approval, took a breath and continued.

"Since it is Mister Blankenship's belief that Shakespeare is at the core of the humanities, it follows that Shakespeare will be at the core of the archive. You know, of course, that Mister Blankenship recently purchased a copy of the First Folio?" This was safe ground. He nodded firmly. "Over the years, Mister Blankenship has acquired many other items relating directly to the Elizabethan and Jacobean theatre. The First Folio is what I guess you might call the crown jewel of the archive." She frowned. "Or rather, was."

"I hope that doesn't mean something unfortunate has happened to it?"

"Not at all." She smiled. His stomach lurched. "It is kept in conditions of maximum security."

"That's all right, then."

"The reason I say *was*, is that recently Mister Blankenship acquired an item he believes is of great importance. I might say of the greatest importance, Doctor Searle. Mister Blankenship believes the item is unique. He would like very much for you to examine it and to know if your opinion agrees with his."

He rubbed the back of his neck. "This item — what is it exactly?"

"A manuscript."

He frowned. "I'm not an expert on orthography. There are people far better qualified than me. People who would be glad to…"

She lifted a hand. Her fingers were long and tapering with polished silver nails. There was an emerald ring on the third finger. Of her right hand, thank God.

"Mister Blankenship has read your book, Doctor Searle. He admires it greatly. He has no doubt you are the person he needs."

He shrugged. "That's very flattering. What can I say? If he cares to let me see it, I'll be happy to let him know what I think. But honestly, there really are lots of other…"

"Mister Blankenship has authorised me to ask if a fee of twenty-five thousand dollars is acceptable."

He blinked. "I suppose…well…ah…Yes."

"That's great, Doctor Searle. Mister Blankenship will be delighted. We all will." She gave him a dazzling smile. His stomach contracted. She leaned down, picked up the briefcase and placed it on her lap. "How soon can you leave?"

He coughed. "I beg your pardon?"

"How soon can you leave? With Mister Blankenship, time is of the essence."

He stared. "You mean you want me to go to – wherever it is?"

"The archive is housed at Mister Blankenship's Foundation in northern California."

"I'm sorry. Let me get this clear." He made a sound like a stifled laugh. "You're saying you want me to go to northern California?"

"That's correct."

"Now? This minute?"

"Ideally, yes."

He laughed again, more loudly this time. "I can't possibly."

She frowned. "There is something else on your schedule?"

"No."

"Then why not?"

A moment passed. He looked at her and shrugged. "I just can't."

"Why not?" Ms. Kamali said again. She looked at the gold wafer on her wrist. "If we left now – which I don't mean literally but let's suppose – if we left now we could be in the air in two hours, at the Foundation by nine this evening – Pacific time is eight hours later than here. You can have three or four days to study the manuscript. Longer if you like. Your choice. But however you figure it, you can be back home inside of five or six days. Easily. Where's the problem, Doctor Searle?"

From the garden outside came the sound of a mower starting up. Was it the same gardener, the one with the straw hat? Or one of the others?

He shook himself. "Ms. Kamali, it's really most kind — extremely — of Mister Blankenship to think of me. And his offer is most — um — most generous. But given the…"

The sound of the mower swelled and faded through the half-open window. It would be cutting lines of geometrical precision on the already-perfect turf.

"What I mean is…"

How long had he been sitting here, gaping at her like a halfwit? "Look, I'm sorry. It's just not possible," he said.

Ms. Kamali nodded as if she understood completely. The locks on her briefcase flipped upwards and she took out a large envelope.

"You will understand this is shown to you in the strictest confidence."

The envelope was fastened with a thin red string wound in a figure-eight around two flat, circular studs. Inside, were two American quarto-sized sheets of paper.

"They are photocopies, naturally," Ms. Kamali said.

He looked at the top sheet. After a while he looked at the second sheet. Outside, the mower came and went. He looked up.

"Is this a joke?"

"Does it look like a joke?"

He looked down at the second sheet. Then he looked at the top sheet again. He placed them together, slid them back into the envelope, re-wound a careful figure-eight and handed it back to Ms. Kamali.

"I'll need to make a phone call," he said.

 **FOUR**

SO THIS WAS HOW the rich travelled. The very rich, that is. He put down the little gold-rimmed cup with its royal blue monogram, *WB*, and sat back in his seat. Seat? It was more like a sculpture, a contoured throne that swivelled and tipped and swung and reclined to any angle you fancied. He felt a deep inner glow. Scott Fitzgerald was right and bullying Hem, as usual, wrong. The rich *are* different. Bullseye, Scottie. Got it in one.

He looked out of the window. Far below, great ice fields stretched to the horizon, edged by a brilliant sea. What did the colour of that vivid water remind him of? A no-brainer: it had to be Ms. Kamali's eyes.

"Doctor Searle, are you okay?"

She was sitting opposite him, in the depths of an equally luxurious throne. A silver tray on the low table between them bore what was left of the tea he had just wolfed: sandwiches, patisseries and a whole pot of Earl Grey. Ms. Kamali had contented herself with an eggshell cup of hot water flavoured with two wafer-thin slices of fresh ginger. Now she leaned forward, a look of enquiry on her – *gorgeous* – face.

"Is something wrong?"

"Not in the least. I'm fine." He smiled broadly to prove it. "Why? Don't I look it?"

Ms. Kamali gazed at him. "You seemed... I'm not sure. Worried. Concerned."

"Did I?" He manufactured a grin. "I can't think why."

"Would you like some more tea, maybe?" Her hand moved towards the button that would summon the steward.

"No, really. I assure you, Ms. Kamali, I'm absolutely fine. First rate. In the pink."

Why had he said that? Bloody fool. Get a hold of yourself, Searle. She's only a woman, for God's sake. Jesus. Next thing, they'll be asking you to join the PCC.

"The fact is…"

What to say? Not: I was thinking about your heavenly eyes, obviously. His mind tumbled. Come on, man. *Think.*

"The fact is…" He looked out of the window. "Down there. Those glaciers. They're so amazing. I couldn't help thinking of a hymn my grandfather used to sing."

"A hymn?" Ms. Kamali looked puzzled.

"*From Greenland's icy mountains, From India's coral strand.* Do you know it? No, why would you? It's one of those old-style Victorian ones, probably written by a bishop. The kind that celebrated the British Empire. You know – God is an Englishman. Well, looking down there reminded me of it."

She still looked puzzled. Don't let her think you're an idiot, man. He cleared his throat, sat back and quoted:

> "*What though the balmy breezes*
> *Blow soft o'er Java's isle,*
> *Where every prospect pleases,*
> *And only man is vile.*"

He laughed. "They don't write them like that anymore."

"Do you think it's true?" Now her look was serious.

"What – that only man is vile?" He frowned, pressed his lips together and pretended to think. "Not necessarily, although it can be, I suppose. Lord knows, we can think of enough examples. I hope not, anyway. What do you think?"

She sat in silence for a few seconds and then nodded her head slowly.

"Yes, I think it *is* true." She looked sad. "I'm afraid your Victorian bishop was right. Man is vile."

He wasn't sure if he ought to reply. A moment passed. She sat up straight and smiled. "Are we all done here?" She pressed the button and almost immediately the steward appeared from the galley at the rear of the plane to remove the tray. Beyond the galley was a bathroom with a shower and beyond that, at the very rear, a curtained space with a bed where, Ms. Kamali had told him, he could take a nap if he felt like it. A nap? Fat chance.

He had never flown in a private jet before. His flying experience was limited to cut-price trips from Exeter or Bristol, crammed knee-to-knee into a narrow, head-threatening space with a hundred or so others, courtesy of Flybe or EasyJet. It wasn't glamorous but what the hell. It was cheap and they got you there. He had never taken a proper long-haul flight, though. And when the chauffeur in Cambridge had held the door open for him to slide into the back of the limo next to Ms. Kamali, he had imagined vaguely they would be going to Heathrow to catch a normal, scheduled flight.

Instead, they had turned off the M11 at Stansted and driven not to the terminal building but to a gate somewhere on the chain-link perimeter, where they had stopped to be looked over by four policemen in bullet-proof jackets and with automatic weapons hanging round their necks. Then they had passed through onto the airfield and driven to where the plane was waiting, its rear-mounted twin engines already whispering to go. A customs official had checked his passport, nodded his bags on board and all that was left was for him to climb the steps, buckle up and enjoy the ride. Which he was doing. Tremendously. It was great.

He picked up the envelope and took out the two photocopied pages. It must be the twentieth time he had looked at them. He still couldn't quite credit what he saw. On the first sheet, a single line in Tudor secretary hand said:

The Booke of Loues Labors Wonne

Lower down, a series of dark splotches looked like damp-stains and there was a tear in the bottom right-hand corner. The second sheet read:

Actus primus
Scaena Prima

Sounde a Flourishe. Enter Ferdinand King of Nauarre attended at one doore. Enter Berowne, Longauill, and Dumane at another doore.

King   *Now greete we lordes yn happy meetynge heere*
       Despyte of envyous wynters sneapynge hande,
       A twelvemoneth and a daye synce last we mette
       Yn thys same plotte our kyngdome of Nauarre,
       Twelve barren moneths of abstynence and tryal
       Remote from alle the pleasures of the worlde
       Tyll now we stande newborne and shryved of synne
       Guiltlesse of guilte and purged of perjurye,
       Welcome Dumane and welcome Longauill
       And you Berowne, thryce welcome to us alle.

The speech continued to the bottom of the page. Halfway down, three-and-a-quarter lines seemed to have been crossed out and three more were underlined. There was some smudging, and some words towards the bottom were heavily blurred by the damp-stains and the tear, which matched the blemishes on the first page.

"Doctor Searle?" Ms. Kamali was leaning towards him. "Is it all right if I ask you a question?"

"It's perfectly fine, Ms. Kamali." He put the pages down, sat back and smiled encouragingly. This was familiar ground. Tutor and student. He could handle it. "Fire away."

She hesitated. "As you've probably figured out already, I don't know much about Shakespeare." Her cheeks took on a subdued glow. Ms. Kamali was blushing. It was delightful. "In fact, the truth of it is I don't know anything, except what Mister Blankenship has told me, which isn't a whole lot. So what I'm wondering is…" Her gaze lowered to the pages on the table between them. "What exactly *is* that, Doctor Searle? And why is it so special?"

"What is it?" He gave a little, self-deprecating cough. "To be frank with you, Ms. Kamali, I don't know – and I may not, even when I've seen the original. But I can tell you what it looks like. This…" He picked up the first sheet and held it out to her. "This seems to be what's called a wrapper, the title page or cover for a playscript. This…" he gave her the second sheet, "appears to be the first scene of the play itself."

"You can read it?" Her eyes widened. He was thrilled.

"It's not too hard once you've had some practice." He leaned forward and tapped the pages. "What it looks like is the book-keeper's copy. It's fairly typical, in fact. You see, what happened was, playscripts were kept in the theatre, in a chest or cupboard somewhere backstage or in the company offices, and the book-keeper was the guy responsible for them. They were valuable property, don't forget, and were guarded pretty closely. There would have been a stack of them, the company's whole repertoire, each one carefully preserved from its first run of performances and taken out to be used again when the play was revived. Does that answer your first question?"

"I guess so." She nodded slowly. "This is an Elizabethan playscript."

"It *seems* to be." He sat back. "As to your second question: what makes it so special? Well, a number of things. First, a bit of background. In 1598…" He broke off and made a face. "Sorry. I'm being pompous. This is starting to sound horribly like a lecture."

"No! It's fascinating. I never knew any of it. Please don't stop."

"You're sure? Okay, then. In 1598 a guy called Francis Meres published a book called *Palladis Tamia*. It was a sort of anthology of proverbs and moral precepts, bits of wisdom mostly copied from the classics, nothing original, pretty ordinary stuff. But what makes the book special is that in one section Meres talks about contemporary writers and ranks them according to how good he thought they were. One of the writers is William Shakespeare and he lists a number of his plays. One of the plays is called *Love's Labour's Won*. What's interesting about that is we have no knowledge whatsoever of a play with that title. We know *Love's Labour's Lost* – but *Love's Labour's Won*? Nothing. Zip. It isn't in the First Folio; there is no single printed copy; it's a total blank."

He paused for a moment to let the point sink in and give her the chance to ask questions but she sat perfectly still, her eyes fixed on him gravely. Splendid.

"Now Meres could have made a simple mistake and got the title wrong. In which case, end of mystery. Or *Love's Labour's Won* may be a play we know by another name. Some people think it's *Much Ado about Nothing*, which I think is just possible. Others go for *All's Well that Ends Well*, which I'm pretty certain isn't. A lot of people once thought it was *The Taming of the Shrew*, which Meres doesn't mention and we're sure had been written by 1598. But then someone found a sixteenth-century bookseller's list of stock in which *Love's Labour's Won* was mentioned – as well as *The Taming of the Shrew*. So we are back to our original possibilities. Either Francis Meres made a mistake…"

"Or *Love's Labour's Won* is a lost play by William Shakespeare."

"That's right. And what's interesting here…" He picked up the second sheet and stared down at it. "Is the way this first scene begins."

"The way it begins?" Ms. Kamali looked bewildered.

"Let me explain," Adam said. He put the sheet in front of her. "At the end of *Love's Labour's Lost* these characters – the King of Navarre and his friends Berowne, Dumain and Longaville – all take a vow to spend a year of penitence as a sort of punishment imposed by the girls they're in love with – the Princess of France and her three ladies. Well..." He pointed to the opening lines. "This seems to start twelve months later, when the boys are being reunited, presumably before meeting up with the girls again."

"You mean it's a kind of sequel?"

"That's what it looks like."

"And that's why it's called *Love's Labour's Won*!" Ms. Kamali's eyes were radiant. "Doctor Searle, that's so exciting! Whoever would have thought it, after all this time!"

"Hold on a minute." He lifted a hand. "That isn't the end of it."

She stared. "Are you saying there's more?"

"Yes, I think I am." He sat back and crossed his legs. His chair tilted alarmingly. He sat up straight again. "You haven't read my book, have you?"

She blushed once more. Honeygold cheeks. Positively heart-stopping. "I mean to. Truly I do. I just haven't gotten around to it."

"It's all right. I didn't expect you had." He gave her a reassuring smile. "Well, what I try to do in my book is consider Shakespeare primarily as a man of the theatre, as a professional actor and working writer in a company of other professional actors, his colleagues and partners. I talk about the day-to-day business of rehearsal and performance, the writing and delivering of scripts, play production, casting, stage management, styles of acting, costumes, the demands of the box office, repertoire, the problem of censorship, the need for a patron." He paused for breath.

"Wowee. That sounds like some book," Ms. Kamali said.

"Thank you. It has been quite – ah – quite well received." Another little smile, modest this time. "Well, anyway, I try to discuss everything that went into being part of a working commercial enterprise, which the Elizabethan theatre most certainly was."

Ms. Kamali looked doubtful. "But it was a bit – you know – highbrow, wasn't it?"

"Highbrow? Whatever gave you that idea?" He laughed. "It was the movies, Soraya! Is it all right if I call you Soraya? Just think of the movies and how they started. What an impact they made, how quickly it all happened, how popular they became. The Elizabethan theatre was not unlike that — it was a new means of mass entertainment that people were hungry for. They couldn't get enough of it. Everybody went! If you could satisfy them, deliver the goods, you could make a seriously good living. Shakespeare did."

"He got rich?"

"Very. Just about every other Elizabethan playwright we know of died in poverty or something close to it. Not William. He was a canny soul. At one point he was earning money in four different ways: as an actor and playwright, obviously; but also as a sharer in the overall profits of the company and part-owner of the theatre — in fact *two* theatres when they opened another one in Blackfriars. It meant he could buy the second biggest house in Stratford plus another one in London, and build a fair-sized estate of land and rents to pass on to his kids."

He shook his head. "Don't ever listen to the stupid people who say all we know about Shakespeare can be written on the back of a postcard, Soraya. It just isn't true. Oh, sure there are gaps — missing years, personal stuff, possible lost plays that we'd give our eye-teeth to know about. But all in all, we know more about him than any other writer of his time, except maybe Ben Jonson, who had a pretty high opinion of himself and published his autobiography. Oh yes, we have a great deal of information about William Shakespeare.

"What we don't have, though..." He leaned forward, frowning in emphasis, "is anything he actually *wrote*. I mean, there's nothing in his handwriting — apart from a few signatures on legal documents and three pages from a play he may have collaborated on with three or four other writers."

"They did that? Collaborated?"

"Sure they did. All the time." He grinned. "It was the movies, like I said. But that's not the point." He took the pages and placed them side by side on the table in front of her. "Take another look, Soraya. Does anything strike you about these?"

She leaned forward, frowning. After a moment she shook her head. "You'll have to show me."

"Well, like I told you, I'm not an expert on orthography. But it seems to me there are two different sets of handwriting here. Look…"

He tapped his finger, indicating. "The title on the wrapper is in one hand. The same hand seems to have made some notes, stage directions, in the margin on the second page…*there*." He pointed. "But otherwise, the second sheet, the play-text itself, is in another hand. Which, of course, could be a copyist's. There was a guy called Ralph Crane, a professional scrivener, who we know they hired to copy out several of the plays." He coughed. A moment went by.

"There is one other possibility, of course," Adam said. He cleared his throat. "That the hand is – ah – the playwright's himself."

It took a moment to register. Then Ms. Kamali stared. Slowly, she looked down at the second page. "Are you saying this writing…*is William Shakespeare's?*"

"Not yet. How could I? All I can say is, there's a possibility – just a faint one – that this might be Shakespeare's foul papers."

"His *what?*"

"Sorry. It's the term we give to the writer's own manuscript. His original draft. What probably used to happen was, he would finish the play and then hand it over to the book-keeper – who was responsible for copying it out fair, dividing it into actors' parts, stuff like that. He was often the prompter and what we'd nowadays call the stage manager, so he'd write in the margins details of props, music cues, sound effects, sometimes the names of the actors who played the different parts."

"Like this?" Ms. Kamali pointed to the notes in the left-hand margin. He nodded. "Like that."

"So is that what this is?" She lifted the second page with a care that was almost reverent. "A lost play by William Shakespeare?" Her voice sank to a thrilled, husky whisper. *"In his own original handwriting?"*

"It may be. I emphasise *may be*." He took a deep breath. "Look, the odds are it's nothing of the kind. That at best it's a clever forgery, at worst an obvious con."

"But if it is? If it really and truly *is*?" Ms. Kamali's lovely eyes regarded him gravely.

"If it *is*, Soraya, your employer has got hold of literary dynamite." He gave a quick laugh. "What did he pay for the First Folio? Seven million dollars?"

"Seven-and-a-half."

"Seven-and-a-half million dollars. For a single copy. Of which there are two hundred and thirty-two other copies in existence. The Folger Library alone owns eighty-two of them. Well, with *this*…" he tapped the pages, "there would be nothing comparable. Nothing in the whole world."

"I guess it would be worth a stack of money."

"If it's genuine?" He rubbed the back of his neck and blew out his cheeks. "How much gold is there in Fort Knox?"

The hills below were a tawny brown and growing closer by the minute. They were heading south, following the coastline, with an ocean that must be the Pacific on their right-hand side. On the left, towns spread randomly on each side of a central highway, while a pattern of ribbon-roads led to smaller settlements up in the hills. Then there was water on both sides and they were flying over a huge bay. There were lines of stakes in the water and a distant road bridge. Now he could see waterside developments with neat marinas and ordered ranks of moored boats.

And suddenly there was the famous bridge, the Golden Gate, with the city beyond just like in the photographs. The bay itself, flecked with white sails and the tracks of larger vessels, glinted in the late-afternoon sun. And here came the steward to touch Ms. Kamali gently on the shoulder to wake her from her light slumber and remind them both to bring their seats to the upright position and fasten their seat-belts as they were shortly about to land.

 **FIVE**

FROM DOWN HERE, THE bridge was even more impressive. You didn't appreciate the scale of it, the plunging-rising swoop of the huge cables, the height of the towers, its sheer *span*, from the air. It wasn't golden though but a kind of red-orange, he thought, or deep rust-brown. No matter. It was a beautiful thing in a beautiful setting. It had taken the best part of an hour to get here and Ms. Kamali — Soraya — had said it would be at least another hour before they arrived at the Foundation. He didn't mind.

The landing at San Francisco airport had been as easy as the departure from Stansted. (More thrilling, though: they had swept in from the south, low across the bay, closer and closer to the ribbed water, to touch down on a narrow runway stuck out from the land like a spear.) Once again, he was met by an immigration official at the foot of the plane's steps, his passport was dealt with, and a moment later he was stepping into the dark blue limousine parked a short distance beyond.

It was wider and longer than the car that had driven him from Cambridge and had a much softer suspension — when Enrique the driver got in it had gently rocked up and down like a partly moored boat. But it was at least as comfortable and much better equipped. There was a small fridge (icebox?) in the bulkhead in front of him containing an array of bottles that Soraya invited him to choose from. His immediate thought was he wasn't thirsty but what the hell. He selected a small tonic water and settled back, sipping slowly, letting the burnt-flavour quinine bubbles prickle gently at his nostrils as they headed north across the great bridge.

The six-lane highway narrowed to five and then four as they swooped into a tunnel. The road surface was terrible, he noted, with huge splits in the tarmac: badly-patched bumps and fissures that caused the big car to pitch and shudder as they gathered speed. Out from the other end there were glimpses of water on the right, wooded hills on the left and up ahead the rounded outline of something Soraya told him was Mount Tam. He finished the tonic water and sat back against the padded leather. A sudden wave of light-headedness came over him and he glanced at his watch. Three o'clock. In the morning. No wonder he was starting to feel shattered. He took it off and wound the hands back eight full turns. Seven in the evening. That was better. All the same, it was going to be an effort to keep his eyes open much longer.

"Ms. Kamali?" Enrique spoke from the driver's seat. "At the house they told me to give you this." He handed an envelope back over his shoulder. She took it, tore it open, scanned the contents and frowned.

"When did this come through, Ricky?"

"Sometime this afternoon, I guess."

"And this is all?"

His shoulders lifted and dropped in a faint shrug. "I guess."

Enrique spoke to the windshield, his eyes fixed on the evening traffic flow ahead. He was in his late thirties or early forties, Adam thought, and partly or wholly Mexican: what they called a Latino – or was it Hispanic? He wasn't sure. A big, wide-shouldered man, not tall but bulky, well-muscled, with sallow skin, high cheekbones, long combed-back hair and a heavy down-swept Zapata moustache, you could imagine him in an old Hollywood movie as a bandit or pirate, the hero's best friend who saves his life early on and dies in his arms just before the credits roll. Soraya had introduced him as Mister Blankenship's personal driver. Bodyguard too, by the look of him, Adam thought. Beside him, Soraya clicked her tongue in dismay.

"Mister Blankenship isn't at the Foundation yet. Something came up. He's in New York City, or ..." she glanced at the message, "maybe Vermont. He hopes to be here by tomorrow. I'm so sorry, Doctor Searle."

"It's not important."

"Maybe not. But I know Mister Blankenship wanted to welcome you personally. He'd set his heart on it. Oh well, that's how it goes, I guess. He sends his apologies. You'll just have to make do with me." She smiled. "I hope that's not a problem."

"Not in the least. Provided you stop calling me Doctor Searle."

"It's okay to call you Adam?"

"It's essential."

She laughed. "Anything you say."

He couldn't think of a reply. Another wave of light-headedness washed over him and he sat back again. His eyelids felt heavy and he must have dozed for a while, because when he opened them it was to find they had turned off the main highway and were following the steep curves of a minor road as it climbed out of a small valley. At the crest there was an unfolding vista of brown hills studded with irregular stands of trees, their green sharp against the scorched earth. Dry watercourses each side of the road were part-filled with the debris of small rockfalls, and at one point they passed a huge boulder, purple-shadowed and dramatic against the fading evening sky. Like the granite tors he knew on Dartmoor? Perhaps this was the California equivalent. Different, obviously, but the same kind of thing.

"Not long now," Soraya said.

Twenty minutes later they turned off the road and stopped, facing a massive iron-barred gate. Enrique's window slid down and he leaned out and spoke to a pile of rocks by the gatepost. There was a short pause and then the rocks replied in a clipped, metallic-sounding voice. Enrique reached out and pressed some buttons inset below the speaker. Another brief pause, then the huge gate quivered and swung slowly inward and they passed through. Three hundred yards later they slowed again through a narrow chicane and came to a stop by a small cabin-like building where a man in a dark blue uniform stood waiting. Inside the cabin, another man in dark blue sat in front of a row of television screens. The man outside leaned down to look carefully at Adam before smiling at Soraya and nodding them through.

"Your security is impressive," Adam said.

In front, Enrique gave a little snort. Soraya laughed. "That's the least of it," she said.

They drove on through the thickening light, over a rumbling covered bridge and through dense stands of tall trees. He got the impression of a low greystone building and a distant small lake but it was hard to be certain, partly because the light was so poor, mainly because he was so tired. Then, at last, they were turning in a half-circle and stopping in front of a building where lights shone from mullioned windows and through the wide-opening doorway as someone came out to meet them. He had the impression of a timbered façade with two flanking wings and then the car door was held open and he was climbing out to the sharp smell of pine in the air, Enrique was hefting down his luggage, and Soraya was arriving to stand beside him and lay her hand lightly on his arm.

"Welcome to the Foundation, Adam," she said.

He had been certain he would sleep through the night, but when he looked at the clock by his bedside the red-glowing numerals said 12:32. Or just gone half-past eight in the morning. He groaned. Bugger. His body was still on British Summertime. He lay still for a while, staring up at the dark ceiling, hoping he would drift back to sleep; but it didn't happen, so he swung himself down from the thick mattress and padded across to the window.

He had been right about the lake. He could see where the moonlight glinted palely on its dark surface about half a mile away. Clouds were passing fitfully. The lake came and went. In a funny way moonlight was different here – but then so was everything, he thought, even when it looked the same. Or was it simply that he was still stupid from the journey and everything would make sense once he had adjusted? Wait and see.

What time was it now? One a.m. Maybe he should have eaten something before going to bed, like they suggested, but he really hadn't felt like it and said thank you but no. The housekeeper, a stout, middle-aged Hispanic lady called Marisol, had said there was a meal ready, but all he wanted was to crash and when they showed him his bed he could hardly stay upright. Soraya offered him some pills called Melatonin that she said were natural and organic and would help him sleep, but he laughed and said that was the last thing he needed. *Wrong.*

There was movement in the darkness somewhere in front of the house. He stared hard. Movement again, about fifty yards away. A small herd of deer, seven or eight of them, moving slowly across the grass, stopping briefly to graze and then moving on, tails flicking across their white scuts. He watched them disappear across the drive and into a small clump of trees. He yawned. His eye-balls stung. He felt a hundred years old. He turned from the window and groped his way back into bed.

"How did you sleep?"

"Not – ah – not too well."

"I'm sorry."

"It was my fault. I should have taken your pills."

"I'll have Marisol put some in your room."

"Thank you."

"You're welcome. How's your breakfast?"

"Delicious. Aren't you having any?"

She laughed. "I had mine hours ago."

"Oh lord, it's nearly eleven, isn't it? Sorry."

"Don't worry about it. It's quite normal."

She was wearing jeans and a cream silk shirt. Her hair was caught up at the back with a scarlet band. If anything, she looked even lovelier than yesterday, which he wouldn't have thought possible until now.

"When you're done, I'll show you the library if you'd like."

"I would like." He pushed his plate away, took a last sip of coffee, wiped his mouth on the thick linen napkin and stood up. "Lead on."

He followed her from the breakfast room, with its view of sepia, tree-scattered hills, and out into the hallway, where the stone floor, wide staircase and carved floor-to-ceiling panelling looked just like a Tudor entrance hall — except that, instead of age-blackened oak, the wood was a deep, glowing red.

"California redwood," Soraya said. "From an old railroad bridge they didn't use anymore. Mister Blankenship had it brought in specially."

They crossed the hallway to a long sitting room with sofas and a grand piano and entered a panelled corridor with a pale rose carpet and heavy doors at the end.

The library made him blink. It was a kind of medieval tithe-barn, at least two stories high, which he guessed took up the whole of one wing. Great wooden posts like old-style crucks rose from the floor to the timbered roof, where they were jointed and pegged to the central ridge beam and the double tier of curved wind-braces. There were about eight bays, he reckoned, stretching the length of the huge room and, like the entrance hall, the wood was the same rich, glowing red. So were the book-filled shelves that lined the walls, and the little curved staircase leading up to the gallery that ran around three sides of the room, where there were many more book-crowded shelves. It was slightly weird, he thought, to see something at once so familiar and yet so strange: a bit like finding a blue daffodil. But then, why not? There was no law he knew of that said tithe-barns couldn't be constructed from California redwood instead of English oak.

High on the wall at the far end, light filtered through a great rose window, bordered with a garland of fruit and flowers surrounding the monogram *WB*. Midway along the left-hand wall, a huge open fireplace was topped with a greystone mantel carved with the motto *Non Sans Droit*. A bust of Shakespeare stood in a niche above the mantel. It looked like a copy of the Davenant bust, the one that was in the Garrick Club in London. Beyond the fireplace, a line of Shakespeare portraits was ranged along the wall. He recognised the Chandos, the Flower and the Grafton portraits and a large framed photograph of the Darmstadt death-mask. Some painted china figurines, rather pretty, of Shakespeare characters were grouped in a nearby display case: commemoration souvenirs from David Garrick's Stratford Jubilee of 1769. Desks and work tables with chairs and computer screens were placed around the room, and four or five deep leather armchairs stood by the enormous fireplace.

"What an amazing room," he said.

She frowned. "You don't find it too dark?"

He looked around. "A little, maybe. But I could live with it."

"Not me." She gave a little shiver. "I need light. Fresh air. Space."

She took a deep breath. Her cream shirtfront swelled. He coughed and looked away.

"Perhaps I could take a look at the manuscript?"

"Oh, the manuscript's not here. Mister Blankenship has it. He doesn't let it out of his sight."

He nodded. It made sense. "Where do you keep the First Folio?"

"I'll show you."

Across the room from the fireplace was another redwood door, smaller this time, with a metal keypad set in the wall beside it. He watched her tap out some numbers, heard the *click* as the locks turned, and then she swung the door open and he followed her inside. It was a small room, only about ten feet square, with metal shelves and a bank of thermostats by the door.

"Temperature and humidity controls," Soraya said.

There were some boxes and several volumes in slip-cases on the shelves; half a dozen black leather briefcases like the one she was carrying yesterday —and the First Folio, lying on its side, covered with a blue cloth. She handed it to him and they went out to the nearest work table where he put it down and took away the cloth. It had been re-bound – beautifully, he noted – in dark blue leather with gold-leaf tooling. He opened it at the title page:

Mr. WILLIAM
SHAKESPEARE'S
Comedies,
Histories, &
Tragedies.
Publifhed according to the True Originall Copies

And below, taking up the rest of the page, the famous Droeshout etching: the high, domed forehead; the thinning hair neatly combed and bobbed over each ear; the crescent eyebrows; the little moustache; the tuft of beard under the lower lip; the cool sideways glance.

LONDON
Printed by Ifaac Iaggard, and Ed. Blount. 1623

"That's our William," he said.

She put her head on one side. "He was quite a little guy, wasn't he?"

"By our standards, possibly. He was probably about average for the time."

She frowned. "You know something, Adam?" She hesitated. "No, you'll think I'm terrible."

"I'm sure I won't. Go on. What were you going to say?"

"It's just – well – he looks like a little old lady to me."

He laughed. "There's an old-maid look, I grant you. But you have to remember this was done years after he died, by an artist who almost certainly never met him."

"So how could he draw his picture?"

"Shakespeare's friends, the guys who published the Folio, would have described him. And there may have been a portrait from when Shakespeare was still alive that he could copy from."

"One of those, you mean?"

He looked at the line of portraits and shook his head. "Oh, no." He pointed to the Grafton portrait. "I don't want to disillusion you, but that one is almost certainly not Shakespeare but someone else. That one…" he nodded to the Flower, "is a nineteenth-century fake. And that one…" indicating the Chandos, "obviously wasn't used for the Folio — even though I wish it was." He looked round quickly, as if checking that no one else could hear. "Shall I tell you a secret, Soraya? I think that's really him."

She walked slowly to where the picture hung and stood looking up at it. "This is Shakespeare? That's how he looked?"

"I like to think so." He went to stand beside her. The man with the untied, open-neck collar and little gold earring, looked back at them. "The story is it was painted by his friend, the actor Richard Burbage. It's just a story, though. No one really knows."

"Then why do you think this is him?"

"Because he looks like a writer. It's the only picture in which he does." He shrugged. "I can't prove it, of course. Nobody can. It's just a feeling. But something about it says to me it's authentic." He stared up at the portrait. "Maybe it's the cunning look in his eye."

She laughed. "Anyhow, it's not important. *This* is what's important," Adam said. He went back to the First Folio and turned to the contents page:

A CATALOGVE

of the feverall Comedies, Hiftories, and Tragedies contained in this Volume.

And then the thirty-five titles, with *Troilus and Cressida* left out, probably because there was some temporary dispute about the rights, but printed in the main body of the text.

He tapped the page. "Ben Jonson got it right, Soraya: Look not on his picture, but his book."

A telephone rang. "Excuse me." She went to a low table by one of the fireside armchairs and picked it up.

"Mister Blankenship? Good morning, sir! …Yes, he's here right now… Would you …? Yes, sir… Yes, sir, I surely will."

She held out the receiver. He took it. Their fingers touched.

"Mister Blankenship?"

"Adam? Good to hear you." The voice was musical, fairly high-pitched. "They taking care of you at the Foundation?"

"They most certainly are."

"I'm happy to hear it. Now listen, Adam: Something came up here and it doesn't look as if I can get away till tomorrow. It's a goddamn nuisance, but there's not a whole lot I can do about it."

"I hope it's nothing serious."

"No, it's not serious. Just a goddamn pain in the ass. Means another day before we can get together. Is that going to be a problem for you?"

"I don't think so."

"That's fine. Alright, Adam, it's good to talk with you. I'll see you tomorrow."

"I look forward to it, Mister Blankenship."

"Let me speak with Soraya, will you?"

He handed back the telephone. She listened intently.

" …Yes, Mister Blankenship. I will, sir… That's a great idea… Yes, I will… Yes, very. He's absolutely charming." She looked at Adam and smiled. "I surely will, Mister Blankenship. Goodbye." She put the telephone down.

"Things sound pretty hectic in New York. Or is it Vermont?" Adam said.

"Oh, he isn't there anymore. He's in Montana."

"Montana?"

She nodded. "Mister Blankenship has many interests." She put a hand on his arm. "Now tell me true: how are you feeling?"

"Okay. Still a bit — you know — not quite here."

She nodded. "I don't wonder. It's so gloomy inside." She looked round the room and made a face. "What you need is daylight, Adam. Blue sky. Sunshine!" She laughed. "How about we take a little swim?"

 **SIX**

THEY STOPPED HALFWAY DOWN the drive and he turned to look back at the house. It was three stories high, a timber-faced manor house built in the traditional Tudor E shape: a long central section with a jutting entrance porch in the centre and two flanking wings, each with a little tower and onion-shaped cupola. The ground floor was red herring-bone brick, while the upper floors were faced with white-painted plaster and great patterned timbers. Banks of tall, leaded windows gleamed in the sunlight and he picked out his own room, high up to the left. Instead of tiles, the steep-pitched roof was made of wooden shingles, with several small dormer windows that by rights oughtn't to be there sticking out at odd angles, and clusters of tall, barley-sugar chimney stacks rising from the centre and at each end.

The stone path to the entrance porch was flanked with little trees in white tubs that he'd been too tired to notice last night, and the whole front of the house was bordered by a low, clipped hedge, dark green and glossy, about four feet high, where a shirtless man – Enrique, wasn't it? – was working with a pair of long-handled shears.

Adam frowned. From where he stood, the house seemed slightly askew, higgledy-piggledy, as if bits had been added at random or as late afterthoughts. Was there a touch of Disney about it? Yes, there was. Did it matter? Not really. It was someone's idea of what a Tudor manor house ought to be, and even though they hadn't quite got it right — and its setting among these brown California hills was extraordinary — somehow it didn't matter. Forget Disney. It worked.

"Do you think it looks silly?" Soraya said.

"Not a bit." He shook his head. "In fact it's rather impressive. How old is it?"

"About fifteen years." She smiled at his surprise. "Mister Blankenship designed it himself. He's very proud of it. But you'll see some real old houses — what we call Victorians — when we go to the city tonight."

"Are we going to the city tonight?"

"Oh, *rats!*" Her hand flew to her mouth, her eyes wide in dismay. "I'm sorry, Adam. It was going to be a surprise. Now I've spoiled it. Oh, well." She shrugged. "There's a performance at the opera. Would you like to go?"

"If you're going, I would. Very much."

Her cheeks glowed. She was blushing again. He was delighted. "What's the opera?" he said.

"I forget." Now she was positively flaming. She struck herself on the forehead. "Stupid! There I go again!"

He touched her arm lightly. There was a faint down on her skin. "Don't worry about it," he said.

They continued their walk. The air was bright, clear, sharp; he could smell pine and freshly turned earth. On a nearby hillside he made out a group of slow-moving cattle and it looked as if vines had been planted on the slopes lower down. High above, several huge birds circled the rising thermals. He squinted upwards.

"Turkey buzzards," Soraya said.

He thought of the buzzards over Dartmoor. They were nothing like the slightly sinister black shapes up there.

"They look more like vultures."

"I think they are. Only, people call them buzzards."

He looked ahead to where water glinted through a stand of willows and nodded towards it. "Looks inviting."

She gave a little squeal. "The lake? We're not going to swim there!"

"We're not?"

"Heavens, no! There are all kinds of things — snakes and stuff! I'd rather die!"

The path led them round the base of a low rise. "This is where we swim," Soraya said.

He saw that the low rise was actually a piece of artful landscaping. Around the other side, at the foot of the slope and out of sight of the house, was a single-storey wooden-frame building (light-coloured wood this time; fir or pine). They went inside and through a glass partition-wall he saw a gym and what looked like half a basketball court with a marked floor and single basket at one end. Soraya reached into her straw bag, took out a navy-blue swimsuit and handed it to him.

"Down here."

He followed her past a water-cooler, down a short flight of steps to a small lobby with two doors.

"This one's you. That one's me."

She went through the second door. He went through the first and found himself in a white-painted room with a row of metal lockers down the middle. To one side there were shelves with mirrors and heaps of folded white towels. The wall opposite was lined with benches and a row of blue-painted hooks. At the end nearest him, two or three wooden stools stood by a clothes rail where white terrycloth robes hung on wooden hangers. Through an archway he could see a longer tiled room with basins and showers and lavatory stalls. He hung his clothes on the rail and put on the swimsuit she had given him. Should he wear a robe? He decided against. Instead, he took a towel from one of the heaps and hung it round his neck, hesitated for a moment, then picked up another one, draped it over his arm and went out.

There was a set of glazed doors on the far side of the little lobby. He pushed them open, followed a little curved, upward-sloping path bordered with yellow flowers and found himself at the edge of a blue-and-white tiled swimming pool. The glare on the water made him blink. Some loungers with opened sunshades were set out along the near side of the pool. He dropped his towels on the closest one, walked to the edge, looked towards the far end for a moment, took a deep breath and dived.

He prided himself on his swimming. He was pretty good, he knew. He started at a fast crawl, reached the far end, turned and started back. This was great, his chance to look good. Any minute now he'd be into his stride and really motoring. A couple more lengths and…a half-submerged shape moved smoothly past him and he stopped, treading water, staring.

She was wearing a green one-piece swimsuit and she swam like a dream, cutting through the water with firm, stylish strokes to reach the far end where she flipped into a neat tumble-turn and started back, long legs beating an effortless rhythm as she flowed past. It was no contest. She was miles better. He turned on his back and floated. Give up.

"How are you feeling now?"

"Terrific. This was a great idea. Positively inspired." He stretched his arms wide and yawned hugely.

She looked concerned. "So long as you don't overdo it." She raised herself on one elbow and looked down at him. "Something tells me you need a little protection." She reached under her lounger and came up with a small yellow bottle. She sat up, shook it and unscrewed the cap. "Turn over."

Did it get any better than this? How could it? He rested his chin on his forearms and peered dreamily into the distance. *Such heavenly touches.* Something moved on the other side of the bushes screening the pool.

"Don't be so tense. *Relax.*"

"Sorry. Only someone seems to be watching us."

"Where?"

"Over there."

Her hand on his back was still for a moment. Then, "It's just Ricky," she said. "Don't mind him."

"He seems to be taking a lot of interest in us."

"He's just doing his job."

Her hand started to move again. He grunted softly. He didn't want it ever to stop.

"Don't go to sleep now."

"I won't."

But his eyelids grew heavier, the bright sunlight dimmed to sepia, then to black, and the next thing he knew she was shaking him gently and telling him to wake up because it was time for them to go back to the house and get ready. Otherwise, what with the evening traffic and all, they were going to be late.

Going south it was even better. You came out of the tunnel and there it was below you, the beautiful bridge, reaching out from the headland to the opposite low-lying shore. Over there lay the city, tall buildings gleaming in the late sunlight, streets and houses flowing down to the water. At this moment, seeing it like this, he understood completely why so many people said they loved this place.

"What time does Mister Blankenship get in tomorrow?" he said.

"I don't know yet. It's usually a last-minute thing. Do you know, Ricky?"

"From Montana? Not till early evening, I guess."

They drove along a bustling street. The bay was on one side, steep-rising hills on the other. He saw wharves, boats, people, cars, buses, trucks, restaurants, cafes, shops.

"Do you think I could come here tomorrow?" he said. "In the morning, perhaps, before Mister Blankenship arrives? Once he gets here I don't expect there'll be much time for sightseeing and I'd hate to miss out on all this."

"That's a great idea," Soraya said. "We could catch the ferry from Tiburon, take a look at North Beach, visit Chinatown, have lunch there – no, better! Go to Sears and eat pancakes. Do you like pancakes, Adam?"

"I adore pancakes."

"That's settled, then. After that we'll take a walk around downtown, catch the ferry back or have Ricky pick us up somewhere, and be back at the Foundation in good time to say hello to Mister Blankenship. What do you say?"

"I say yes. Most definitely yes."

"How does that sound to you, Ricky?"

The broad shoulders lifted a fraction and dropped. "Your call, Ms. Kamali," Enrique said.

The Opera House was a tall, classical building, heavy-looking and rather gloomy, that seemed to occupy a whole city block. Inside, the wide foyer and broad staircases were swarming with chattering people, all of them elegantly dressed. Quite a few of the men were in dinner jackets (tuxedos?). Clearly, going to the opera here was a formal event. His grey worsted trousers and corduroy jacket were just about acceptable, he reckoned, and he was glad he had decided to pack a tie. She, on the other hand, was absolutely stunning in a black silk-jersey dress and gold-threaded evening shawl. In those amazing heels she was nearly as tall as he was.

"You look wonderful," he said.

She smiled. "Thank you."

That was one of the nice things about American women, he thought. They knew how to take a compliment. None of that English mix of embarrassment and false modesty that made you hesitate to say something nice about a woman's appearance in case she thought you were lying or, worse, making fun of her. A bell rang. Soraya took his arm. They joined the moving crowd.

The opera was *Faust*. She asked him if he knew it and he said he'd seen it once, a long time ago, when he had been taken as a kid to the Opera House in Covent Garden. But he knew it well because it was a favourite of his parents. They had an old nineteen-fifties recording with Victoria de Los Angeles and Nicolai Gedda and it was played often at home. His mother, especially, had loved it, playing the garden scene over and over and sometimes singing along in near-perfect French.

They were shown to a box in the centre of one of the lower tiers.

"Terrific seats," he said.

She nodded. "Mister Blankenship is a generous patron."

He leaned forward and looked around. The auditorium was disappointing, huge and featureless, rather drab, with none of the gilding and over-the-top opulence he'd expected. A bit like an enormous town hall, he thought. And to his surprise, rather shabby: the upholstery on his chair was fraying and the carpet underfoot wearing thin. The stage, a vast proscenium, looked forbidding. He wondered what the acoustic was going to be like. The lights dimmed. Applause started and swelled. A bald head appeared above the rail of the orchestra pit and bowed several times to the house. Then it turned, the clapping died, the baton lifted. He was about to find out.

It wasn't bad. A bit cavernous but that was to be expected. Perhaps that was why the orchestra seemed a little ponderous, not as light-footed as Gounod ought to be. Most of the cast were eastern Europeans: Marguerite was a Czech, Faust a Croatian and Valentin a Bulgarian. They sang well enough, but without any real feeling for the piece or the spirit that was needed for it (it was *French*, for goodness sake). Each note was produced and hammered home without much regard for what was happening, while the acting was of the basic one-foot-forward, stand-and-deliver kind. The exception was Mephistopheles, an ageing Italian bass-baritone who was well past his best, who had only the shadow of what once had been a great voice, but whose wonderful technique and marvellous stage intelligence put him in a different class from the others. He was still great, even though he couldn't really sing any longer. Adam watched him in delight.

The production, he thought, was pretty good. Instead of the traditional medieval Germany, the director had opted for a nineteenth-century Paris that was straight out of *Trilby*. So the rejuvenated Faust was a kind of left-bank Little Billee, Marguerite was Trilby herself and, best of all, Mephistopheles was a sardonic Svengali in a great fur-lined coat and silk hat, with a cigar and silver-topped stick.

The Calf of Gold scene was set outside a little café in the Latin Quarter where everyone got smashed on absinthe; the soldiers marching off to war were *Poilus* going to fight the Prussians, complete with canteen cart and two saucy *Vivandieres*; only the garden scene was disappointing. *Salut! Demure chaste et pure* could have been the recital of a laundry list, and though the Jewel Song was better (and brought the house down; they roared for at least a couple of minutes), the love duet didn't move him as it usually did.

> *Je veux t'aimer et te cherir!*
> *Parle encore!*
> *Je t'appartiens, je t'adore!*
> *Pour toi je veux mourir!*

"What do you think?" he said to Soraya at the interval.

"I love it," she said. "I absolutely *love it!* What's going to happen? I mean, what happens next?"

"You don't know the story? Oh, then I'm not going to spoil it by telling you."

"Please, Adam. *Please*."

"I wouldn't dream of it. Wait and see."

"That's really mean of you."

"Can't help it. Look, I'll buy you a glass of champagne instead."

He fought his way successfully to the bar and they took their drinks outside, standing at the head of the broad steps, not saying much, watching the lights of the city until it was time to go back.

The second half was disappointing. The director was clearly one of the breed that liked to shock (he was a Spanish film director, according to the programme) and in the Cathedral scene a heavily pregnant Marguerite appeared to abort herself on the steps of the altar – or was it the font? Pointless, anyway. Adam sat back and let his mind wander, thinking of Marlowe's version of the Faust story and wondering why Shakespeare never used it.

Why hadn't he? Surely not because Marlowe had already triumphed with it? If anything, that would have been an incentive, a spur. Christopher Marlowe had been the great star of Shakespeare's early years in the theatre. He was the yardstick to measure yourself against, the guy you had to beat. Shakespeare would have been envious – how could he not be? – of the other man's success.

They were almost exact contemporaries, both middle-class provincial grammar-school boys. But where the shoemaker's son from Canterbury had gone up to Cambridge and brilliant early success, taking London by storm with *Tamburlaine* and delighting the elite with *Hero and Leander*, the glover's son from Stratford had had to content himself with the anonymity of the lost years and the life of a humble jobbing actor. And when he started to write, reworking speeches, spatchcocking scenes together, adapting other men's plays (out of sheer necessity? Because the company needed a new play quickly and the ones they had weren't good enough? Because they had to establish ownership of some older plays they had picked up?), he was attacked as an ignorant, conceited plagiarist, the Upstart Crow. And by the time he was truly making a name for himself, Marlowe was dead, stabbed in the eye in a quarrel over a pub bill.

But dead or not, Marlowe was still there, the outrageous exemplar, and there was no avoiding him, even if he wanted to. On some level, conscious or otherwise, Shakespeare set out deliberately to compete with him – and outstrip him if he could. So where Marlowe had written *Edward II*, Shakespeare came up with *Richard II*; against *The Jew of Malta* he offered *The Merchant of Venice*; and to rival *Hero and Leander* he gave them *Venus and Adonis*.

So then why no counter to *Doctor Faustus*? Was it because by now Shakespeare was established, recognised as the leading playwright of the day and there was no longer any need? Possibly. Applause is a great healer. Although it was more likely, Adam thought, that on the deeper level, the one all artists draw upon, the one that really *mattered*, he didn't need the verdict of the public. He *knew* he had measured himself against the other man and equalled if not surpassed him. It was enough. There was no longer any fear of comparison. It was a pivotal moment, a turning point in English drama: when Shakespeare the player became Shakespeare the playwright, once and for all.

All the same, it was fun to imagine Shakespeare's alternative *Doctor Faustus*. What would he have done with it? Answer: a hell of a lot. The whole central third of the play would have been transformed, with none of that silly Pope and Emperor stuff; or, if he'd kept it, it would have been infinitely more than the crude knockabout of Marlowe's play. Did Marlowe actually write that? Was it really what he intended, or was it just a sketch for the actors, a scenario for them to take and improvise upon?

How often did Shakespeare do that? How much did a playwright, particularly one who wrote for a permanent company, depend upon his actors, feed off them, build on their strengths? Answer: a great deal, obviously. Parts were written especially for them, tailored to what they could do best. (Which meant, surely, that the text was certain to be full of private jokes. A book about that would be interesting, wouldn't it? Difficult to write, though. The more private the joke, the harder it would be to recognise. Still, it was an intriguing idea and might be worth spending some time on. *Shakespeare's Shadow Plays.* Yes! File it away for future thought.)

But if you were part of a company there would be drawbacks, too. Minuses to balance the pluses. How could there not be? Personality problems, rivalries, jealousies. Tempers to be soothed, egos massaged. Actors! Sometimes William couldn't stand it any longer. *Let those that play your clowns speak no more than is set down for them.* They'd got up his nose once too often, with their face-pulling and their anything-for-a-laugh improvised gags. The hell with them. He'd had enough. Was that why Will Kempe, the leading comic, left the company? Were there huge rows and a final him-or-me bust-up? He wouldn't be surprised.

Onstage, the ballet sequence was in full flow as Mephistopheles distracted Faust with Cleopatra and Helen of Troy, presented as Second Empire trollops. Clothes were shed; a naked odalisque was carried on lying on an enormous silver tray. *Une grande horizontale.* He was smiling at the image when suddenly beside him Soraya caught her breath and gave a little sniff. She sniffed again. And again. Then she reached into her little evening bag and took out a tissue.

He leaned towards her. "Are you all right?"

She nodded, sniffed and dabbed her eyes. It did no good. By the final scene in the madhouse, when a half-crazed Marguerite, surrounded by slobbering sexual deviants, found redemption and God — *Anges purs! Anges radieux!* — the tears were streaming and she was clutching hotly at his hand. Adam was delighted. God bless you, Charlie Gounod, he thought, clutching hotly back.

 SEVEN

"ADAM, I'M SO *SORRY!* I'm so *ashamed!*"

"Why? There's no need to be."

"There *is*. You must think I'm a total fool!"

"Don't be silly. Of course I don't."

"I couldn't help it. I just *couldn't*. I tried to stop myself. I did every-thing I could think of. I pinched my arm. I even tried biting my tongue. It didn't work. I just couldn't stop crying. Poor Marguerite. It was so beautiful. So *sad*. Oh, rats! What must you be thinking?"

He reached across the table and touched her wrist. His fingertips tin-gled. "I think I'm very lucky," he said.

From where they sat, close to an enormous window, he could see out across the bay, where lights blinked fitfully on the dark water and threaded the low hills of the opposite shore. This must be one of the tallest buildings in the city, he thought. The very tallest? Perhaps it was. There was nothing out there taller, as far as he could tell. They had driven here straight from the opera, stepping from the car onto a carpeted sidewalk that led directly to a private elevator, whose uprush caused his stomach to clench fright-eningly before delivering them to this hushed, candle-lit space, where the Maitre d' conducted you smoothly between the tables and waiters appeared at your elbow before you even thought to look up.

She had excused herself and disappeared to the powder room, returning in less than ten minutes, as composed and lovely as at the beginning of the evening, except perhaps for a slight mistiness in the eyes. Even so, she was without doubt the most beautiful creature in this beautiful room. And she was with him. He lifted his glass and tasted the wine the sommelier had suggested: a Pinot Noir from the Napa Valley, apparently. It was superb. So was the food. Soraya said it was a good example of California cuisine. He thought of the Feast of Benefactors and decided that when it came to scoff, California left Cambridge for dead. He drank some more wine. *The life in banquets,* he thought.

"Pardon me?" She was looking at him inquiringly.

"I'm sorry?"

"You said something."

"Did I?"

"Something about blankets?"

"Did I really? Good Lord, I didn't mean to. It was just something I was thinking. A line from a poem."

"Well?" She waited a moment and made a tiny, lip-pouting face. "Aren't you going to tell me what it is?"

He put down his glass, his wrist loose on the tablecloth, fingers moving gently up and down the crystal stem. "There's a little poem by Sir Thomas Wyatt."

"Was he a friend of Shakespeare's?"

"No, he was earlier. He died more than twenty years before Shakespeare was born. He was a friend of Henry VIII, a courtier and a poet, and probably one of Anne Boleyn's lovers before she married the king."

"Fantastic!" Her eyes were shining.

"Anyway, the poem is called *In Court to Serve*. It's about what it was like being one of Henry's courtiers, the way they lived, what I suppose you'd call their lifestyle. It's very short, only seven lines."

"Can you say it?"

"Well...ah... It starts like this:

In court to serve, decked with fresh array,
Of sugared meats feeling the sweet repast,

And then it has this wonderful line, the one I was thinking about:

The life in banquets and sundry kinds of play."

"The life in banquets! Oh, I like that!"

"Yes, it's good, isn't it? Well…" He picked up his glass. "I guess that's pretty much how I feel at this moment."

"It's a happy poem, then?"

He hesitated. "Well no, not exactly. In fact, it goes on to say that in the end it all turns sour; that life in court is like being in prison, only with golden chains."

"Oh." Her face fell.

"But it was the first bit I was thinking of. The bit that says how fantastic it all is. Because it is. At least, from where I'm sitting."

She laughed. He finished his wine and looked out of the window again. Far below, strings of diamonds and rubies flowed past each other along the waterside that she told him had once been the notorious Barbary Coast.

"What about Enrique?" he said.

She frowned. "What about him?"

"Is he all right?"

"Sure he is." She looked puzzled. "Why shouldn't he be?"

"I feel a bit guilty. I mean, sitting up here having this fabulous meal, while he's stuck down there in the car."

She smiled. "Bless your heart, Adam, there's no reason to feel guilty. Ricky's fine. He's probably in some all-night diner right now, eating tacos with all the other drivers and watching baseball on TV. Don't trouble yourself about Ricky. Ricky does what he's told. Besides…" She gave a little shrug, pouting again. "It's what he's paid for."

The Maitre d' appeared from the shadows and asked if they had enjoyed the meal and was there anything else he could suggest? A little co-
gnac, perhaps? They told him the meal was better than excellent and no,
thank you, they really didn't need anything more. Not even a brandy.
Well, a very small one, maybe.

He lifted the balloon glass to his nose and savoured the pungent, oily
bouquet. He closed his eyes and sipped. Who was it first thought of
brandy after a meal? Give that man a gold star. He felt its slow warmth
unfold inside him. He opened his eyes. She was looking down at the tablecloth, her face half-turned away from him. Her skin glowed in the candlelight. Her mouth was touched with a faint smile. This has to be the
moment, he thought. Go for it, Adam. He put his glass down and leaned
forward. "Tell me about yourself," he said.

"Me?" She blushed slightly.

"I want to know all about you."

She hesitated for a moment. "You first."

He laughed. "That won't take long. It's very simple and very boring.
Born and grew up in Devon. Went to school and then university. Been
there ever since. There. I told you it was boring. Now you."

"Oh, no. You don't get away that easily. What about your parents? What
do they do?"

"My mother was a teacher in what we call primary school. She taught
little children. She died when I was fifteen."

"I'm so sorry. You must miss her."

"Yes, I do. She was lovely."

"Was she sick a long time?"

"Yes, I think so. She must have been. Only, I never knew. They kept it
from me, you see. Which was quite easy because I was at boarding school,
had been since I was eight."

He made a face. "One of the great crimes the English middle-classes
commit is sending their kids away to be educated. It's a terrible thing to
do. It has ruined whole generations of children. The only excuse you can

give their parents – the only thing you can say in their defence, I mean –
is that they genuinely believe they are doing the right thing. It's what mine
believed, I know." He shook his head. "And it still goes on."

"Did you hate school?"

"No, not really. I don't think I ever questioned it. It was what you did.
And because I was one of the clever boys the masters approved of me and
I had quite an easy time."

"What about your father? Is he still alive?"

He smiled. "Very much so. He was a solicitor – what you'd call a
lawyer, but he didn't appear in court or argue cases or anything like that.
He handled wills, probate, family law, that kind of thing. He's retired now,
of course."

"I bet he's proud of you, isn't he?"

"Yes, I suppose he is."

"Do you see him much?"

"Quite a lot. In the vacations, that is, when I'm home. He's getting
on a bit and isn't as active as he was. I was a late child, you see. My parents
were quite elderly when they had me. I think they'd just about given up
and I was a surprise. Abraham and Sarah, you know? Anyway, Dad's getting a bit doddery, a bit forgetful. Sometimes he can be a bit of a pain."

"You're lucky to have him, though."

"Yes, I am." He pushed his glass away and sat back. The brandy had
done its job. He felt *good*. "Your turn."

She was silent for a while; then she gave a little sigh and looked up at
him. *If I could write the beauty of your eyes.*

"My parents were Iranian. You must have figured that out already. My
father was a government official. He wasn't a big shot, not high up or important, nothing like that. He was what you'd call a minor functionary, I
guess, no big deal, nothing to boast about." She broke off, looking down
at the tablecloth again.

He waited, saying nothing. A couple at a nearby table got to their feet.

"He was a good man," Soraya said. "He believed in the Shah and the reforms he was trying to bring about. He hated injustice. He loved his country. He knew what Khomeini meant, and the kind of bigotry and intolerance the ayatollahs would impose. So when the Shah fell, my parents left the country. They were only just in time, I guess. I can't be sure, but I think my father would have been arrested if they hadn't gotten out when they did. My mother was pregnant with me and I was born here in America. It wasn't easy for them. They were very poor."

On the tablecloth in front of her were some scattered breadcrumbs the waiter had missed. She touched them with a long finger, gathering them together, rolling them into line.

"You hear stories of people coming away with fortunes – smuggling diamonds out or with money that's been salted away in Switzerland. Maybe some people did that. Not my parents. They had it tough. My father worked at anything he could get, from bagging groceries in supermarkets to selling shoes in Macy's. He was an insurance salesman once, door-to-door, but he wasn't very good at it. I don't know how they survived. But they did, and eventually he got taken on by one of Mister Blankenship's companies. He worked hard. Mister Blankenship took notice and promoted him. Things got better. I remember one day my mother saying that at last the future was looking good, and how it proved what a wonderful country America was, that would take in people like us and if you worked hard enough would reward you with a good life, because everything is possible here." She shook her head slowly and frowned.

"Then in my last year of high school, just before graduation, my parents were killed in an automobile accident. A truck went out of control on the freeway, you know? And…it was so sudden. So final. I couldn't believe it. I couldn't understand how someone could be here one minute and then – *gone*. I couldn't get my mind around it. And then, when I did, I thought I would die, too. Do you know what I mean, Adam? I thought everything had come to an end. And it would have too, if it hadn't been for Mister Blankenship. He took care of me. He put me through college, and after college he gave me a job. I guess you could say he saved me."

She flicked the line of breadcrumbs, scattering them, and looked up at him, smiling. "And tra-la, here I am."

The room was silent. When finally he looked around, he saw it was empty except for their waiter and the impassive Maitre d'.

"Heavens, look how late it is! Time we were leaving." She pushed back her chair and stood up. "Or Ricky will be getting worried about us."

They didn't speak much on the way back. High up on the bridge, great tendrils of ocean fog were being sucked into the bay, and at one point near the Foundation Enrique swore and braked hard to avoid three deer that had strayed onto the road. At the house, Marisol had set a bottle of wine by the fire in the big room with the piano but they didn't touch it. He told her again how much he had enjoyed the evening. She said it had been one of the best she could remember. They stood and looked at each other. Then his courage failed. He wished her goodnight and went up to his room, scowling at the carved staircase. Bloody fool.

He stood looking at the big bed. Why wasn't he tired? There was no way he could have got through his jet-lag by now. He ought to be on his knees. Or had he gone through exhaustion and was out the other side into another twenty-four-hour cycle? Damn and blast. Maybe a shower would do the trick. It was worth a try, anyway. Anything to avoid another night staring at the ceiling or blinking painfully at some ancient black-and-white movie on TV.

He undressed and stepped into the shower, turning the temperature control as high as he could bear, and stood for a long time under the downrush. It felt good, no question. The trouble was, after he had towelled himself dry he was wider awake than before. The hell with it. He was going to have to get through the night the best way he could. He dropped the towel on the floor and headed back to the bedroom. He stopped in the doorway.

Candles burned on the little tables by the bed, on the dresser and along the low windowsills. There was the smell of shadowed sandalwood. She wore a nightdress of lace and ivory silk, her hair spread across the pillows like a dark, rippling fan. She reached up and caressed him. Her mouth opened softly. Her tongue drew him in. *If it were now to die, 'Twere now to be most happy.*

 EIGHT

YOU GOT A DIFFERENT perspective from down here, a clearer impression of how steeply the hills rose beyond the bustling wharves and crowded ocean terminals. And you realised how high the span of the Golden Gate was, way out there to the right. No wonder it was a favoured spot for jumpers. You wouldn't have much chance if you went off from up there. Plus you got to appreciate the length of the Bay Bridge too, the one out to the left, hinged on an island on the other side of the city, that seemed to go on for miles and carried such a huge volume of traffic. It wasn't as beautiful as the Golden Gate, how could it be? But it was at least as important, maybe more so, Soraya said.

They caught the ferry at Tiburon, almost directly across from the city. It looked a pleasant-enough place, especially if you lived in one of those houses on the cliffs above the marina. How much would one of them cost? A fortune, you could bet. There was a little street edging the water, with cafes and shops and an old movie house, and a Mexican restaurant which she said was worth a visit sometime. He said how about tomorrow? And she laughed and said there wouldn't be time because he would be busy with Mister Blankenship, and he squeezed her hand and said we'll make time.

When he had woken this morning she was gone. And when they met at breakfast she gave no sign of what had happened between them, what they had discovered about each other, what they had whispered during the night. Instead, she was formal, polite, a little distant even, discussing with Marisol the day's schedule, arranging for Enrique to pick them up at the Presidio after lunch, running over the details of Mister Blankenship's arrival that evening and asking to be called on her cell phone the minute they heard what time he was due in. It was only after the ferry had cleared Angel Island and they were well into the bay that she put her arms around him and kissed him and told him how happy she was.

That was when he said she was wonderful and last night was fantastic, he could hardly believe it had happened it was so good. She said he was a great lover. He said it wasn't true but if it was it was because she made him one, and if she'd like to step into that corner out of sight of the other passengers he would be more than happy to prove it. She laughed and said don't tempt me and he kissed her again and said how beautiful she was and how amazing her body was, and when she blushed he reminded her of some of the things they had done and some of the things she had said to him and how incredible they had made him feel.

But some of it had been in another language. Was it Farsi? What did she say? What did it mean? That was when she blushed hotly and said she couldn't possibly tell him, not here in front of everyone, and he said take no notice of any of them, they don't exist, there is only you and me. But she shook her head and turned her face away and it was only after he had kissed her a lot more that she said she would whisper it. Which she did, blushing even more hotly, after which he said *No! — Really?* And she hid her face in his shoulder and said *I promise you it's true.*

After that there was a lot more kissing and whispering, which is why he missed a closer view of Alcatraz, but looking back across the water from the city terminal it didn't seem all that interesting. She said there was a tour with an audio guide if he really wanted to visit it. He said under the circumstances he'd be happy to give it a miss. If he was going to be a tourist he'd much rather do something like ride a cable car, which made her pull a funny face and say oh no, Adam, that is so *corny!* But if he really and truly wanted to they should maybe save the cable car till later and meantime how about taking a look at North Beach?

He had to remind himself to look left before stepping into the road, even though the sign on the traffic lights had turned from red to a little green walking man. The morning rush spewed a rising haze of exhaust fumes, with blaring cars punishing their suspension in the network of cracks and potholes. Strange that a nation so dependent on the automobile should have such lousy roads. They reached the opposite pavement and stopped for a moment. The cross-street ahead fell away sharply. At the far end, a great span of the Bay Bridge filled the void. A sudden breeze rippled the store-front awnings the length of the street.

"It's like the whole city is flying," he said.

She frowned, looking puzzled for a moment, and then she nodded. "It can seem that way sometimes." She turned to look at a shop window. "Do you need any hardware?"

"Hardware?"

"Scissors? A pocket knife? This is a good place."

Inside, it was tiny, more like a kiosk than a proper shop, its narrow walls lined with fitted drawers and crowding stacks of brown cardboard boxes. At its heart, behind a wooden-flap counter, a fat old woman presided over glass-topped display cases full of more kinds of scissors than he imagined existed. She had scissors for everything, from cutting lengths of heavy sailcloth to trimming the hairs in your nose.

"I need something for my nails," Soraya said.

And there were knives of all shapes and for all purposes: tiny penknives to hang on your key ring or massive bright-bladed things so wicked-looking he marvelled they were legal.

"This is cute."

She held it up for him to see. It was no more than three inches long, a kind of miniature tool kit that, when you opened it out, was a pair of pliers, a screwdriver, a file, a hole-puncher, a corkscrew and at least three other things as well as a very sharp knife.

"That's clever," he said.

"It's a present. From me to you." And when he began to protest she put a finger to his lips. "You can thank me later."

In Chinatown the sidewalks were so busy it seemed every ten yards or so they had to step into the gutter or flatten themselves against a wall to let the barging people past. The riot of stores and restaurants with their flaring neon characters and teeth-on-edge Chinese music were bewildering. First it made him stare and then laugh out loud.

"I never realised there was so much of it. It's so big."

She shrugged. "And getting bigger all the time."

He stopped at a sidewalk grocery where baskets were piled high with vegetables and spices, and was bending low to peer at a heap of small, strangely shaped fruit, when he felt her hand pull away from him sharply. He heard an engine racing, then a quick door-slam. He straightened fast, turning to catch a fleeting impression of her shocked face staring back at him through the window as the car pulled away. Then a hand gripped his arm.

"This way, please, Doctor Searle."

Another hand gripped his other arm and he found himself half-led, half-carried into the back of a car with an abruptness that gave him no time to protest. As they accelerated down the street he realised dimly that it had been done so swiftly, so expertly, not one of the Chinese crowding the pavement had noticed anything unusual or out of the way.

The man in the rear-facing seat opposite him was in his seventies or maybe eighties. It wasn't easy to tell. He was thin, neat, birdlike, dressed in a blue business suit with a faint pinstripe. He looked delicate, fragile even. Unlike the two Orientals on each side of Adam, still holding tight to his arms. There was nothing fragile about either of them. Bruisers. Were they all Chinese? Even the driver? There wasn't time to think.

"What the hell's going on?"

"Please do not be alarmed," the little bird-man said.

"Who are you? What do you think you're playing at?"

Even as he said it he realised how pathetic it sounded. Bird-man took a handkerchief from his jacket pocket. "I wanted a few moments to talk with you, and this seemed the simplest way."

"Are you crazy? Let me out of here now!"

"As soon as we have talked, Doctor Searle. I assure you I mean you no harm."

"No? What about these two? Do they mean me no harm?"

The little man said something in a language Adam didn't understand. The bruisers let go his arms.

"Where's Soraya? What have you done to her?" he said.

Bird-man wiped his palms carefully with the handkerchief. "Ms. Kamali is perfectly safe, Doctor Searle. As are you."

The little man smiled. He felt a surge of anger. "Now look here, Mister whatever-your-name-is —"

"My name is Ch'a Min-su. Ch'a... Min... su. Which should tell you that no, I am not Chinese as you may have been wondering. I am Korean."

The man on Adam's left leaned forward, reaching up to take hold of the grab-handle above the door. His unbuttoned jacket fell open and Adam saw there was a gun strapped below the man's shoulder. The car speeded up. Looking out, he saw trees and open spaces. Where were all the buildings? Was it a playground? A public park? Or had they left the city already?

"Where are we going?" he said.

Mister Ch'a dabbed his palms. "We are driving, that is all. When our conversation is finished you will be taken back to the Foundation where you will rejoin Ms. Kamali." He began to fold the handkerchief. "I do apologise, most sincerely, that we should have to meet this way, but I understand Willard Blankenship is due to return very soon and I am anxious we should talk before he is back." He folded the handkerchief one more time, put it back in his pocket, smoothed the flap carefully, patted it and smiled. "It is about the manuscript, of course."

"The manuscript?"

"Why do you look surprised, Doctor Searle? What else could it be about? Do you think I am trying to deceive you? Believe me, I have no wish to. All I require is that we should understand each other. And you should know precisely where you stand."

There was another man in the front, sitting next to the driver. Thick necks, big shoulders. That made four bruisers – all with guns? – and one bird-man. Koreans. Adam felt very lonely.

"I'm listening," he said.

"Thank you." Mister Ch'a smiled again. "Now: the manuscript. I take it you have not seen it yet? I thought not. When you do, I think you will be impressed. Excited, even. As a scholar, I mean. That is wholly understandable. Mister Blankenship is a man of great persuasion. He will tell you many things. Most of them will be fascinating. Some of them may even be true."

"Look, Mister Ch'a, I don't know what any of this is about, but I've got a pretty good idea that grabbing people off the street is illegal. So if I were you —"

Mister Ch'a lifted a twig-like hand. There was a yellow band round his wrist. Not gold. Copper, maybe? A protection against rheumatism? A lucky charm? "Let us get to the point, Doctor Searle. Mister Blankenship has asked you to examine and possibly authenticate a Shakespeare manuscript, is that not so? Well, it is my duty to tell you that Mister Blankenship has no right to do this."

"How do you figure that?"

"Because the manuscript does not belong to him. He obtained it fraudulently and by force. In other words, he stole it."

"How do you know?"

"I was the person he stole it from." Mister Ch'a put his hands on his knees and leaned forward. His breath smelled faintly of peppermint. "Let me be clear: The manuscript does not belong to Mister Blankenship, Doctor Searle. It belongs to me."

The car slowed and he saw they were driving beside what seemed to be a cliff top with the ocean on their right. Ahead was a low, classical-looking building with a row of columns along the front and a Greek-style pediment. They followed the semi-circular drive past the entrance and picked up speed again, driving back the way they had come.

"If that's true, why not go to the police? Tell them what you've just told me and let them sort it out."

Mister Ch'a smiled sadly. "Doctor Searle, you are a scholar and an Englishman. The law in this country operates differently. Or at least, those who administer it do."

He stared at the fragile-looking little man, feeling the pressure build inside him. What a little creep! Who the bloody hell did he think he was?

"So that's it, is it?" he said. "The manuscript belongs to you and not

Willard Blankenship? That's what you wanted to tell me? Well, fine. You've told me. Is it over? Are we done?"

The two men beside him stirred. Mister Ch'a said something and they sat back in their seats. Mister Ch'a looked at Adam and smiled politely.

"Yes, Doctor Searle, we are done. Unless you have any questions for me? If so, I shall do my best to satisfy you."

"Yes, I have. What have you done with Soraya?"

"The lovely Ms. Kamali?" Mister Ch'a looked down at his left wrist. "By now she will be back at the Foundation and waiting anxiously for your return."

"I hope for your sake that's true."

Mister Ch'a smiled again. Adam wanted to hit him. "I see she has made a deep impression on you, Doctor Searle. That is hardly surprising. She is a beautiful woman. Did she tell you much about her background?"

"Some."

"About her parents and how they came to leave Iran?"

"She told me her father was a minor government official who got out when the Shah was deposed."

"She made no mention of Savak?"

He stared. "Savak?"

"The Shah's secret police. She didn't? That does not surprise me. It is not something a young girl would be likely to boast about."

"I don't know what the hell you're talking about," Adam said.

Mister Ch'a nodded sympathetically. "Her father was called Hamid Kamali. He was a Colonel in Savak. It is said, correctly, he was trained by the CIA. He was one of the most ruthless – no, that is incorrect." Mr Ch'a frowned. "Hamid Kamali was the most ruthless, the most cruel and most feared of all the Shah's secret policemen. It is not known how many deaths he was responsible for, but if there was one man who symbolised everything that was evil about the regime it was Hamid Kamali. To this day there are people who spit at his name. Others curse. I see you do not believe me, Doctor Searle. Well, you do not have to take my word for it.

What I have told you will not be difficult to verify."

There was silence inside the car. He was vaguely aware of buildings outside the windows. They were in the city again.

"Even if that's true, she may not know it. Parents hide things from their children. And anyway, she wasn't born till after they left Iran."

Mister Ch'a sighed. "That is very fair and very English of you. I congratulate you, Doctor Searle."

The man next to the driver turned round and said something in Korean. Mister Ch'a nodded and sat back. The man said something to the driver. The car slowed. Mister Ch'a buttoned his jacket.

"Now I will take my leave. These men will see to your safe return. Once again, I apologise most sincerely for the manner of our meeting. It was not the way I would have preferred, but circumstances gave me no other choice. Even so, I hope you will believe me when I say it has been a privilege. I have not yet been able to read your book, but I saw a most excellent review recently in the *Times Literary Supplement* and I am greatly looking forward to it. I trust next time we meet it will be under much more agreeable circumstances."

The car stopped. The man on Adam's right got out and held the door open. Mister Ch'a got out, the man slid back into his seat and the car moved forward. Adam turned to look out of the rear window, catching a brief glimpse of the trim little figure before it disappeared in the bustling crowd.

She came running down the pathway between the little tubs of trees. "My God, Adam, are you all right? We've been so scared!" She threw her arms around him and hugged him tightly.

He could feel her heart. Behind him, the big limousine drew up. Enrique got out quickly and opened the rear door.

She pulled him towards the car. "You can tell me on the way to the airport."

"Airport?" He stared. "I don't understand."

"When I called Mister Blankenship and told him what happened he said to leave immediately."

"We're leaving? Where to?"

Enrique got into the front seat. The car started forward. She squeezed his hand. "Don't worry, darling. Everything's taken care of. We're going to Montana. You'll meet with Mister Blankenship there."

 NINE

MONTANA WAS DEAD FLAT. At least, that's what it looked like when they came down through the clouds and he was able to see the ground. The farm land immediately below was scored with ruler-straight roads that all seemed to intersect at ninety degrees. Boring. They flew lower and the port wing dropped as they circled, preparing to land. The airport, at a place called Kalispell, looked dead flat and boring, too. Then, as the plane levelled out, he saw the great jagged walls that loomed in the near distance, realised his mistake and understood at once how Montana got its name.

Neither of them had talked much during the flight and there had been very little to see. Once they had taken off from San Francisco it had been clouds all the way during the three-and-something hours' flight and So-raya had been asleep most of the time. Or that's what it looked like, with her seat almost horizontal, lying still with her eyes closed, taking a single deep, sighing breath from time to time. Maybe she was in shock. Or maybe it was Enrique, sitting silently behind them in the space near the galley. Did his presence inhibit her? Surely not. Or was she was taking her cue from him, Adam? He had said very little after they left the Foundation. When she asked what happened, he told her about Ch'a Min-su and his Koreans and said it had to do with the manuscript. He left out the bit about who owned it and said nothing at all about Colonel Hamid

Kamali, the butcher of Savak.

Once they were on the ground and inside the little terminal, Enrique disappeared to collect their bags and find the transport he said was nearby. As they stood waiting, he put his arm around her and said cheer up, darling, it's not as bad as all that. She smiled wanly and said she would feel better once they were there. He asked how much longer it was going to be and she said hopefully not more than three or four hours. She excused herself and went to the ladies' room, and he spent the next fifteen minutes staring at a brightly coloured tourist map on the terminal wall.

It was dotted with little pictures of bears and deer, mountain sheep and eagles and leaping, red-throated trout. He found Kalispell, high up and to the left; not far, it seemed, from the border with Canada. According to the map, the country around was mainly forest and mountains with hardly any towns. But that seemed to be true of most of Montana. To the north east was a great stretch marked *Wilderness*. He wondered vaguely what it was like. Above the map was a clock that made him adjust his watch again because apparently they were now on Mountain Time, which was one hour ahead. It was all slightly confusing and he was relieved when Enrique returned to say everything was ready and let's get the fuck out of here, boss.

Outside on the tarmac was an enormous black four-by-four Cruiser. He handed Soraya into the rear seat and went around the back to climb in beside her. Enrique took the wheel, the engine gave a belching diesel-throb and they were off, wheeling past the signs to Departures and Car Parks and finally out onto the featureless highway. It was only when they had passed through the nothing-looking little town and were heading north along one of the ruler-straight roads that Soraya took his hand and gave him a brief smile.

"I'm sorry. I'll be okay once we've arrived."

"Me, too." He took a deep breath and let it out slowly. "What a day."

She looked out of the window where, at the end of an unpaved track, a steep-roofed farmhouse was flanked by a couple of red barns. "It's just,

I feel so responsible."

"Nonsense." He leaned across and kissed her cheek. "Relax. And stop fussing. I'm quite capable of looking after myself."

Was that a look of doubt in her eyes? If so, it passed quickly because she gave him a little nod, squeezed his hand and settled back in her seat. He looked at his watch. Three more hours. Did that mean it would be dark by the time they got there? He slumped against the padded leather. Jesus. Why was this bloody country so bloody *big*?

Half an hour after leaving town, they came to a rushing, dirty-green river with a railroad track running beside it. They followed it for several miles before turning sharp right onto a minor road with a rutted surface that caused Enrique to swear and slow down. Fifteen minutes later they arrived at a village – no, not a village, it wasn't big enough; more a hamlet, really: a clutch of stained wooden houses on each side of the road, with rusting trucks parked out front and a group of kids standing around another kid straddling a motorbike. They looked up as the big car went past: stained t-shirts, dirty baseball caps, flat faces, dead eyes.

"They don't look very friendly," Adam said.

Enrique snorted. "Fucking no-good rednecks."

Then they were past the splintered houses and suddenly the road ended. Clouds of dust rose behind the rear window, stones leaped and spat, as they followed what was now a dirt track with a great stand of trees immediately ahead. The mountains looked much closer now. Were they heading directly towards them? The track narrowed and before he knew it they were into the forest, trees on all sides, with an occasional break that showed the great peaks looming ahead.

"Is this the Wilderness?"

Enrique snorted again. "Not yet."

The track grew narrower and Enrique drove more slowly. Even so, Adam felt the big car slide on some of the bends as they lost traction on the loose dirt.

"I wouldn't fancy driving along here in the dark. Or at anytime, come to that."

Enrique didn't bother to reply.

It was nearly two hours later when they came to the river. It happened suddenly, without warning, a shock. One minute they were driving through thick forest, the next moment the trees on their right ended, the ground dropped away — and there it was below them: a great ribbon of water, copper-coloured in the setting sun. He sat up quickly and reached for the door-handle. "Stop the car. I have to see this."

He stood on the edge of the bluff, staring out. Far below, deep and slow-moving, the great river unwound. Was it a hundred yards wide? Two hundred? It must be, surely, if not more. Great whirls and eddies marked the passage it had gouged through the valley; massive boulders stood clear of its surface, creating runs of tumbling white water whose rushing sound he could make out even from up here; and wherever he looked, he saw the widening circles of rising fish. Trees grew down to the water's edge, with the occasional little beach of gravel or bright sand. Beyond, above the tree-line, the mountains stood halfway up the sky, their red-gold peaks shading to indigo in the evening light. A solitary bird rose from a tree-top close to the water. An osprey? If so, it was the first he had ever seen. He held his breath, watching it climb.

Soraya came to stand beside him. "It's called the Flathead River," she said. "The north fork."

He didn't say anything. She took his hand and they stood for five more silent minutes. He would have stayed longer but Enrique tapped the horn a couple of times so they climbed back into the Cruiser, Enrique switched on the headlights against the gathering dusk and they set off again. Not long after, there was a wooden sign at the side of the track and a cluster of huts off to the right among the trees.

"A fishing lodge," Soraya said. "Sportsmen come here from all over."

"I can see why," Adam said.

A little later there was another sign and a single hut close to the track.

"The ranger station. Last outpost of civilisation. And last place it's possible to make a phone call from."

"What about mobiles – cell phones?"

She shook her head. "They're no good up here in the mountains. They don't work. No reception."

"How did you manage to talk to Mister Blankenship?"

"He called the Foundation when he got to the airport, as he always does, to let us know when he was due to arrive. Otherwise we'd have surely missed him."

The Cruiser jolted. The ranger station disappeared into the dark trees behind them. "So it's pretty isolated," he said.

Enrique laughed. "You can say that again."

Soraya frowned. "Mister Blankenship values his privacy. He prefers it that way."

Not long after, the dirt track gave out and they were driving through what looked like virgin forest. It seemed endless. He felt defeated just looking at it. And totally exhausted. His head throbbed, his back ached. Weren't they ever going to arrive? Then, at last, there were lights up ahead, Enrique sounded the horn and the big car slowed and stopped.

"We're here," Soraya said.

He got down stiffly and stretched. Three or four cabins were set under the trees, with the dark outline of another Cruiser parked by one of them. There were lights in the windows and he smelled woodsmoke. The door of the nearest cabin opened and a man stood framed in the sudden spill of light. He came quickly across the ground, smiling widely, hand held out.

"Adam! Great to see you!" He took Adam's hand and shook it firmly. "Willard Blankenship."

Prospero, Adam thought.

"How do you like the stew, Adam?"

They were at the table in the first little cabin, snug in the light of kerosene lamps and the wood-burning stove in the corner.

"Delicious," he said.

"Glad to hear it. Made it myself. Had to. Let the help go yesterday and been on my own here since I got back from the airport." Willard Blankenship grinned across at Soraya, showing wide-spaced teeth. "Good thing you brought Ricky along."

She got up and collected the dishes together, stacked them and went to the door.

"Don't be too long now," Willard Blankenship said.

"I won't."

The door closed behind her. There was a dull sound from the corner as a log stirred and fell inside the wood-burning stove. Willard Blankenship got up and went to it, hooked the front open and tossed in another log.

He was a tall man, six-foot-two or three, Adam guessed, with a long skull and yellow, slab-like teeth. His hair was dark brown shot with grey and cropped close around his ears which were remarkable, with long, pendulous lobes. His beard was darker, with tufted white patches at the corners of his mouth. His eyes were slate-colour and there were deep lines across his forehead and down into his beard. He must be in his late sixties, Adam thought. Or early seventies maybe. He wore a heavy dark

tan woollen coat, full-length and belted loosely over an unbleached cotton
shirt and matching cotton trousers. There were sandals on his feet and a
necklace of coloured stones on a leather thong around his throat.

Did he always dress like that, Adam wondered, or was it his Montana
costume, worn only when he was in residence here? It didn't matter. On
someone else it might well have looked ridiculous. Not on this man. There
was something Old Testament about Willard Blankenship. Something pa-
triarchal. It wasn't hard to imagine him on Shakespeare's island with his
staff and magic book.

He closed the stove and came back to the table. "You want another beer?"

"No, thank you."

He opened a small box and held it out. "Smoke?"

"No, thank you."

Willard Blankenship frowned. "These are damn fine cigars."

"I'm sure they are, but I don't smoke."

The tall man shrugged. He took a cigar and bit the end off, spat it towards the stove and struck a match. He held the cigar an inch above the
flame, rolling it slowly between long, stained fingers; then he put the
cigar between his lips and drew on it. He shook out the match. His chair
creaked as he sat back exhaling, long legs extended, watching the smoke
drift to the ceiling.

"Well, now. I guess it's time we talked," he said.

Adam didn't say anything. Moments passed. Willard Blankenship sat
up. The chair creaked again as he leaned forward. "They tell me you ran
into Jimmy Ch'a."

"This morning." Was it really only then? It seemed a week ago. "I was
in San Francisco with Soraya — Ms. Kamali. We were in Chinatown. He
— or rather, some men with him — pushed me into a car and drove me
around the city."

"Were you scared?"

"It happened so quickly I was more startled than scared. He said he
wanted to talk."

"About the manuscript?"

"Yes."

"Said it belonged to him, did he?"

"Yes."

Willard Blankenship chuckled. "Gotta hand it to the little bastard. He never gives up."

He lifted the can and poured beer into his glass. The pale liquid seethed and settled, tiny strings of bubbles rising to the surface. He drew deeply on the cigar. "Jimmy Ch'a and me go way back. So what I'm going to give you, Adam, is the edited version. If I tell you the whole story we'll be here the rest of the month." He chuckled again and drank.

"To start with, we were partners. This is years ago, before you were born. Jimmy was one of the first Koreans to go international – I'm talking about after the Korean War, in Syngman Rhee's time, when the rebuilding had begun and South Korea suddenly had a future. I was out there with the military. I wasn't much more than a kid, still wet behind the ears, I guess; but I could see pretty damn well what was going to happen and I wanted a piece of it. As big a piece as I could get. So I got in touch – doesn't matter how – with some local ... let's call them businessmen." Willard Blankenship looked over his cigar and winked.

"A few of them – young ones – saw there were possibilities opening up – big possibilities – and Jimmy Ch'a was one of them. He was sharp in those days. Truth is, he was damn good. I had a stake in one or two things – things of interest – in that part of the world and was looking for a partner. Someone who knew the territory and could open a few doors for me. Someone who knew who counted and who didn't; who to bribe and how much to bribe them with. And don't pull that face, son. That's how business was done out there in those days. Still is, for that matter. And not just out there." Willard Blankenship showed his teeth and grinned.

"For a few years it worked fine. We were a good team and made some money. A hell of a lot of money, tell you the truth. If you knew what you were doing, the stuff was there for the taking, and I don't mind admitting we took our share. I tell you, Adam, it got so it felt like we could take on the world." Willard Blankenship frowned. "Then Jimmy got greedy and the next thing you knew the whole damn thing had fallen apart."

He lifted the glass, drained it and put it aside. He leaned forward, one elbow on the table, fat cigar slanted between two fingers. "If you listen to Jimmy, he'll tell you the exact same thing. Except, in his version it'll be me who got greedy and screwed everything up. Well, you know something? I'm not going to argue. What's the use? In fact, I'll even go so far as to say he could be right. A little bit. That's right, son. I'm prepared to admit there was some wrong on my side, too. Let's be generous and say fifty-fifty. Each as bad as the other. How does that sound to you?"

It was clearly a rhetorical question. Willard Blankenship was not expecting a reply. Adam sat waiting while the tall man reached out to tap his cigar against the lip of his beer glass. A grey cylinder of ash fell to the bottom, hissed briefly and broke apart. Willard Blankenship shook his head.

"Since that time it's been war. Every chance Jimmy Ch'a's had to cross me, do me down, he's taken it. That little bastard's fought me fair and he's fought me dirty. And you know something?" The bearded mouth split open in the widest of grins. "I've fought him back. Given as good as I've got and then some, you bet your ass." Willard Blankenship chuckled. "Way things are at the moment, I'd say I'm four lengths clear in the home-stretch and going away."

The door opened. Willard Blankenship beamed. "Come on in, honey," he said. "I've just been briefing our friend here about Jimmy Ch'a. Bringing him up to speed, you might say."

She nodded and sat down at the table. She was breathing quickly, as if she had been hurrying, and her face was flushed. *Beauty's ensign yet Is crimson in thy lips and in thy cheeks.*

"So now it's the manuscript," Willard Blankenship said. "The latest round in our war. Jimmy says it's his and I stole it, right?" Adam nodded. "Did he tell you how he got it?"

"So he did have it at one time?"

Willard Blankenship frowned. "For a little while only," he said. "A month or two. Not long. And I'm not going to pretend I didn't cut a few corners to get it away from him." He leaned forward and thumped the table. "But I had every right, goddammit! Jimmy Ch'a's not interested in Shakespeare. He doesn't give a damn about the manuscript except as something to beat me with. He isn't like us, Adam. He doesn't lose sleep at the thought of it. His heart doesn't beat faster at the sight of it. He doesn't want to see it preserved and published for scholars to study and everyone to learn from. He has no idea of its worth. He thinks its value is just a matter of dollars and cents. Men like that don't deserve to own it because they can never appreciate it, never know what it truly is. I'm right, aren't I, Adam? You know damn well I am."

Adam stared. This man could be insane.

Willard Blankenship got up and went to the far side of the cabin, outside the circle of lamp light. There was the creak of timber as he slid back a small section of the wall. He reached into the cavity inside, picked something up, came back and placed it on the table between them.

"There's the proof."

 TEN

IT WAS A SMALL metal case, the kind businessmen sometimes carry; silver-coloured, about eighteen inches by twelve and no more than six or seven inches deep, with two combination locks. Willard Blankenship rapped the shell with his knuckles.

"Titanium. Had it made specially."

He turned the combination wheels. There seemed to be eight of them, four to each lock. He grunted, snapped the locks open, lifted the lid and spun the case towards Adam.

"Take a look."

Adam leaned forward. Why was he finding it hard to breathe? Why was his hand shaking? He rubbed the back of his neck. For God's sake man, relax! You're a scholar. Act like one!

The inside of the case was blocked with green baize. There was a rectangular recess in the centre, filled with sheets of yellowed vellum. The top sheet was familiar. A single line in Tudor secretary hand said:

The Booke of Loues Labors Wonne

Lower down the page was a series of dark splotches and there was a tear in the bottom right-hand corner.

Willard Blankenship settled into his chair. The cigar tip glowed. "Go ahead, son. It's on the house."

Adam lifted out the sheets and placed them gently on the table in front of him. How many were there? Thirty-five? Forty? He couldn't tell. Anyway, now wasn't the time to start counting. He turned them slowly, at random. Words leaped out at him. Characters' names: *Queene, Rosaline... Wench... Clowne.* And was that *Don Armado?* Yes, it was! The fantastical Spaniard! *Enter yn hys shyrtte,* according to the note in the left-hand margin. That made sense. There was a joke about him losing his shirt at the end of *Love's Labour's Lost,* wasn't there? This could be the follow-up.

Somewhere near the middle, a page had been torn right across and stuck back together (fairly recently from the look of it) with discoloured Scotch tape. A botched job but it could be repaired. Some pages were heavily underlined; others were almost completely crossed out. By the playwright as he wrote? By the book-keeper in rehearsal? If so, when? Was that a list of props? And were those actors' names in the left-hand margin?

His head swam.

He turned to the end. Was the last scene a wedding? It looked like it. *King and Queene, Ber and Ros, Dum and Kath, Long and Mar. Hymen above attended with Musique.* A dance. A song. Was this Shakespeare's first use of the courtly masque? In which case, was it written for private performance? For a nobleman's wedding? Whose? Questions fought for space, multiplying, tumbling, crowding his mind. Suddenly he felt very tired.

"Well, sir? What do you think?"

He sat back and looked at the tall man. Prospero with a Havana cigar.

Adam took a deep breath. "I think I need time to study it. Quite a long time, I'd say."

Willard Blankenship nodded. "You'll get all the time you need. That's a promise."

"And I want to start as soon as possible."

Willard Blankenship grinned. "That, too." He reached forward and took the papers, put them into the silver case and closed the lid. "Anything else on your mind?"

"There is one thing."

The locks snapped shut; the little wheels turned; the silver case was placed to one side. "Shoot," Willard Blankenship said.

"How did you come by it in the first place?"

"You want to know its history?" Willard Blankenship nodded, leaned across and patted Soraya on the shoulder, his fingers lingering for a moment, brushing the down on her neck. "Honey, why don't we all have a proper drink?"

She got up and went to a shelf in the far corner opposite the wood stove, returning with a bottle and three small glasses. Willard Blankenship thumbed the cork from the bottle.

"You like bourbon, Adam?"

"I've never tried it."

The tall man grinned. "Now's your chance."

He filled the glasses and pushed one across the table. Adam picked it up. "Down the hatch," Prospero said.

It tasted good. Not as smooth as a single malt, perhaps, and without the peaty flavour of a fine scotch. But it had a charge to it. He felt gentle fire at the base of his throat and suppressed a rising cough.

"What's the verdict?"

"It's good. Very good." He put the glass down on the table. "But you were going to tell me about the manuscript."

"I'll tell you as much as I know." Willard Blankenship lifted the bottle to re-fill the glasses.

"The first time I heard of it was over a year ago. Nearly two years, in point of fact. A friend of mine in San Francisco — a dealer, antiquarian — got in touch with me one weekend. He knew of course about the Foundation, about my purchase of the First Folio. He'd acted for me in several other transactions — material I'd bought for the Foundation archive — and figured I'd be interested in a sixteenth-century manuscript, even though it was most likely a fake. I said let's find out some more about it. It could be interesting, who knows? Turned out I was right." The tall man showed his yellow teeth, reached out and lifted his glass.

"At the time, it was in the possession of an antique dealer in Sonoma. I'll tell you later how it got there. Seems it was part of a whole bundle of papers, most of it trash. And the guy was a complete amateur. One of those panty-waists who rents a little store, puts a few sticks of furniture in the window and calls himself an expert. Asshole. He had no idea what it was." He frowned and put the glass down. "But I'm getting ahead of myself. You want the history. To begin at the beginning, right?

"Well, I guess the first thing you want to know is who it first belonged to. After it left the playhouse, that is. Sorry, I can't tell you because I don't know his name. But I think I can tell you what his profession was and how it got here. To the USA, I mean." Willard Blankenship drained his glass, lifted the bottle and refilled it. "He was a ship's captain, and it came in his sea-chest, maybe with some other plays he carried for the amusement of his crew."

"Like William Keeling."

"Exactly!"

"Who is William Keeling?" Soraya said.

Prospero laughed. "Tell her."

Adam turned to her. Her cheeks were still flushed. (He was wrong. She hadn't been hurrying; it was excitement that made her catch her breath.) "William Keeling was the captain of a ship called the *Dragon*. In 1607 he was on a trading voyage for the East India Company in convoy with two other Company ships. In September that year, after a storm, they were becalmed off the coast of West Africa near Sierra Leone, and he wrote in the ship's log that he ordered his men to act *The Tragedy of Hamlet*."

"He did? That's *amazing!*"

"It seems to have been a success, because a few weeks later he invited the captain of one of the other ships aboard to see a repeat performance. Apparently, they did *Richard the Second* as well."

"Oh wow, that's fantastic! The guy must have been a real fan!"

"Possibly, but he didn't do it just because he liked plays. According to what Keeling wrote in the log, it was *to keep my people from idleness and unlawful games, or sleep.*"

"Smart guy." Her eyes shone. "But don't you just *love* the idea? Acting *Hamlet* on a ship, near Africa? It's so cool! How well do you think they did it? Were they any good?"

"We can only guess. And we don't know how close they were to the original script. They were just sailors, ordinary seamen, don't forget. Most of them couldn't read."

"I figure Keeling told them the story and they acted their version of it," Willard Blankenship said.

"It's a possibility." Adam nodded. "But more likely, one or two of the officers, who certainly could read, played the leading parts and taught the others. Maybe they had some gentlemen adventurers aboard and they were in it, too. However you look at it, my feeling is there's a good chance that what they did was pretty faithful to the text."

"Where did they act it? In the captain's cabin?" Soraya said.

"There wouldn't have been enough space. No, I think they performed it on the after-deck, which would have served very well as a stage. Think of the stern of an Elizabethan galleon and imagine yourself sitting facing it. You've got one or two doors at deck level, and steps each side going up to the poop-deck above, which is like a gallery with a rail across the front. It's not a million miles from what you'd see in the playhouse. And if you wanted some kind of basic scenery it would be easy to paint some canvas and hang it across the back."

"Incredible! *I love it!*"

"The point is," Willard Blankenship said, "it proves playscripts were used at sea. Think about it. Keeling could have taken other plays as well as *Hamlet* and *Richard the Second*. In fact, it's almost certain he did. They had a practical use, after all. And if one captain did it, why not others?"

"We can't prove that. All we can say is it's a possibility."

"Which Keeling's evidence supports," Willard Blankenship said.

Adam thought for a moment. "Assuming you're right, how do you think he got hold of the manuscript? Our captain, I mean?"

"Not possible to know for sure. Someone in the company – the book-keeper, maybe? – needed cash, so he stole it. Or a printer had it and our man got it from him. My guess is different, though. And a hell of a lot better." He leaned across the table, bringing his long face close. Adam smelt the bourbon on his breath.

"It's sometime in 1598-99. We know *Love's Labour's Won* has been writ-ten and performed. Francis Meres has told us that. The players need money. As much as they can raise. So for once they're prepared to break one of their most important rules and sell a playscript. Not because some sonofabitch printer has pirated it and there's no longer any point in hang-ing onto it. Or because the play was a flop and no one wants to see it – but because *they need money*. Why, Adam? It's 1598-99, remember. Why do the players need a whole heap of dough?"

Adam stared. The idea was so amazing it just might be true. "Because they are leaving the Theatre in Shoreditch. They are crossing the river to Southwark…to build the Globe."

"Right!" Willard Blankenship brought his fist down hard on the table. "Which also explains why the play doesn't appear in the First Folio. They had sold it. It wasn't theirs anymore."

For a long time the cabin was silent. Outside, a bird called. An owl? Or was there another bird of prey that hunted in the night? He didn't think so.

"You mentioned a sea-chest," Adam said.

"That's how the manuscript came to the U.S., sometime early in the eighteenth century, long after our captain was dead." A match flared to re-light the cigar. Willard Blankenship turned to Soraya. "Sea chests were important. They carried a sailor's possessions, just about everything he owned. Very often they were beautifully made. Works of art. A good ex-ample, if you can find one, will cost you several thousand dollars. Any-thing a man had that was valuable would be kept in his sea-chest, which is why a lot of them had a secret compartment or a false bottom. In fact, most of them did. It was common. And I believe that's where our guy kept the play: in his sea chest with a whole lot of other stuff.

"Then he died and the chest stayed at home and the play was forgotten; and after a while the chest was passed on or sold to some other seaman who didn't know where the secret compartment was or how it was operated. Maybe it had several owners and went around the world. Maybe it stayed with the one family and they brought it with them when they emigrated, who knows? But in 1836 it was in New England, in a place called Duxbury, Massachusetts, up the coast from Cape Cod. Used to be pretty important back in the old whaling days. It was owned by the local schoolteacher, whose name was Enoch Perkins. My guess is he inherited it or maybe bought it from a sailor; it doesn't matter which. Then, in the Civil War, Perkins – or his eldest son, who was also called Enoch – enlisted in one of the Massachusetts regiments and took the chest with him when he went with McClellan on the Peninsula Campaign, where he was killed at Gaines Mill in June of 1862. We know that because Army records show the chest and his other personal effects were eventually shipped home to Duxbury in early '63.

"And that's where it stayed for the next thirty-forty years, according to the provenance of the guy in Sonoma. How it got to the West Coast, God alone knows. Maybe by wagon train or railroad; more likely on another ship, and came ashore at San Francisco, where it kicked around for a few years, probably stuck away in someone's barn or attic, until at last – hey! – they realise it's a beautiful bit of work that'll make a fine piece of furniture. Which is where the panty-waist from Sonoma eventually comes in. Who was an asshole, I'm happy to say." The cigar was a damp stub between his fingers. He tossed it in the direction of the wood stove.

"He found the secret compartment by accident, when the chest was in his workshop being renovated. So far as he could tell, what it contained was just a bunch of old papers. They didn't interest him. All he cared about was how much he was going to get for the chest. So he let it be known on the circuit what he'd found, and pretty soon word got to my friend in San Francisco. The antiquarian. Who contacted me."

"And Ch'a min-su? Where does he come in?" Adam said.

Willard Blankenship frowned. "Ah, yes. Jimmy Ch'a." He reached up to finger the coloured stones at his neck. "Here's what happened. My friend in San Francisco? — well, it turned out he wasn't as much of a friend as I thought he was, because as well as contacting me he got in touch with Jimmy Ch'a. And Jimmy being Jimmy made him one hell of an offer, sight unseen. Which my former friend accepted. Don't mind telling you I was pretty mad when I heard."

"What did you do?"

"I took…certain steps," Willard Blankenship said. "What they were doesn't matter. Unless you really need to know. Do you?"

Adam looked into the slate-coloured eyes. "I don't think so," he said.

Willard Blankenship nodded. "That's why the little bastard claims the manuscript is his and I stole it from him. Which technically, I grant you, may contain a grain or two of truth. But who gives a damn about technicalities? The thing is mine, bought and paid for, and that's all that counts."

"The antiquarian?"

The slate eyes fixed him again. "No longer in business."

There was silence in the little rom. Soraya picked up her glass. The first sip she had taken all evening, Adam thought.

"What happened to the sea chest?" she said.

"The fruit in Sonoma sold it. Damn fool didn't even get a good price for it. Else I'd have been delighted to give it to you, sweetheart." Willard Blankenship shrugged. "An asshole, like I said."

Adam's eyes blurred. He tried to focus but they blurred again. He grasped the edge of the table and pulled himself to his feet. "Sorry, but I'm exhausted. If I don't get some sleep I'll pass out."

Willard Blankenship laughed and pushed back his chair. He touched Soraya lightly on the arm. "Show him his bed, honey," he said.

It had a bright patchwork quilt and a king-sized mattress, and for a moment he wondered if she was going to stay. But she gave him a quick kiss, said she knew he'd understand, darling, but she had to get back to Mister Blankenship, and was gone. He felt slightly relieved. He really was exhausted. He splashed his face in the little bathroom at the back of the cabin and climbed out of his clothes. There was a wood stove in the corner with logs and kindling but he didn't try to light it. There was no need. The night was warm and he found he was sweating. Because the other cabin had been too hot? Or was it from excitement? He was too tired to think. He pulled back the quilt, climbed into the big bed and fell asleep.

It was still dark when she woke him. She was in a flame-coloured nightdress and for a confused moment he thought she had come to share the bed with him. But then he saw the fear in her face and heard the terror in her voice and at once he came awake. He pulled on his clothes and stumbled after her through the black trees to the main cabin where Enrique was standing by the open door.

The room where they had been sitting only a couple of hours before was in chaos. Splintered chairs lay on their sides, the table was upended, the shelves in the corner had been ripped from the wall and their books scattered across the floor. Even the wood-pile by the stove had been turned over, the logs tossed around as if by some frantically burrowing creature.

The door at the far end stood open. Inside, Willard Blankenship lay across the bed, one arm stretched out in the lamp light, pointing into the shadows. He was naked, his face half-covered by the pillow. His neck was circled with a string of bright colour, not pebbles but blood, stiffening the sheet where his throat had been cut.

No rough magic could help him. Prospero was dead.

ELEVEN

"I DON'T KNOW WHAT it was! A noise? I don't know. *Something!* But it woke me. I got up and saw his cabin door was open. And there was a light inside. That's not like him. He never... So I came over and I looked in. And saw everything was broken. And this door was open, too. So I came in. And I saw... I *saw*..."

She began to gasp for breath, hyperventilating. He put his arms around her and held her.

"It's all right. You're safe now. Listen to me, Soraya, do you hear me? You're *safe*."

She nodded, still trembling but breathing more easily. After a moment, he let her go.

"So I went to fetch Ricky. Then you."

"Did you see anybody?"

"No one! But the cabin door was open and there was a light inside the bedroom, which is why I came over."

"What about you?" he said to Enrique. "Did you see anyone?"

Enrique shook his head. "I sleep good."

"What are we going to do?" Soraya began to cry.

"Call the authorities – the police – whoever it is we're supposed to notify. From that ranger station. We can phone from there, can't we? Someone will have to go. How far is it?"

Enrique looked towards the open cabin door behind them. "What if the guy's still out there?"

They stared at each other. Enrique was in his nightwear, Adam realised: the thin khaki singlet and scarlet underpants. His chest and shoulders were thick with matted black hair and he was barefoot. They all were. He looked at the dead man, at the soaked sheet, at the arc of bloodstains on the wooden-plank floor. And suddenly it hit him. "*The manuscript!*"

They went into the main room. The wall on the far side looked undisturbed, solid. Adam pushed at it. Nothing happened.

"I can do it," Enrique said.

He reached down, leaned his weight against the wall and pushed. There was a creak. Enrique grunted and pushed harder. There was a low, scraping sound and a section of the woodwork slid away. Enrique stepped back.

Adam reached into the cavity. His fingers groped the empty darkness. Then they touched the smooth metal. "It's still here."

He lifted out the titanium case and held it out to Soraya. She flinched and stepped back. "I don't want it."

They stared at each other. There was a sudden creak from the wood panelling and she gave a little cry. Enrique stepped between them and shoved the wall closed. He looked at her, lifted his arms and then dropped them. "Don't worry, Ms. Kamali. *Todo va bien.*" He turned to Adam. "What do we do now, boss?"

It was time to take charge, make decisions. Someone had to. These two were helpless. Clearly, it was up to him. He took a deep breath. "We'll go together. Get dressed, both of you. We'll go now."

"What about the other Cruiser?" Enrique said.

"We'll leave it here."

Enrique looked worried. "Suppose he hot-wires it?"

"*No!*" Soraya flinched again.

Adam put his arm around her. "I'll drive it," he said. "Darling – you go with Enrique. I'll follow you."

"But Adam –"

"Don't argue. You'll be safer with him. Please – just do as I say."

Enrique looked towards the bedroom. "What about him?"

They went back inside. Willard Blankenship's outstretched arm still pointed beyond them into the darkness. The sheet near his throat was dark with stiffening blood.

"It's up to the police now," Adam said. "We mustn't touch anything."

"We can't just leave him. Not like that." She started to cry again.

The dark tan woolen coat was tumbled in a heap just inside the door. Adam picked it up, shook it open and spread it across the body. Only the long-fingered hand stuck out.

"Now get dressed and let's go. Be as quick as you can."

Ten minutes later he turned the wick down, killing the soft lamp light in the wrecked cabin, and went outside. He locked the door and crossed to where the others stood waiting.

"Here." He gave the key to Soraya. "Are you ready?"

She nodded and slipped the key into her jacket pocket. She was calmer now, he was pleased to see. She was wearing chinos and a soft sweater under the jacket. Her hair was brushed and tied at the back. She had washed her face and put on a little makeup. The tears, thank goodness, were gone.

He lifted the silver case. "What about this?"

She gave a little shudder and shook her head. "You keep it. It's better with you."

He turned to Enrique. "See you look after her."

"Right, boss."

He looked at his watch. "How much longer till daylight?"

"Two hours. Three, maybe."

"Then let's get going."

He opened the passenger door and helped her climb in. He turned away and walked across the soft ground to where the other Cruiser was parked close to the cabin. He reached up to the door.

"Adam — !"

She came running across to him. He took her in his arms and she clung to him fiercely, her arms tight around him. "Don't be frightened," he said. "This will all be over soon." He felt her shudder and kissed her forehead. "I promise you."

Across the clearing, the Cruiser rumbled into life. She kissed him, pulled away and ran back. Adam climbed into the big car, put the silver case on the passenger seat beside him and threw his jacket across it. He switched on the engine. The cabin shook briefly and the little dials on the dashboard sprang to life. Enrique's rear lights came on, a startling red in the darkness, then flaring white as the Cruiser reversed. Adam switched on the headlights.

The glare bounced back at him from the thick screen of trees. High beam. Damn. He clicked the stalk on the steering column and switched down to full. Up ahead, Enrique's tail lights dipped and swung as he drove out of the clearing. Adam took off the hand brake, moved the gear lever to Drive and the big car moved forward, bumping gently over the ground as it gathered speed. He was gripping the wheel much too tightly. He sat back, flexed his fingers and tried to relax.

It wasn't the first time he'd driven a four-by-four. He'd had some experience with a Land Rover on Dartmoor, herding sheep with a local farmer and following the annual drive when the wild Dartmoor Ponies were brought in. But this thing was different: heavier, softer; more comfortable certainly, but much more ponderous; a diesel behemoth on huge balloon tyres.

A branch smacked the windshield. He spun the wheel to the right, braked sharply to avoid a rock, stopped, reversed and started forward again, hunched over the steering wheel, staring hard into the darkness where the tail lights dipped and swayed up ahead. Mustn't lose them. God knows what would happen if he did.

Had it been an hour since they left the cabin? Two hours? More? It felt like it. Every so often he took a deep breath and tried to sit back in the huge leather seat; but within seconds he was bending forward again, clutching hard at the wheel, shoulders rigid, eyes narrowed, peering ahead. Sometimes he was close – too close – to the other Cruiser and was forced to hang back as Enrique slowed or stopped to negotiate some sudden obstacle. Sometimes the red lights seemed too distant, flickering and disappearing momentarily through the trees, and he was forced to tread hard on the accelerator to catch up.

The Cruiser lurched and swayed. Was it his imagination or was it getting lighter out there? Was the sky paler in that break above the canopy? Shouldn't they be at the ranger station by now? It couldn't be much further, surely? Where was Enrique? Oh yes – there. Up ahead. Way ahead! Jesus. He was being left behind! He floored the accelerator. The Cruiser surged forward. There was a sudden, bone-jolting crash, the wheel spun in his hands and the big car slewed crazily and lurched to a halt.

For several moments he did nothing, too shocked to think. Then he hit the horn and flashed the headlights a few times. Would they hear it, see it? He pushed the door open, climbed down and walked around the car to the passenger side.

A ten-foot sapling had caught under the front wing and jammed hard in the wheel-arch, trapping the nearside tyre. Bugger. He should have seen it. Served him right for staring at the sky when he should have been concentrating on the ground ahead. He squatted by the wheel and reached in where the sapling was lodged between the tyre and the steel bodywork. It felt pretty solid. Not much joy there. He stood up and pulled at the thin trunk. Nothing. He took a breath and pulled as hard as he could. It shifted slightly. Not enough. He let go and stood up, breathing heavily. He looked around. Yes, he'd been right: it *was* getting lighter. No sign of Enrique, though. He frowned and squatted down again beside the big, earth-crusted tyre.

He located the valve stem, unscrewed the cap, found the nipple and pressed down hard. Air hissed past his finger. What sort of pressure did these tyres take? Why were they so enormous? How long before this bloody thing started to deflate? Several minutes, as it happened; but at last the tyre had flattened enough so that when he tugged at the sapling it shifted more easily. He stepped away and looked at the base of the slender trunk. Would it pull free? It had better. If not, he was buggered. He climbed back into the car.

He settled behind the wheel, and as he reached for the ignition his stomach tightened and he froze. The passenger seat was empty. *Shit!* Then he saw the silver case on the floor, half under the seat where it had fallen. He picked it up, wrapped his jacket around it and replaced it on the passenger seat. He started the engine and put the Cruiser into Drive. The car inched forward a few feet, there was a shriek of metal and he braked, reversed and drove back. He stopped and drove forward, stopped and reversed, repeating the operation until – five minutes later, was it? Ten? – there was a last screech from the wheel-arch, the Cruiser tore free of the sapling and he was able to drive on.

But where? In which direction? Where was the ranger station from here? He had no idea. But it was getting lighter, that was certain. He could see without the headlights and if he kept going he was bound to arrive at somewhere eventually, wasn't he? He put his foot down and ploughed forward, not troubling any longer to avoid small trees or low bushes, smashing through the undergrowth, scraping past low rocks – who cared about the Cruiser's paintwork now? – pounding the horn from time to time in case they were near enough to hear.

He drove into a small clearing and braked halfway across when he saw sudden movement to his left. A herd of deer took off fast, bounding high into the forest. Such grace! It was amazing. He drove on. The half-flattened front tyre made the steering much heavier and the car handled atrociously, slewing hard to the right. Keeping straight was an effort. He felt sweat between his shoulders. But the trees ahead began to grow thinner and the ground started to slope upwards. Was he coming to the end of the forest? Was he nearly there? He felt a great rush of relief. He stamped down, flooring the accelerator, the engine kicked down a gear and the Cruiser shot forward, surging to the crest of the slope.

And suddenly he was in space… Freefall… *Incredible!* The Cruiser dipped to strike the uprushing ground. Everything turned over. Something flew past his head. He heard an explosion of glass. And then nothing.

 TWELVE

HE WAS IN A tent. He could see the ridge pole above his head and the olive canvas stretched over it. He could see the unlaced flaps in the door-way moving slightly in the breeze. He was in Scout camp somewhere. Yes. But where were Skipper and the rest of the Troop? And his Patrol, the Buffaloes, where were they? Out map-reading, probably; or practising woodcraft; or playing British Bulldog. But why wasn't he with them? Why was he still here in bed? And why was he naked under the blankets?

The door flaps were pulled aside and a red-haired boy came into the tent. He stood by the bed looking down at him. "Hey, Adam. How you doing?" he said.

Adam frowned. There was no red-haired boy in the Troop. And why was this one talking with that stupid accent?

"Need anything?" the boy said.

Adam thought for a long moment. "A drink."

"You got it."

The boy grinned and went outside. Adam looked around the tent. Funny tent. Its walls were made of wood — logs, that is, about five feet high, piled lengthways on top of each other and caulked with dried mud. It was only the pitched roof that was made of canvas. He frowned again. He didn't remember anything like this at camp.

There was movement in the doorway and the red-haired boy came in again. He was carrying a white mug and there was a man with him. He sat on the iron bed and held out the mug. Adam heaved himself onto his elbows.

"Easy," the boy said.

Adam took the mug. It was made of very thick china and filled with very sweet coffee.

"Taste okay?"

Adam nodded and tried to say delicious, but it didn't come out right and he spluttered and coffee ran down his chin onto his bare chest. He yelped and the boy laughed.

"Ain't much wrong with him," the man who had come in with the boy said.

The man had a stupid accent, too. He was middle-aged and thin; ferrety-looking with sandy hair and little ears. His eyes were set close together each side of his nose and Adam decided he didn't like him.

"Where are the others?" Adam said.

"Others?" the man looked puzzled. "What others? Who you talking about?"

Adam realised he didn't know and for a moment he felt scared. He drank the rest of the coffee and handed the mug back to the boy. "Time I was on my way." He started to push himself upright.

"Whoa there, Adam."

The boy put his hand on Adam's chest and pushed him backwards. Adam tried to stop him but found he couldn't. The boy must be very strong. He lay back on the pillow staring upwards. The boy leaned forward and put his hand on Adam's forehead.

"You just take it easy." He stroked his forehead gently.

And then Adam saw it wasn't a boy but a girl. A red-haired girl.

"You just sleep a while," she said.

What was a girl doing at Scout camp? It was most confusing. Adam closed his eyes to think about it. Something was wrong here, he was certain. Only, he couldn't put his finger on what it was. Oh, well. Perhaps it would come to him if he didn't think too hard about it. If he just let it take its own time. Yes. That seemed a good idea. So in the meantime, all things being equal, maybe it would be better to do as the red-haired girl said.

The next time he woke he knew at once where he was. America. Montana. *But where, exactly?* In bed, in this strange tent. With no clothes on. *Where were they?* He rubbed his face, sat up and looked around. The girl was sitting on a low stool by the wall opposite. She grinned at him.

"Adam, I gotta tell you. You sure do snore."

She wore jeans and a plaid shirt and her red hair — more bright-copper, really — was cropped short in a kind of pudding-basin style. That was probably why he had mistaken her for a boy. She had hazel eyes, a wide mouth, snub nose and a spray of freckles.

"I'm awfully sorry," he said.

She shrugged. "Don't make no difference to me. Anyways, I guess you needed the shut-eye."

He thought for a moment. "How long have I been asleep?"

"Most of two days."

"Two days!" He was shocked. He let himself fall back against the pillow and lay staring up at the canvas roof.

"Must've hit your head when you drove off that ridge. Automobile's a wreck. Total write-off. Way I figure it, you got thrown out when it rolled. Else no way you'd be here, no sir. I tell you, it was a *mess*."

And then he remembered it: the dead man in the cabin; the night drive through the forest; the crash.

"How did I get here?"

"I was on my way back to camp and just happened by. With supplies, you know? So I got you on one of the horses — that was the hard part, believe me. I had to tie you real tight — and brung you in."

A faint memory stirred in his mind: the smell of horsehair, sweat and leather. Then it was gone.

"You saved my life," he said.

She made a little face. She was really quite pretty. Or rather, what they called cute.

"I'm very grateful. Thank you."

"You're welcome, Adam."

"I mean it."

She nodded and smiled. Her mouth was wide, with very white teeth. This country must be an orthodontist's paradise.

"How do you know my name?"

"From your passport. Had to look in your coat to find out who you were."

His corduroy jacket was hanging from a peg on the nearest tent pole. It was dark with dried mud and there was a tear in one of the sleeves that someone had sewn up. She leaned forward, hands together, pressed tight between her knees. "You're a Brit, right? I never met a Brit before."

She was clearly impressed. This could be useful. Better play up the accent. Lay it on a bit thick. Because let's face it, you never knew when – a sudden thought gripped him, clenching his stomach horribly.

"There was a case. In the car with me. Silver. It –"

She got up and came to the bedside, bent down and reached under the iron frame. "This it?"

The handle was half-wrenched off, but apart from a bit of scuffing on one corner, the titanium shell seemed unharmed. He turned it over. Not a scratch. He let out a deep breath and almost hugged it.

"Looks like it's pretty important, huh?"

"Yes."

He didn't say any more. The girl frowned for a moment and then nodded to herself. She put her hands into the back pockets of her jeans and looked towards the doorway; then she looked down at him.

"How you feeling? Ready to get up?"

"Good idea." He reached to pull back the blankets and stopped.

"Where are my clothes?"

"Had to dump them in the garbage." She made a face and turned away. "Your shirt was all ripped and your pants were soaked in oil. *Yuk*." She made a being-sick sound, came back and placed some folded things at the foot of the bed. "Try these."

He started to get up and stopped again. He looked at her. There was a moment of silence. He looked away.

"What's up, Adam? You bashful or what?"

"Of course not." He cleared his throat. "It isn't that. It's just…"

She laughed. "You *are* bashful. Why, bless your heart. Who do you reckon put you into that bed?"

He stared. The girl laughed again. "Suit yourself, mister." She went to the doorway. "Got nothing to be ashamed of." She went out.

He waited a moment before looking at the little pile of clothes she had left. There was a pair of jeans, recently washed by the fresh smell of them, and a denim shirt, faded to duck-egg blue. It, too, had been recently washed and ironed. His underpants were clean and neatly folded. So were his socks. He got out of bed, stood up straight – and gasped at the sudden stab in his side. Had he broken a rib? He prodded carefully. It didn't feel like it. More like a muscle in spasm. All the same, he'd better be careful. He took a deep breath, winced and started slowly to dress.

The shirt fitted well: plenty of room in the shoulders. The jeans were a little tight. He had to suck in his stomach to fix the top button and pull up the zip. Still, they'd give a bit after he had worn them for a while. And they were too long by a couple of inches. Never mind: he could always turn the bottoms up. There was no sign of his shoes, but a pair of boots stood on the rough floorboards at the foot of the bed. They were made of black leather, not new but well cared-for by the look of them, with a design of red, green and white flowers tooled on each side. The heels were odd. They sloped forward and looked to be at least three inches high. Why were they sloping? For digging your heels in, obviously. When you were lassoing a steer and going *yee-haw!* or whatever it was you were supposed to shout. Would the boots fit?

He sat down and tried them. It took a fair bit of tugging, and two more wincing stabs in his side, but there were loops to hang onto as you worked your foot in, and eventually he was able to stand up and stamp to the opposite wall and back. They weren't too small; that was good. If anything they might be a bit big. And with those heels there was no need to turn the bottoms of the jeans up. He wiggled his toes, looking down at the squared-off tips and the pattern of stitching across the insteps. Cowboy boots. Extraordinary. He couldn't help smiling. Then his eye fell on the silver case and the smile wiped. He sat on the bed, picked up the case and put it on his lap.

There were eight little combination wheels, four to each lock. He looked at the eight random numbers showing and drew in his breath. There was a chance – it was a crazy idea, he knew, but still a chance – that Willard Blankenship hadn't broken the combination when he put the manuscript back last night. Please God, let it be true! He put a thumb to each lock. Come on, God. Do your stuff!

He pressed. Nothing happened. God hadn't done his stuff. Pity. Given the circumstances, he might have helped out a bit. Adam reached up to his jacket and took out his wallet and ball-point pen. He found a credit card receipt, smoothed it out and wrote on the back:

0 1 2 3 4 5 6 7 8 9

He stared at the numbers. How many permutations could you get out of that? Factorial ten, was it? He groaned.

It was a meadow of bright grass, a wide clearing ringed by tall trees. It reminded him of an Alpine meadow, only not so self-conscious, not so manicured – no, that wasn't the right word. Not so *domesticated*. Yes. This was wilder, more natural. More beautiful, too. On the far side, some thirty or so horses were grazing. There were several other tents nearby, nudging the edge of the clearing, with log walls and canvas roofs like the one he had slept in. Deeper into the trees he could see the outlines of some cabins that looked as if they were made entirely of logs. Figures were moving about, chopping wood or carrying buckets. Smoke rose slowly from several fires. The girl was bending over one not more than twenty yards away, pouring something into a large pot. She straightened up, watching him come.

"How's the boots? They fit?"

"Quite well, thank you." He stamped the grass lightly. "They're a little big, possibly."

She nodded. "Thicker socks oughtta do it."

"That was my thought."

A man came out of a nearby tent and crossed the grass to them, stepping lightly with quick strides. It was the sandy-haired, ferrety one with little ears and close-set eyes; the one, Adam remembered, he didn't like.

"Everything okay, Nonnie?" the man said.

She nodded. "Sure, why not?"

Nonnie. Weird names these people had. The man hooked his thumbs in his belt and looked at Adam. "Howdy."

"This is my daddy," Nonnie said.

"How do you do?"

Adam put out his hand. After a moment the man unhooked his right thumb and took it. Their hands went up and down.

"Name's Burt," he said. "How're you today?"

"I'm quite well, thank you. All things considered." (How stupid that sounded! But at least he hadn't said in the pink.) "Your – ah – daughter was just telling me how I got here. And I was trying to thank her for what she did. I mean, finding me, getting me out of the smash-up. If it weren't for her, it seems I wouldn't be here."

The man nodded. "You're one lucky sonofabitch."

"Yes, I suppose I am."

There was movement on the other side of the meadow. The little herd of horses bunched together and turned, walking towards some fencing rails near the cabins. A man walked behind them with a coiled rope that he swung slowly from side to side.

"Where exactly were you heading?" ferrety Burt said.

"I was trying to get to the ranger station."

"Ranger station? My Lord, that's more'n forty miles away!" Nonnie said.

"Closer on fifty." Burt gazed at Adam. "Seems like you got yourself well and truly lost, boy."

"It does, doesn't it?" Adam said. "And look, you've been most kind, and I don't want you to think I'm not grateful, because I am. More than I can say." He smiled at Nonnie and put a hand on her shoulder. She went pink around the freckles and looked at the ground. He took his hand away. "But I don't want to trespass on your hospitality any more than I have to. You've done enough for me already. What I mean is: How soon can I leave here? It's – ah – rather important I get back."

Burt looked across the meadow to where the horses were being herded into a space surrounded by the rail fencing. It was a pen, Adam realised. A corral.

"Trail's not easy. Gonna take you five-six days at least."

"Four," Nonnie said. "If we make good time."

Her father looked at her. "You aiming to guide him?"

The girl lifted her chin. "Well, he sure can't guide himself."

Burt gave a ferrety snort. Or was it a sneer? The girl scowled and stared back at him. Burt shrugged. The silence was broken by the whinnying of some horses as the corral gate was swung shut and the man with the rope called to someone who had come out of the nearest cabin.

"Can we go now?" Adam said.

"You kidding?" Burt laughed: a thin, yelping, unpleasant sound. "To-morrow, maybe. If you're lucky." He turned and walked away.

"It really is important," Adam said. Burt kept on walking. Adam looked at the girl. "I don't think he understands."

She gave a little sigh. "Don't worry about it. Ease up. Ranger station ain't going nowhere."

"You don't understand either." He had a sudden picture of Soraya. Her hair on the pillow. Her perfume. Her touch. Where was she now? Wherever it was, she would be frantic, surely? "This is — ah — well. You could say it's a matter of life and death."

"Don't look so grouchy, Adam. Lighten up a little. *Smile*." She picked up a large metal spoon and bent to stir whatever it was simmering in the pot. "Oh, and there's something else. Did I tell you?" She looked up at him and grinned, showing happy white teeth. "On account the season's just opened, we're having a little party tonight. And guess what? You're invited," Nonnie said.

 **THIRTEEN**

THERE WAS A MAN with a fiddle and a man with a guitar, sometimes two men with guitars. A man played a washboard and another man played drums on a cluster of upended pots and pans. There was even a man who played the spoons, only he wasn't very good and he soon quit, joining the others to drink or dance or just listen. Every so often someone would get up and sing. It was called CW, Adam knew. Country and Western. Not exactly concert-hall stuff and you wouldn't care to record it – or would you? It was rough around the edges (that was putting it kindly), but it had energy, *life*. You couldn't help smiling. His fingers tapped out the rhythm on the table top. He drank some beer.

They were ballads, of course, part of an old tradition going back hundreds of years. To Chaucer and even further. The tales they told were universal: same stories, same characters, same themes. That song the little fat guy had just sung; the one about how his wife ran off with a truck driver and now he was all alone except for their little daughter, who reminded him of his lost darlin' every time he looked into her baby-blue eyes. Wasn't it just a version of *The Foggy Foggy Dew*? Undoubtedly. Did the little fat guy know that? Undoubtedly not. Did it matter?

Adam frowned. He must stop it, this habit of looking at everything academically, of classifying things, fitting them into categories, compartments, doing a quick mental compare-and-contrast. It was getting in the way. There was a danger he was becoming an old fogey. (That he was *already* an old fogey? Surely not!) What was it the girl had said? Lighten up a little. He must make the effort. He drank some more beer. It was gassy and tickled his nose, making him sneeze.

"Bless you," the girl said.

"Thank you."

"You're welcome."

The beer was nicely cold though, from a tin bath packed with ice, and it tasted pleasant enough. A bit sour maybe, but it was pretty strong. Was that why he could hardly feel the pain in his side? He drank some more. He was feeling better, no question. Not so tense. More relaxed. Oh, yes.

The setting helped, obviously. The setting took your breath away. The dark forest; the immense, silent mountains; that three-quarter moon in a sky of stars so brilliant and so close you could reach up and pluck them. And the glow from the three huge fires; the way the sparks flew; the way the firelight played on people's faces. Chiaroscuro. Yes, incredible. He watched the dancers out in the middle, turning in slow circles or staying on one spot, arms enfolding each other, heads on shoulders, moving their weight from foot to foot.

"Who are these people?" he said to Nonnie.

She looked at him across the table. "Just guys."

Her hair was red-gold in the semi-darkness. She had washed it especially for the party, he knew. He had watched her this afternoon rinsing and drying it, and then spending ages combing and brushing, pulling it this way and that, clicking her tongue with impatience until at last she had fixed it with two little butterfly hair-slides, one above each ear.

"What sort of guys?"

She frowned slightly. "I told you: guys."

"But what do they do?"

"Oh…" She picked up her beer can and moved it in quick little circles, swirling the beer inside. "Some of them do guide work at the fishing lodges. Some of them are wranglers with the outfitters."

"Outfitters?"

"It's a business that caters for folks who come here on vacation. Who want to explore the Wilderness. Least, that's what they think they're doing. Season started beginning of June. That's why we're here now, just arrived mostly. Can't live up here in the winter on account of the snow." She looked around the tables. "Some outfits have gone out already. People come from all over to ride the trails, sleep in tents, live rough for a while. They're mostly city folks. Getting back to nature, you know?"

"It sounds wonderful."

"Does it?" She thought for a moment, head on one side. "Well, maybe so. Sometimes it's whole families, dads and moms with all their kids. Sometimes it's a group from a particular firm or company – they think it's going to help them *bond*, okay? So their business is going to make a shitload more money?" She grinned. "Sometimes it's a bunch of assholes getting in touch with their inner man. Iron John, that kind of crap." She made a face. "Well, someone has to look after the horses, see the tents are pitched and the camp set up each night. Someone has to cook their food, wipe their noses, pick them up and dust them off when they fall over. And that's where these guys come in."

"You sound as if you don't approve."

"Ain't that. It's just the whole thing's gotten so phony." She swirled her beer and drank. He looked at the crowd of dancers, the people eating and drinking at the tables.

"What about the rest of them?"

"How do you mean?"

"They can't all work as guides or wranglers. So what do the rest of them do?"

She put her empty can on the table. Her chin set firmly and she stared out into the darkness. "I guess that's their business."

It seemed clear she wasn't disposed to tell him anything more. Why not? Was there something illegal about this place and these people? Or was it simply that he was being nosey and she was telling him to back off?

He cleared his throat a couple of times and drummed his fingers on the table. He hummed along with the band for a few seconds but she didn't respond.

He felt in his jacket pocket and took out the folded credit card receipt. He opened it, moved his beer can to one side and placed the slip of paper on the table. He looked down at the row of figures he had written this morning:

$$0\ 1\ 2\ 3\ 4\ 5\ 6\ 7\ 8\ 9$$

He frowned, took out his pen and underneath wrote:

$$1\ 0\ 3\ 2\ 5\ 4\ 7\ 6\ 9\ 8$$

He studied it for a few moments. Then underneath he wrote:

$$1\ 3\ 0\ 5\ 2\ 7\ 4\ 9\ 6\ 8$$

He looked at what he had written and a great tide of weariness came over him. He gave a soft groan.

"What's up, Adam?"

"Nothing."

She leaned across. "What're you writing?"

"Nothing." He put the cap back on his ball-point.

"Don't look like nothing to me. Looks more like a bunch of figures to me."

He folded the little paper. "You wouldn't understand."

Her mouth twitched and he saw he had hurt her. "I'm sorry," he said. "I didn't mean to be rude. But I have this problem."

"What kind of problem?"

He hesitated. How much should he tell her? Not the whole story, obviously. Still, now that he'd started he was going to have to say something.

"You know the – ah – silver case? The one that was in the car with me?" She nodded. He cleared his throat. "Well, it contains something rather important, and I'm – ah – I'm extremely worried about it."

"You are?"

He nodded. "I'm scared it may have been damaged in the crash."

Nonnie shrugged. "Why don't you open the case and check it out?"

"That's just it, I can't," Adam said. "It has these special locks that only open if you know the right combination, and I don't know what the right combination is."

She gazed at him mildly. "Why don't you just bust it open?"

"I can't. It's too dangerous. I mean, I daren't take the risk of damaging what's inside even more."

She looked at the folded slip of paper. "So is that what you're doing? Figuring out the combination?"

He made a face. "Trying to."

"It's only numbers." She sat back in her chair and stuck her legs out in front of her. Her boots were black leather too, he saw, only without the fancy flowers. "Seems to me it shouldn't be so tough."

"Shouldn't be so tough?" He felt a surge of real anger at her stupidity. "It's an eight-figure sequence and there are ten numbers to choose from, from zero to nine. Do you have any idea how many permutations you can get from ten numbers? Do you?" She shook her head. "Well, for your information it's over three-and-a-half *million*. And since you need only eight numbers, which ones do you leave out? And what if some of them are repeated? How many million more permutations does that add up to, do you know? Because I certainly don't." He stuffed the credit card receipt back in his pocket. "So perhaps now you can see why trying to work it out is *tough*."

She started to say something but stopped herself, scowled and looked away. Damn. He'd upset her again.

A woman got up from one of the nearby tables, walked across the grass and stood in front of him. Her bosom was huge. "I'm Charlene." She took his hand and hauled him upright. "Let's dance."

"So what do you think of the Bob?" Charlene said.

Was it the name of the band? The song? The dance they were doing (if that was what you could call being squashed tight against a pair of outsize mammary glands)? He decided to look stupid.

Charlene grinned. "You don't know what the Bob is?"

"Sorry. Is it a person?"

She laughed. Her enormous front went up and down. "Was once. Long time ago. Bob Marshall was one of the first conservation guys, back in the thirties. Spent his life trying to convince the government this whole territory ought to be protected. So Congress finally passed an Act and now it's officially the Bob Marshall Wilderness, only everybody calls it the Bob."

"I see. That's good to know. Thank you."

"My pleasure."

Her hand moved around his back and took a tight handful of shirt, pulling him closer. My God, he thought. If I turn sideways I'll disappear.

"What do you do?"

"I – ah – teach. At a University. In England."

"You're a prof?"

"Sort of. That is, yes."

Her breasts were like bolsters. Being held against them wasn't so bad. In fact it was rather nice. For a moment he thought of Soraya's body. How voluptuous it was. How incredible that night had been. He was a great lover, she said. When was it? Only five days ago? He could hardly believe it.

"Some of the guys had you figured for a narc."

"A narc?"

"With the DEA. You don't know what that is?"

"Not the slightest idea."

"Drug Enforcement Agency. Narcs are federal officers."

"Is that bad?"

"Well, let's just say if you had been a narc, you wouldn't be here right now. And they'd never have found you. No, sir. No way."

She was joking, he thought. Then he saw the way she was looking at him and realised she wasn't. Was that why Nonnie had clammed up on him just now? Were these people somehow involved in drug trafficking?

The music stopped abruptly. Some couples nearby whooped and clapped.

"Thank you, Charlene," he said. "That was really..."

The fiddler struck up. The drummer bashed some pans and one of the men with guitars started to sing. Charlene's arm clamped his waist firmly. There was no point in resisting. He was engulfed once again. They shuffled a slow half-circle, stopped, and shuffled a slow half-circle back. Charlene let out a big sigh and rested her head on his shoulder. He listened to the song.

It was another one about a faithless, two-timing woman. Her name was Chrissie. Was it an echo of Cressida? That was intriguing because if it was, the story was ancient. Not truly classical, though. It doesn't appear in Homer. No, the tale of Troilus and Cressida was a medieval invention. French. Picked up by Boccaccio and later by Chaucer and later still by Henryson. So by the time Shakespeare came to use it – *Stop!* He had vowed not to do this. Get a grip, Searle!

Across the trampled grass he saw the table where Nonnie sat on the edge of the firelight, the two little butterfly grips glinting in her hair. No one had come to sit with her. He smiled across at her but she seemed not to notice. He lifted Charlene's arm in a sort of wave, but she looked away. Deliberately? He feared so.

"You banging Nonnie?" Charlene said.

"Am I *what?*"

"I said, you banging Nonnie?"

"Certainly not!"

"Don't matter to me." Charlene shrugged. Her chest heaved and settled. "Only if you are, you better hope Sonny don't get to hear about it."

"I just told you I'm not. And who is Sonny?"

"Ask Nonnie. And hope to hell Sonny don't get mad at you."

"This is crazy," Adam said. "I got lost and had a car crash. She pulled me out of it and brought me here. I was unconscious for two days. What possible reason could this Sonny have to get mad at me?"

She lifted her head from his shoulder. She was grinning. Pleasantly or maliciously? He couldn't tell. "Well, for one thing, you're wearing his boots," Charlene said.

"Before we start, there's a couple things we need to get straight."

It was well after ten. Nearly eleven, in fact. It was his fault. He hadn't woken until half-past nine. She had been up and ready, he guessed, for hours. The two horses were saddled and loaded with their supplies and stood with lowered heads tied to a nearby rail. Hardly anyone else was about. The place seemed almost deserted.

"Fire away."

Nonnie scowled. Oh, dear. Had he upset her? If so, how much? It was hard to know. She had been remarkably silent last night, saying she was tired and leaving the party early. Odd, when she had seemed so keen on it yesterday morning. After she left, he had sat by himself for a while until invited to join some people at their table, where he had drunk some throat-scalding liquor as well as several more beers and danced with two or three of the women when they asked him to.

The liquor was home-brew, they told him, and laughed a lot when it made him splutter and cough. Later on he had some more and got a little bit squiffy. Perhaps more than a little bit, if the way his head ached this morning was anything to go by, but last night no one seemed to mind. Last night everyone was very jolly. They clapped him on the back and told him he was a really great guy. He told them they were great guys, too. And at the time he meant every word.

All the same, these people were different, weren't they? You couldn't fail to be aware of it. Just when you thought you were beginning to understand them, something happened or was said or they looked at you sideways and suddenly you were a stranger again. *Strange fowl light upon neighbouring ponds.* Forget the common language. This is the most foreign place I've ever been to. This is the other side of the moon.

A fly buzzed the space between them. Nonnie took off her hat and swatted it away. "First off: on the trail I lead, you follow. And that don't mean some of the time, it means all of it, okay?"

He nodded. "Fair enough. I mean, okay."

"And I don't want no backtalk, no argument, either. If I say something, that's how it is. I say do something, you do it. I say don't, you don't."

"Absolutely."

She glared. "And we stay quiet. No talking, you got that?"

"Not a word shall pass my lips," Adam said. Then, quickly, "No, sorry, I don't mean to be facetious. I'll do everything you say. That's a promise."

She pursed her lips. There was silence for a moment. She nodded. "How well do you ride?"

"Not well at all. I've been on a horse a few times but I can't say I'm an expert. I didn't fall off, though."

"Don't really matter," Nonnie said. "Your horse is a trail pony. He knows what he's doing. Just don't try and second-guess him is all."

"Right."

"One last thing. It's important. If I hold up my hand and stop..." She held up her hand like a traffic policeman. "You stop, too. And stay still. And stay quiet. And don't move till I say."

"I won't. But why?"

"Because there's a bear on the trail ahead of us."

He stared. "A bear? Are you serious?"

"There's black bears and grizzlies out there. Probably more grizzlies than anywhere else in the US outside of Alaska, and they're mean critters, believe me. You don't argue with 'em. You do, you're dead. And here's a thing: if something goes wrong and you find yourself looking at one, whatever you do don't try and run. Over a short distance a grizzly'll out-run a horse. So you hit the dirt and play dead, you hear me? Stay still as you can – and maybe you'll be lucky and it'll move on."

He looked at the rifle in the crook of her arm. "Couldn't you just shoot it?"

She made a face. "Answer's no. Bear don't take kindly to being shot at. Being shot at'll prob'ly make him even madder'n he is already. So you remember what I say."

He thought of the little pictures on the map in the airport. All those animals had looked rather pretty. This was different. He took a deep breath. "I won't forget."

"Okay, then. Let's do it."

The titanium case lay in the grass at his feet. He picked it up by the broken handle and they walked to where the horses were tethered. The case bumped awkwardly against his leg and he changed his grip, lifting and holding it against his chest. His side twitched briefly. The muscle pain was almost gone, thank goodness. Now if only his head would stop aching... Nonnie unhitched the nearest horse and reached up to where a black cowboy hat hung from the saddle horn.

"Here. Try it."

He put it on. "It's a little snug."

"Better'n nothing, though." She looked at the silver case. "How you aiming to carry that?"

"I thought I'd tie it on somewhere."

He lifted the case and held it balanced behind the saddle. Nonnie frowned. "That ain't gonna work."

She turned to the second horse and slid the rifle, barrel first, into its long sheath-like holster. She undid one of the saddle bags, reached inside and took out two narrow strips of leather. "Give it here."

She took the silver case and tied the leather strips around it, hitching them tight but leaving two loops on one side. She held it up. "Put your arms through."

One loop was tight, cutting into his armpit. "Hold still." She re-tied the knot. "Try it now."

The case sat comfortably between his shoulders like a backpack. Rather fancy. *Time hath, my lord, a wallet at his back.* "Oh, well done," he said. "That's absolutely brilliant."

She made a growling noise and scowled, but he could tell from the faint blush around her freckles that she was pleased. She muttered something, turned her back and got onto the horse. "Moving out," she said and rode past him. He reached up, looping the reins over his horse's neck. It shook its head. The metal bit jangled.

"Good boy," he said. "Nice horse."

He took hold of the saddle-horn, put one foot in the stirrup and swung himself upward. For a moment he couldn't find the other stirrup and leaned over, peering down, almost losing his balance. The horse shifted under him and he nearly fell. Then he found it, planted his foot firmly and faced forward. She was already thirty or forty yards away, heading out across the clearing. He jammed the hat down on his head, shook the reins, said walk on, and the horse started forward. A woman came out of a nearby tent and stared at him, shading her eyes against the morning sun. Was she one of the women he had danced with last night? She might have been.

He touched his hat brim with two fingers like the cowboys did in the movies, smiled and said morning, ma'am, but she didn't respond. He rode past her, following Nonnie across the bright meadow into the tall trees on the other side.

 **FOURTEEN**

SHE WAS RIGHT ABOUT the horse. It knew exactly what to do, following her pony at a steady, easy-paced walk. All he had to do was sit there and not fall off when it shortened stride and stretched its neck, scrabbling upwards over a rise; or threw its weight back onto its hindquarters, sliding in a shower of earth and pebbles as it negotiated a sudden downward slope. Once or twice it stumbled but that was no problem; the western saddle supported him easily. It was deep and contoured, nothing like the ones at home. Those were little pads you perched on; this was like an armchair. He relaxed and looked around, taking in the Wilderness for the first time.

It was dense here, the forest crowding in on you, with the occasional torn-apart gash where a great tree had fallen, its rotted trunk half-split, its upflung, matted roots still crusted with dark, rich-smelling soil. *This is the forest primeval. The murmuring pines and the hemlocks.* But these were fir, weren't they? Douglas fir, from the look of them. And he recognised spruce and the flaring green of larches. There were rushing streams and splashing rivulets and occasional little cascades that were too small to call waterfalls. And many birds, most of which he didn't know, although he was pretty sure he saw a nuthatch and some of them could have been jays.

After about an hour he realised his head had stopped aching. And his cow-boy hat didn't feel so tight against his forehead. Maybe that was why.

He looked around at the tall trees, grinning. He felt like whistling but didn't dare. He thought of Soraya naked and a thrill stirred his groin. He began to hum silently to himself, following Nonnie's slim, tartan-shirted back ten yards ahead.

Je veux t'aimer and te cherir!
Parle encore!

Around early afternoon the trees thinned, light grew and they came out of the forest to the crest of a ridge where, after a moment of sheer, wide-eyed disbelief, he hauled on the reins — too hard but he couldn't help it — bringing his patient horse to a sudden stop. His breath caught in his throat.

They were on a mountainside. Halfway up? Three-quarters? It didn't mat-ter. What he was looking at was incredible. They were on the lip of a great valley, an enormous fissure that ran to the horizon as far as he could see. High peaks circled them, filling half the sky. Thick-wooded slopes, their vivid silver-greens broken by rockfalls and steep ridges, ran down to where, it seemed miles below, a river wound between the mountains, shining like polished metal in the afternoon light. Across the valley on the opposite slope, a waterfall broke and fell hundreds of feet down the rockface. Mist rose from it like smoke, wreathed at its foot with a rain-bow. *Beautiful* wasn't adequate; it wasn't a big enough word, because the scale here was staggering. It was simply *immense*.

He thought of Dartmoor and the couple of times he had visited the Lake District. Those places were puny, insignificant, mere pimples. Com-pared with this they didn't exist. What would Wordsworth have said if he had seen — no, not seen — *beheld* it? Or Shelley? This wasn't lyrical; it was epic in a way he had never imagined. *Most wonderful wonderful! And yet again wonderful!*

He became aware of Nonnie, sitting her horse alongside him. He hadn't noticed her ride back.

"Continental Divide," she said. "Some view, huh?"

So that's what it was: the great geological split dividing the North American landmass, east from west. No wonder it was *mighty*. The air was so sharp it stung his nostrils. How high were they? Four thousand feet? Five? He stared out over the great silent valley. This is how it was just after the Creation, he thought. This is what it must have looked like when it all began.

He nodded slowly. "Yes... Some view."

She pointed upwards. He looked and saw a huge bird a hundred or so feet almost directly above their heads. A bald eagle. He could see it clearly: the dark plumage, the white neck and head, the curved yellow beak. An *American* eagle. He laughed out loud. She grinned. Then she laid the reins across her horse's neck, turned it and started away. He waited a few moments longer before following reluctantly. You will never forget this, he told himself.

As far as he could tell, there was no actual trail she was following, just occasional signs where a branch had been broken or a rockface scored and you realised it was deliberate. They were moving slowly downwards, he noted, traversing the slope of the mountain, crossing open ridges, pushing through stands of forest, splashing through gathering streams, heading roughly south west.

From time to time, there were more wonderful views to stop at briefly and savour, but nothing to compare with that first incredible sight. At one point around mid-afternoon she stopped abruptly and tilted her head, listening. He waited, hearing nothing but with a growing excitement. Was this going to be his first sight of a bear, a cougar or wolverine? Then to his disappointment he heard a faint clatter in the sky.

"Let's get into the trees," Nonnie said.

He followed her into a clump of tall pines where they waited until the helicopter had flown over and the sound finally had died. Then she rode into the open and he kicked his horse's belly to catch up with her.

"Who was it?"

"No idea."

"Then why didn't you want them to see us?"

She shrugged. "No reason."

It was early evening when she called a halt. He pointed out there was still plenty of daylight but she said they'd done enough for the first day. Besides, there was no point overdoing things. He climbed down from the saddle and eased his back.

"How you feeling?" Nonnie said.

"Not too bad." He rubbed the inside of his thighs and winced, immediately regretting it. "A little sore, perhaps."

She grinned. "Gonna be a might sorer in the morning."

He slipped the silver case from his shoulders. The leather straps had worked well. He had hardly been aware of it all day. He took off his saddlebags and bedroll and she showed him how to un-cinch the saddle. He lifted it off and stacked it with the blanket and they pulled up handfuls of the long grass to wipe the horses down. They tethered them to a couple of fallen logs, not because they would wander off in the night, Nonnie said, but in case a critter spooked them. Then they made their fire and ate a meal of barbequed meat with mustard and relish and sourdough bread washed down with beer.

"That was absolutely delicious."

She grinned. "You were expecting beans, maybe?"

He laughed. "I suppose I was." He put down the plate. "Thank you. I'm replete."

She looked startled. "You're what?"

"Full. Stuffed. But nicely."

"There's pie for dessert. You don't want any?"

"Oh. Well. Maybe a little slice."

Afterwards, she made coffee and they sat watching the light fade.

"What's England like?" Nonnie said.

"Compared to this?" He looked out at the Wilderness. "Small."

"Is it pretty?"

"Some of it. Like most places, I suppose."

"Is it pretty where you live?"

"Some of it is. The moors are beautiful if you like moors, and there are some nice places on the coast. There's an area called the South Hams which is lovely, and a town called Salcombe which has a pretty river estuary with lots of creeks where people keep their boats. It's a bit like the South of France – or at least, they say it is. And there's Plymouth, where the Pilgrim Fathers sailed from, but you'd find it very disappointing, I'm afraid."

"It ain't pretty?"

"Not at all."

She nodded, as if unsurprised. "I've hardly ever seen the ocean. I was in Seattle one time."

"Did you like it?"

She thought for a moment. "It was okay. I was glad to get back, though."

"What about San Francisco? Have you been there?"

"Uh-uh." She shook her head. "I'd like to. I hear it's real nice."

"It is. It's great. You must see it."

"One day, maybe." She looked up at the sky where the first stars were showing. "Guess it's time to turn in. So's we can get an early start in the morning."

He got up from the fire, pulling a quick face as he felt his back tweak, and went to fetch his bedroll. He stood with it in his arms.

"May I ask you something?" he said. "Nonnie. Is that your real name? Or is it a nickname?"

A faint blush spread through her freckles. "Ain't no nickname." She unzipped her sleeping bag. "It's short for Winona."

"Winona? That's a nice name. Why don't you use it?"

Her cheeks were beginning to flame. She looked away. "'Cos Nonnie's what folks call me. Always have."

"Would you mind if I called you Winona?"

She turned her back, spread the sleeping bag and sat down on it. "Up to you, I guess."

He unrolled his bag and wriggled into it, working his way down until it was snug around his shoulders. He pulled the zip halfway closed and lay back against the earth. It was dark now. He looked up at the big sky. He hadn't realised how tired he was until this moment. Sleep wasn't going to be a problem.

"Adam?"

"Yes, Winona?"

"Will you do something for me?"

"Of course I will. If I can."

"Will you talk to me?"

"What – now?" She didn't reply. "What about?"

"It don't matter." She turned over in her sleeping bag and he guessed she was blushing. "I just love to hear you talk."

A little wind moved across the ground, causing the flames of their tiny fire to leap and flicker, moving the branches in the trees behind them. He heard the rising whisper of a thousand leaves. Then it passed and everything was quiet again.

"Well, now, that leaves us with a pretty wide choice, doesn't it? I mean, it's like saying…"

"You teach students, don't you? What do you tell them about?"

"My students? William Shakespeare, mostly."

"Okay. Tell me about William Shakespeare. I guess you know an awful lot about him, huh?"

"I know some things," Adam said. "A fair amount, I suppose." His back throbbed. He shifted to a more comfortable position. "But there are quite a few things we don't know. I guess you could say there are one or two real mysteries about him."

"Like murders and stuff?"

"Well, no. Not exactly."

"Then like what?"

"Well, to start with…" He rubbed his neck. Where to begin? At the beginning, obviously. "To start with, we don't really know when Shakespeare was born."

"We don't? My Lord!"

"We know the year. It was 1564. And we know the place: Stratford-upon-Avon in the county of Warwickshire. We know his parents were John and Anne Shakespeare. They had eight children and he was their first son. He had an older sister called Joan and another one called Margaret, who died when she was only a few months old. And though we usually say William's birthday is the 23rd of April, the truth is it's a guess, because we don't know the exact date."

"I know some folks like that," Winona said.

"We do know when he was christened. According to the Stratford parish records it was the 26th of April. Now, in those days children were baptised very early."

"Why?"

"Because infant mortality — babies dying — was pretty common and people didn't like to take chances."

"Makes sense."

"Three days after a child was born is reckoned to be the usual time for its christening, and that's why we say William's birthday was the 23rd. It also happens to be Saint George's day, the patron saint of England, and everyone likes the idea that our national poet and our national saint share the same day."

"We don't have a patron saint," Winona said. "Why is that?"

"I suppose because you don't have an established church. Isn't that part of the constitution?"

She was silent for a moment. Then she nodded. "We do have Washington's birthday, though. I guess it's pretty much the same kind of thing."

"There you are, then," Adam said. "William also died on the 23rd of April."

"On his birthday? How about that!"

"In 1616. And some people like the significance of that."

"Do you?"

"As far as I'm concerned, it doesn't matter. What's important aren't those dates – the day he was born and the day he died – but what happened in between. Am I boring you, Winona?"

"Are you kidding? Don't you dare stop. What happened next?"

"Well, when he was four or five William started at the King's New School in Stratford. At least, we think he did, but the records for that time have been lost, so it's another thing we can't be certain about."

"I hated school."

"Shakespeare might have agreed with you. He once wrote about

> *the whining schoolboy, with his satchel,*
> *And shining morning face, creeping like snail,*
> *Unwillingly to school."*

The bright head nodded. "That says it about right. The snail bit, anyway. Ain't so sure about the face."

"But that was one of his characters talking, not him. I think Shakespeare enjoyed school. He never went to University but he got a very good education."

"I never made it past the tenth grade," Winona said. She yawned and settled down deeper into her sleeping bag.

He went on talking about the Elizabethan school and what the boys would have studied, until he saw her settle and become still. He stopped and listened. He could hear the sound of her breathing.

He was silent for a while. "Goodnight, Winona," he said.

There was no reply. He waited a few moments longer and then eased himself deeper into the quilted bag, zipping it closed around his shoulders. He took a final look up at the night sky. And before he knew it he was asleep.

They broke camp early, like she said, and were on the trail soon after daybreak. Before setting out, she asked him how sore he was. He made a face and said a bit. She took a round tin from one of her saddle bags and said see if this'll help, and when he sniffed the dark green ointment she said it's for your butt, stupid, not your nose. He said just as well because it smells utterly disgusting and she laughed. He went behind a tree and rubbed it in. And he had to admit, his bottom didn't feel quite so bad afterwards. He winced though, when he got into the saddle.

The going was more difficult than yesterday because of the broken ground, a series of ridges that lay in front of them like waves in a stone sea. It was tough on the horses, he thought, hearing his pony suck air and gasp as it struggled over the next crest. Still, they were moving downwards, that was some comfort. It would be much harder if they were going back.

After a few hours they came to a river; not the great one he had seen winding through the valley floor (they were still way above it) but a river all the same. It was about twenty yards across, running fast and growing wider where it was fed by little streams, most likely on its way to join the great one below. It was not unlike some of the Dartmoor rivers, he thought. The bigger ones maybe, like the Upper Teign where it flowed through the gorge below Fingle Bridge, or the Dart above Buckfastleigh, except this was bigger still.

Winona turned in the saddle and pointed across it. Then she rode down the bank and into the water. He followed, feeling his horse strain to keep its footing against the flow, and splashed to the other side.

"Had to make the crossing there," she said. "Too deep further down."

They continued for two hours more, following the right bank of the gathering river. Then Winona called a halt, a half-hour timeout to rest and eat something, because there was still a ways to go. They sat close to the water, eating stale sourdough and processed cheese and drinking the last of the beer. His stomach rumbled and he belched slightly. *Crammed with distressful bread.*

"I hope you don't mind, Winona," he said, "but there's something else I'd like to ask you."

For a moment she looked wary; then she smiled. "Go ahead."

"Who is Sonny?"

The smile wiped instantly. "Who told you about Sonny?"

"I'm not sure. I think, someone at —"

"Was it Charlene?"

"I don't remember."

"Yes, you do. It was Charlene, wasn't it?"

"I really can't —"

"Don't lie to me, mister. It was her, I know it was. Never could keep her goddamn mouth shut. I hate her. Bitch."

She stared at him coldly, eyes hard as pebbles, wide mouth pinched tight. *She's a tough one all right,* he thought. *I wouldn't want to be on the wrong side of her.*

"Look, I'm sorry if I've upset you," he said. "But does it really matter?"

She stared back at him. Then the hardness went out of her eyes, her mouth lost its tightness and she shrugged. "Guess not."

He chewed on a piece of sourdough. "He's your boyfriend, I suppose?"

"Sonny? Lord, no. Sonny's my husband."

"Oh. Oh, I see." He looked at his hands, feeling stupid. "Well, that accounts for it."

"Accounts for what?"

"For someone saying Sonny would be – ah – mad at me for wearing his boots."

"His boots?" She gave a quick laugh. "Sonny wouldn't need no boots to get mad at you. Sonny don't need no reason to get mad at anybody. When Sonny feels like it, he's real *mean*. It's okay, take it easy, you don't need to fret." She reached out and patted his arm. "He's in Deer Lodge."

"Is that a hunting place?"

"Not exactly." Another quick laugh. "State penitentiary."

"He's in prison?"

"Uh-huh." She nodded. "Got another year to go. Would've been free by now only he tried to bust out and lost his remission. Wrecked a car and beat up on two state patrolmen before they got him back inside."

"He sounds quite – ah – quite lively."

"He don't mean no harm. Not really," Winona said. "He's got a good heart, he really does. Trouble is, he can't do anything. I mean, there's nothing he's good at. 'Cept maybe beating up on people." She giggled. "First time I met him, he was trying to rodeo. Only he just weren't no good, you know? He could ride, only not well enough. He could rope and bulldog calves, only not well enough. Same with the Brahma bulls. All he ever done was get his ribs broke and his front teeth knocked out. Poor Sonny. I don't think he's ever going to find something he can do and be proud of. It's a real shame."

"What's he in prison for?"

"He was in a fight."

"Is that all?"

"Not exactly." She looked at the flowing water. "They said he tried to kill a guy."

"And did he?"

She shook her head. "Not really. Sonny wouldn't do a thing like that. He's got a quick temper is all." She sighed. "Poor guy. Sometimes I feel real sorry for him."

"How long have you been married?"

"Must be – what? – eight years now."

"Eight years! You must have been very young."

She looked at him indignantly. "I was sixteen."

They rode through the afternoon and into the early evening, keeping to the river all the way. His crotch felt on fire and he would have been happy to stop earlier, but Winona didn't once turn to look back at him and he was reluctant to ride any closer in case she was upset.

The river was much wider here, wider and deeper, with great boulders and stretches of tumbling white water. The ground rose and they picked their way up onto a ledge with the rushing current some thirty feet below. On their right, the ground rose up steeply, a cliff face studded with hanging bushes and small trees, to the summit a hundred feet above. The ledge was narrow and if he hadn't been so tired he might have been nervous, but he trusted his horse. It had done him proud so far. It wasn't going to make a mistake now.

He looked down at the sliding water. He loved watching the surface of a river. The way it was always shifting, changing, as if it were a living thing… Wait a sec – wasn't there movement in the lee of that rock? Yes, *there!* In the eddy of slack water. A fish! It looked a good one.

He leaned across for a better view, turning in the saddle to look back as the horse moved on past – and something punched him violently in the back, knocking him clean out of the saddle. A *crack* sounded in his ears as he fell. Then he hit the water and heard nothing but its roar as it swept him away.

FIFTEEN

IT WAS THE TITANIUM case that saved him. If it hadn't been strapped to his back he might have gone under for good. But it acted like a buoyancy pack, bearing him up, supporting him, as the fierce current swept him along. Water broke over his face and he choked, gasping for air. God, it was cold! An iron hand gripped him, digging its fingers deep into his bones. He shook the water from his eyes. What was that up ahead? Rocks – big ones! Feet first, he remembered. *Feet first!*

He turned on his back and forced his feet to the surface. Just in time. Then he was fending himself off from a whole line of boulders, thudding and scraping against them, kicking himself clear. The roaring grew louder, white water broke over him and suddenly he was shot into the air.

It was only a short drop, probably not more than five or six feet, but as he plunged downwards he felt a violent blow on his left arm. He swallowed water, choking, until he was born upwards and broke surface again. He couldn't swim, it was pointless. The current was far too strong. All he could do was try to stay afloat until the river widened, the rush of water slackened and he could somehow scramble to the bank.

It was another ten minutes before he found the bottom and dragged himself clear, to collapse onto a patch of earth gouged from the riverbank, where he lay shivering and spewing water until half an hour later, when Winona arrived. And it was at least another half-hour before warmth began slowly to seep back into him as he sat huddled in her sleeping bag while she wrung the water from his dripping clothes. She spread them out on the rocks where they would catch the late sunlight, then came back and stood looking down at him, feet apart, hands stuck into the back pockets of her jeans. He looked up at her and looked away. Neither of them said anything.

She picked up the silver case and set it in front of him. He looked at the diagonal groove the bullet had made across the titanium shell. It was only then he realised it had saved him twice: from the shooter and from the river, both inside a minute.

Nonnie sat down facing him. "My turn to ask questions," she said. "And don't you dare lie to me, mister. Now what in hell's this all about?"

She sat perfectly still, never once stirring the whole time he was speaking. Her eyes held him steadily, her expression serious, solemn even. A little girl in the front row at school, paying attention to what teacher said. After he had finished she was silent for a long time. Then she reached out and touched the silver case, one finger slowly tracing the dark groove.

"And it's all on account of this, huh?"

"It looks like it."

"A bunch of old papers? Is that what's inside?"

"Yes, but they're not just old papers. They're – well, they could be very important. And extremely valuable."

She nodded slowly. "The guy that shot at you – he's the same one killed the rich guy, this Willard Blankenship, right?"

"I suppose so. Who else could it be?"

"Because he wants *this*?" She touched the case again.

"I suppose so. It's the only explanation that makes sense."

She sat back and stared at him. "Who do you think it is — the old Korean guy that snatched you off the street? Chow mein-whoosis?"

"Ch'a min-su. I don't know. But he said the manuscript was his and he wanted it back. He wasn't joking. And neither were the men with him. They had guns. I saw them. And since he and Willard Blankenship have been enemies for years, and fighting each other most of the time, I guess that makes him the most likely suspect, wouldn't you say?"

She was silent for a few moments. Then she got up and went to where his clothes were spread out, picked them up and rearranged them in the setting sun. She stood looking at the river for a while; then she came back and sat down again.

"The two you were with? In the car you were following?"

"Soraya and Enrique. What about them?"

"They'll have reported the killing. And they prob'ly have people out looking for you this minute." She shook her head. "It'll be hard, though. There won't be many of them and it's a big piece of country. You could search for months and never..." She broke off, frowning.

"What is it?" Adam said.

"That helicopter yesterday? It wasn't the first time I seen it. It come over the camp a couple times while you were sleeping."

"The same one?" She nodded. He felt a faint stir of relief. "If that's true and they *are* looking for me, maybe this is going to be over sooner than I thought. God, I hope so."

"Well, it's one possibility. There's always others."

"Like what?"

"Like it's the bad guys up there," Winona said.

They sat looking at each other for a long minute. The only sound was the rushing of water. Adam pulled the sleeping bag closer, sat up straight and stared into the middle distance.

"I am a teacher of English at an ancient university. I specialise in the plays of William Shakespeare and have written a book about them which has been critically well received. A week ago I was preparing to spend the long vacation in a peaceful little village in the South West of England where I live with my elderly father, but I agreed to come to America to give my opinion on a subject of considerable academic interest.

"Since then, I have been kidnapped in broad daylight, become involved in a horrible murder, almost killed in a car crash, shot at and nearly drowned. And now I find myself naked in the middle of the Bob Marshall Wilderness, where I am being hunted so that I may be shot at again. It seems pointless to ask how this happened, and even more pointless to ask why. The only things I want to know, and which I shall be deeply grateful to have answered, are how in God's name do I get out of here and what the hell happens next?"

A bird called from some bushes close by. There was a sudden flutter of wings. He clutched at the sleeping bag.

"You get out of here if we're lucky and real careful," Winona said. "That is, after we turn around and take a different trail. One we're following's too dangerous. He'll be laying up someplace ahead where it's easy to take you out. So we're gonna back up some and then go around. It's gonna take another three-four days, though, and some of it's gonna be tough. Specially with only one horse."

"I lost my horse?" He looked round stupidly. "What happened to it?"

"It run off when you took a dive into the river," Winona said.

"Couldn't you catch it?"

"If I'd gone after it, I might've." The hazel eyes fixed him. "Only, I went after you."

"Oh Lord, I'm sorry," he said. "That was stupid and insensitive of me. I haven't even thanked you. Thank you, Winona. And please forgive me. You're a ministering angel and I'm a bloody fool."

He reached out to touch her hand. She scowled and took it away. The quilted bag began to slip from his shoulders and he grabbed at it quickly, hugging it to his chest. "What about the horse? Will it be all right? I mean, it's not going to get eaten, is it?"

She made a snorting sound. "He'll most likely find his way home. He ain't stupid." She looked around. "Anyways, that answers your first question. What was the second one? Oh, yes — what happens next? Well, the answer to that is we stay here tonight." She scanned the hollowed-out riverbank with its screen of trees and low bushes, frowning slightly. "If we lay low under this overhang we're pretty much sheltered. No one's going to see us unless they walk right over us. Can't risk a fire, though. And there ain't nothing to eat. All the grub was in your saddlebags."

"There are fish in that river."

"Sure there are. 'Cept we got nothing to catch 'em with." She got up and went back to the rocks to gather up his clothes.

"Are they dry yet?"

"Uh-uh. You can maybe wear them in the morning, though."

"I'm sorry about the hat," he said. "And Sonny's boots."

"Boots'll be okay when they're greased," Winona said. "Not like before but you'll still be able to wear 'em. As for the hat..." She shrugged. "Didn't fit so good, anyways. So I reckon it don't... My Lord!" She stared. "That is one hell of a bruise!"

The sleeping bag had slipped from his left shoulder. The skin around his elbow was mottled crimson, already turning to purple.

"Let me see that." She touched his arm lightly with her fingertips. He drew his breath in. "That hurt?"

"A little," Adam said. "That is — yes."

Her horse was tied to one of the low bushes growing out from the riverbank. It raised its head as she approached and snickered gently. She rubbed its forehead and said something to it that Adam couldn't hear. Then she took off the saddle and saddlebags, returning with the blanket, the rifle and this morning's round tin. She knelt beside him.

"Hold still."

He did his best, staring hard at the river, trying not to flinch as she smeared green ointment on his elbow and forearm.

"Don't be such a cry-baby," Winona said.

"I'm trying not to be."

"I'm just teasing. And you're doing real good. There you go." She pressed the top back on the tin, peered at his arm and nodded. "Going to be a whole lot worse this time tomorrow."

"You sound pleased."

"Nope. Just telling you." She picked up the blanket and spread it next to him. "Here. Sleep on this." Her nose wrinkled. "It don't smell so good but it's better'n laying on the dirt."

"What about you?"

"I'll be fine here." She sat down on the pebbles five yards away.

"That's ridiculous. There's room for both of us. Come back here."

She didn't move.

"Look – if I lie on this side there's plenty of space. And if we don't zip up the sleeping bag it will cover us both easily. What are you sitting there for? Come on, don't be silly."

She still didn't move.

"What's up, Winona?" he said. "You bashful or what?"

She gave a little snort, picked up the rifle and came to sit beside him. A minute passed before she lay down. He gave her the edge of the sleeping bag and she pulled it across, turning her back to him.

She was right about the blanket. It smelled pretty strong. Still, it was good to have something between them and the ground, even if it only came down as far as his waist. They lay in silence for a moment. He tugged at the sleeping bag. She tugged back.

"If this is going to work you need to be a bit closer," he said.

Thirty seconds passed; then she shifted slightly. He felt her warmth against his right side. He pulled at the sleeping bag. She pulled back.

"Closer."

She shifted again. He felt the length of her back against him, the roundness of her bottom, her drawn-up feet.

"There you go."

He lay back and stared at the fading sky. A bank of clouds had come up, obscuring the mass of stars. *There's husbandry in Heaven, Their candles are all out.* She wasn't relaxed. He could tell from the plank-like feel of her back. Several minutes passed.

"Adam?"

"What is it?"

"Will you talk to me some more?"

"Like last night, you mean? About Shakespeare?" Her shoulders twitched against him as she nodded twice. "What sort of thing do you want to hear?"

"Stuff we don't know about. Mysteries."

"Stuff we don't know about. Well, let's see… There's a rather nice mystery about his marriage."

"There is? Great! Tell me about that."

"If you can let me have a little bit more of this sleeping bag. A bit more… Thank you, that's fine. Right, then. Listen up – isn't that what you say?"

Her shoulders twitched again, this time as she laughed.

"In November, 1582, Shakespeare got married to a girl called Anne Hathaway. She lived in a village called Shottery about a mile from Stratford. William was eighteen, and legally a minor."

"Sonny was eighteen," Winona said.

"Anne was twenty-six."

"He liked older girls?"

"Possibly. But six months later Anne had a baby, a little girl called Susanna."

"I get it. She was pregnant, right?"

"She was. And the marriage seems to have been something of a rush job, because they had to get a special licence from the bishop's court in Worcester, which was about twenty miles from Stratford. Two men, friends of Anne's family, went with them and posted a bond before the licence was issued, and it seems they…"

"Hold on there! Adam, are you saying Shakespeare knocked up this Anne Hathaway and it was a shotgun wedding?"

"Some people would say that. In fact, quite a few have."

"Wow. Shakespeare was quite a guy, wasn't he?"

"But that isn't the mystery, Winona. The mystery is that, in the court records, the bond the men posted is made out for the marriage of William Shakespeare and Anne Hathaway, which is fine. It's what you'd expect. But on the special licence, the one for the wedding itself, which was issued a day earlier, the names are William Shakespeare and Anne Whateley of Temple Grafton, another village altogether."

"I don't get it." She turned over to face him. "How could it say a different girl from a different place?"

"Nobody is sure. Some people think it means Shakespeare was really in love with a girl called Anne Whateley who lived in Temple Grafton, but he'd got Anne Hathaway from Shottery pregnant and had to marry her instead."

"You mean, he was going to sneak off and marry Anne Whateley in this other town…"

"Worcester."

"But the bond guys turned up at the last minute and forced him to marry Anne Hathaway?"

"That's right."

"Oh, wow! That sounds like it really must have happened! The poor guy!"

"Well, that's one way of looking at it. There is another way, much less romantic but more likely, I think."

"There is? Okay, what is it?"

"The clerk of the consistory court, when he was copying out the licence details into the records, simply wrote down the wrong name."

She made a rude noise. "You serious?"

"Perfectly. There was a William Whateley, whose case they were dealing with on the same day, and the clerk, without thinking, wrote Whateley instead of Hathaway. It's understandable. Busy clerks do make mistakes like that. Sorry to disappoint you, Winona, but it happens every day."

"That's true." She frowned. "Is that what you think, Adam? It was just some stupid asshole of a clerk?"

"On balance, yes."

She was silent for a moment. Then she wriggled onto her back. "You think what you like, mister. I say you're wrong! Way I see it, Shakespeare was in love with Anne Whateley but he had to marry this other Anne because he'd knocked her up and they made him. They even sent a couple tough guys along to make sure. Shit, it happens all the time. And you know something, Adam? I bet it wasn't his kid, anyway. I bet she fooled him real good!"

Adam laughed. "There are people who would agree with you," he said. "But they're the kind who write novels."

"What's wrong with that?"

"Nothing. Only it's not scholarship, and you mustn't confuse the two."

She snorted fiercely. "What about this other place?" she said. "This other village?"

"Temple Grafton?"

"Right. Was that a clerk's mistake, too?"

"There you have me," Adam said. "No one can explain that. It's a total mystery."

"Ha! I was right, see?" She turned on him triumphantly. "I tell you, the thing about you professors, Adam, is you spend so much time reading books and stuff, you don't ever —"

Her fingers touched his naked belly and she broke off quickly. She made a little growling noise and turned away from him, her back rigid again. He tugged at the sleeping bag.

"That's the trouble with scholarship," he said. "Or the beauty of it, depending on your point of view. You have to stick to the evidence. You can't get carried away. So without more hard facts, that's where we have to leave it, I'm afraid. Undecided. In the air. Sorry to disappoint you, Winona."

She snorted briefly but didn't reply, and it was at least twenty minutes before he felt her settle and relax; and it was another half-hour before the whisper of her breathing told him she was asleep.

He didn't sleep much himself, but that was only to be expected. He wasn't cold; the quilted sleeping bag was a good one and the combined warmth of their bodies was enough to keep out the chill. His left arm hurt, though, and there was a dull ache in his elbow. He lay looking at the dark sky, listening to the river, waiting for the night to pass. There was a moment when her horse snorted and moved suddenly, its hooves clattering on the pebbles, and he tensed, raising his head, wondering what it was had disturbed it.

Winona gave a little sigh and turned over to face him. He looked down at her sleeping face. She muttered something that he didn't understand, snuggled into him and put her arm across his chest. He lay motionless, keeping as still as he could, trying not to breathe too deeply. She wasn't heavy and she didn't wake up, but a whole hour passed until at last he dozed off.

 SIXTEEN

HE WOKE LONG BEFORE she did and lay gazing across the valley, where the outlined peaks were beginning to emerge through the dawn mist. *Full many a glorious morning have I seen Flatter the mountaintops with sovereign eye.* She lay close against him, her arm across him, breathing softly. He tried not to move or disturb her. He heard birdsong above the flow of the river, a quick, rising-falling flutter of notes he didn't recognise. He could smell pine needles and wet earth. It would have been perfect, he thought, if it weren't for the pain in his arm. And the knowledge that, somewhere out there, someone was trying to kill him.

He felt her stir and start to wake, and closed his eyes. She murmured something and moved slightly. Then suddenly her body stiffened, she pulled her arm from his chest and rolled away from him quickly. He heard her feet on the pebbles, shifted his position and pretended to wake up. He sat up slowly, yawned and rubbed his face. She was standing by the horse, stroking its nose.

"Good morning," he said. "How did you sleep?"

"Okay, I guess."

Her back was to him but he could tell she was blushing. She went to where his clothes were spread out on the rocks, returning with them in her arms, lifting them to her face.

"Are they dry?"

"Pretty much." She shrugged. "Guess they'll dry on you."

She dropped the clothes beside him and picked up the boots. She squatted down, opened the round tin and began to rub ointment into the cracked leather. The red-white-and-green flowers were soon a shared dirty yellow as she rubbed hard, working the grease in.

He lifted his jacket and felt in the inside pocket. His passport was still there, damp and battered, with some of the pages stuck together, but the laminated section at the back was undamaged. When it was dry it would pass inspection. Big relief. His wallet was a mess; the leather looked to be ruined. Never mind. The credit cards seemed okay. He took out the damp slip of paper that was the receipt and unfolded it carefully. The figures he had written the other evening were blurred and illegible, a pale, blue-black smear. Winona stopped rubbing in grease and looked across at him.

"I been thinking about that numbers thing," she said. "The combination? You know something, Adam? I always use my birthday."

The soggy paper came apart in his fingers. He felt a sharp wave of irritation. "For goodness sake, stop being so bloody stupid!" She went bright red and stood up. "I'm sorry, Winona," he said. "Please don't be angry. I didn't mean to be rude. It's just... It's just I'm so *concerned*."

She looked down at him. A few moments passed. Then she nodded. "Time we was moving."

She put the boots down beside him. He reached for his shirt. "Hold on, there," Winona said. She knelt beside him and peered at his arm where the skin was strawberry-purple with a thin, scummy, darkening edge. "Does it feel a lot worse?"

"Worse. But not a lot. That ointment helped, I think. There's an ache in my elbow, though. And it throbs — *here*." He touched a spot on his forearm, closer to his wrist.

Winona frowned. "Think it's busted?"

"I hope not."

She took his shirt and helped him put it on, doing up the top buttons with deft fingers. "What about my underpants?" he said.

She laughed. "Watch your mouth." She got up and walked over to the horse.

His stomach rumbled. "Winona, I'm hungry."

"Then you better get used to it. 'Cos we ain't gonna eat for the next couple days."

"What about some nice, fresh-caught grilled trout?"

She turned to look at him. "How you aiming to do that, mister?"

"I'll show you, if you think it's safe."

She scanned the line of bushes that overhung the riverbank and nodded slowly. "I reckon."

"Excellent." He fastened the last buttons on his shirt. "Do you have an axe in those saddle bags?"

"No, but there's a pretty damn good knife."

"You see that little tree? The one the other side of your horse? Do you think you can cut it down and trim off the branches?"

She reached into one of the saddle bags and went around behind the horse. There was a chopping sound and the sapling began to quiver. He found his underpants and eased into them. They were nearly dry. She came back with the trimmed sapling. It was about twelve feet long and almost straight. It might do. The hacked-off base, though, was too fat to get his hands around.

"Can you shave that down for me?"

She sliced downwards. The white wood curled and fell away from the heavy serrated blade. It was a fearsome-looking thing. It reminded him of the knives he had seen in the North Beach hardware store. How long ago? It seemed like a year.

"I need something to make a line," he said. "Do you think we could cut up some of those leather strips?"

"I got some nylon line."

"Perfect!"

She went back to the horse, returning with a little red spool. "Use it for hanging stuff on. Ain't but a few feet."

"That's all we need."

He unspooled the length of nylon. There was about nine feet of it, he reckoned. He had no idea what its breaking strain was. Never mind. It would have to do. He reached into his jacket pocket and took out the little tool kit Soraya had given him. He unfolded it and spread the blades.

"That's pretty neat," Winona said.

He selected the corkscrew and twisted it carefully into the tapering end of the sapling, stopping when he felt the metal tip bulge the soft wood. He used the smaller blade to open the hole a little and blew into it, clearing it. He threaded the nylon through the hole and knotted it tight.

"You reckon that's going to work?" She looked doubtful.

"It works for the Japanese. It's called *tenkara*. Basically, it's just a pole with a line tied to it and a fly on the end."

"And that's good enough to catch fish with?"

"It's supposed to be."

"Supposed to be? You ain't never tried it?"

"I've been meaning to." She made a face. "Look, there's always a first time," he said.

Winona sniffed. "Need a fly. Ain't going catch no trout with no fly."

"Quite right. Will you lend me one of your hair-slides, please?"

She blinked. "My what?"

"Hair-slides. Or clips, grips, whatever they're called. You were wearing them at the party. Very pretty." He touched his hair above his ears. She stared. Clearly, he was a lunatic. "With little butterflies on them," he said.

A moment passed. Then she reached into her shirt pocket.

"Thank you."

He took one of the slides and broke off the plastic butterfly. Winona blinked. "I'll buy you another one," Adam said. He looked around. "Is it safe to light a fire?"

"I guess so. No one's going to see it in the daylight. Long as it don't make no smoke."

She got up and moved along the riverbank, collecting scattered pieces of driftwood. He opened the tool kit, selected the cutters and sheared off the hair-slide halfway along its length, where it bent back upon itself. A twist with the little pliers and he had made an eye to thread the line through, with an inch of bare metal left to work into a hook. He got up from the blanket, wincing slightly at the pull in his side, and went to where she had lit the fire in the shelter of the overhang.

"Here we go."

He knelt beside her, the hair-slide gripped in the jaws of the little pliers, and held the sticking-out inch over the flames. After a few seconds he took it away and pressed it against a stone. The metal bent slightly. He held it over the flames again, took it away and pressed. The metal bent further, beginning to form roughly into a hook. *The art of our necessities is strange.* He heated the bent slide again, took it away and pressed – and it snapped.

"*Damn,*" Adam said.

Winona reached into her shirt pocket. "Last try. And this time don't be so hasty."

He tried not to be. The truth was, he wasn't so much impatient as anxious. But after several more attempts and by pressing more lightly, what he ended up with didn't look a million miles from a proper hook. A few strokes with the file and it would be sharp enough. No barb, it was true, but at home he had taken many fish on hooks with no barbs.

"Yay, Adam," Winona said. "Now what?"

"Now we tie the fly. Can you get me some hairs from that horse of yours?"

"Mane or tail?"

"Both."

She came back with a handful. He chose a black tail-hair and placed the rest under a stone so they wouldn't blow away. He gave her the hook and the pliers.

"Hold it as still as you can."

She lay down on her belly, propped on her elbows, the hook gripped between the pliers, held steady in both hands. "That okay?"

"Splendid. Now let's see…"

He wound the dark thread eight turns just behind the eye, working down the shank and back, building a bump like a little head. "You should really do this with lead wire," he said.

"Only we ain't got none."

"Never mind."

He tied off the hair and selected another one. This time he wound further down the shank, carrying the thread to a point more or less opposite the tip of the hook. The next hair was from the horse's mane, lighter brown flecked with chestnut. He wound carefully up and down the shank.

"You sure this is going to work?" Winona said.

He chose another hair. "No, I'm not sure. In fact, at this point I'm doubtful. But I might feel less doubtful if we didn't discuss it."

"I only –"

"*Quiet.*"

He finished winding, sat back and studied the fly. Then he looked at Winona.

"It needs another colour," he said. "Something exciting. Like…ah…*red.*"

A second passed. Then she giggled and lowered her head. He leaned forward and tweaked.

"*Ow.*"

"Sorry."

Ten minutes later he took the fly from the pliers and held it up. It wasn't a complete disaster, he thought. The head and body, black and dark brown with copper-red tints along the shank, wasn't bad at all.

"Is it done?"

He frowned. "It needs a hackle." She blinked. "Something that makes it look like it has wings."

She got up and fetched her hat from where it lay on the rolled-up sleeping bag. There was a small olive-yellow feather in the hat-band.

"I could kiss you," he said.

Her freckles glowed like fever spots. He cut a short length of feather, used the little scissors to trim it and tied it behind the eye with two or three turns of red hair. He smoothed it down along the shank and snipped off the ragged ends.

"You reckon a trout's gonna take that?" She looked unconvinced.

"I have a colleague at the university. An entomologist. Nice guy," Adam said. "His field is actually moths, but he was once sufficiently interested to do a little research into artificial flies. Which ones worked and which didn't. How fish responded and why." He took the nylon line and threaded it carefully through the eye.

"Yeah? So what did he find out?"

"According to my colleague, most flies aren't really necessary. There are five or six traditional patterns, but most of the rest are inventions by the makers of fishing tackle, flash nonsense, just a way of maintaining sales."

"You saying they're a con?"

"Yes and no. Because … and this is the most interesting thing my colleague found out…" He finished tying the half-blood knot, moistened it with spit and pulled it tight. "According to him, when the fish are feeding it doesn't really matter what you throw at them, because hungry trout will take anything, even a scrap of old ribbon." He trimmed the knot. "Interesting theory. Let's hope he was right."

He rubbed a fingertip of grease from his boot, smeared it onto the fly and held it up.

"A fly has to have a name. Can't fish with a fly that doesn't have a name. What shall we call it? Any suggestions?"

"Waste of time," she said.

He grinned. "Good try but here's a better one. How about *Winona's Wonder*?"

Her freckles flamed again. He laughed, picked up the pole and walked to the river.

"Good luck," Winona said.

"You're supposed to say tight lines."

"Okay, I'm saying it. Tight lines."

The water was cold but fairly shallow. He knotted his shirt above his underpants and waded out deeper. His arm throbbed. Good thing he wasn't left-handed. About twenty yards upstream, near the opposite bank, was a large boulder where the main current flowed strongly. In the slack water near the bankside below it was a fish. He had watched it rising since dawn. He waded out further, working his way upstream until he was about ten yards below the boulder. He lifted the pole, the line streamed behind him, he flicked it forward and cast.

The sapling trunk surprised him. It was much more flexible than he expected. All the same, the line flew fairly straight. Not straight enough, though. The fly landed in the main current and came swiftly back. It floated pretty well, he noted. The lick of grease had done the trick. He drew it clear and cast again. And missed again. The third time he managed to hit the slack water but too far below the boulder. The spot he needed was just above it, in the neck of the little pool where the fish was lying. He got it on the fifth cast. The fly bobbed for a moment, began to drift slowly towards him – and then disappeared in a flurry of water as the fish hit.

He felt the electric thrill run down the pole and the sapling bent violently as he struck to fix the hook. A sudden slackening – please God he hadn't lost it! – then an explosion on the surface and the fish leaped clear – Jesus, it was beautiful! – twisting and thrashing before falling back.

"Go, Adam!" Her voice whooped from the bank behind him as he took a pace backwards, struggling to control the fighting fish.

It took nearly ten minutes, and there was another sickening moment when the pole cracked and he thought it was going to snap. But it held – just, and at last the fish lay flapping on the dirt. He dropped the pole, grabbed a stone and killed it with three blows to the head, feeling the shiver run through his fingers as the fish died. It was nearly eighteen inches long and at least a two-pounder. And so beautiful! Its back, fins and tail were marked with a spray of dark spots, and there were slashes of red below its gills that spread in a great flush along its belly. A western cut-throat trout. He had never seen one before. What a fish! He carried it up the bank to where she waited by the fire.

"Way to go!" Winona said.

 SEVENTEEN

THE FIRST COUPLE OF hundred yards were going to be the most dangerous. It was open ground all the way, and if there was a shooter out there they'd be easy meat until they could reach the trees, where there was plenty of cover and they ought to be safe. Or safer, anyways, Winona said. She finished loading the horse, cinched the saddle and slid the rifle into its long sheath. She said how's the arm and he said about the same. She nodded and said okay, you take this side, I'll take the other. Put your arm through the stirrup leathers, grab a hold of the saddle horn and hang on tight, you ready? He said ready, they scrambled up the riverbank, broke free of the screen of low bushes, she slapped the horse hard and they ran.

The titanium case bounced between his shoulders. It wasn't silver anymore – at least, not for the moment. She had smeared it with a thick coating of river mud – so's it won't catch the sun, right? Or the eye of a shooter. The running horse checked and swerved to avoid a jutting boulder. Adam stumbled and would have fallen if his right arm hadn't been looped through the leathers, crying out as pain stabbed his left side. But the horse kept on, hauling him upright, slowing only when they were in amongst the spruce and the larches and she brought it to a halt. He collapsed face-down, sucking air into lungs that were on fire. His mouth was in the earth, half-choked with dark leaf mould. He sat up, spitting, and cried out as pain jagged his arm again.

"You okay, Adam?"

He tried to nod, sucking air, but it was a full minute before his blood had slowed enough for him to reply. "That was quite – ah – quite something."

She stood up. "You ready to move?"

He got to his feet, felt sick and sat down again. "Give me another minute, will you, please? I'm sorry to hold things up. I thought I was fitter than this but it seems I was…"

He broke off as she lifted her head, listening. He heard the far-off clatter from the other side of the valley, becoming louder as the helicopter approached. He looked down at the ground and made himself sit still — which was silly, he realised, because here among the trees they were completely hidden. He looked up at Winona. It seemed she had had the same thought because she grinned at him and shrugged. The sound grew louder and he stood up. The helicopter seemed to be following the course of the river. They waited until it had passed over, heading upstream the way they had come. The time it took was a blessing, because by now his breathing was back to normal. He smiled and took hold of the stirrup.

"What are we waiting for?" he said.

They were in the forest most of the day, breaking cover only occasionally when they had to cross a ridge, or where a natural fire had left an acres-wide scar and there was no easy way around. As far as he could tell, they were heading north or north east, following rising ground all the way. They heard the helicopter twice more, around midday and towards the end of the afternoon, but each time it sounded fainter, overflying the other side of the valley, where they would surely have been if they hadn't changed direction, Winona said.

Every couple of hours she called a halt and he lay on his back with his knees drawn up, following the quick flight of birds or trying to identify the various flowers, shrubs or bushes – anything to distract himself from the growing ache in his arm. Once, she suggested he get up on the horse and ride for the next hour but he said certainly not it was a ridiculous idea, and when she said what's ridiculous about it? he said everything and anyway he preferred to walk. Which wasn't true because he didn't but he wasn't going to say so, and she said suit yourself, mister, and they went on.

By early evening they were resting at the foot of a low outcrop, a stone ship's prow jutting from the mountainside. The temperature was dropping and the air was sharp and pungent. This must be the highest we have been so far, he thought. She passed him the canteen and he took a couple of mouthfuls, watching the horse crop the grasses that grew around the base of the cliff.

"You hungry?" Winona said.

"I wouldn't say no to a steak."

She laughed. "Makes two of us."

He put the canteen between his knees, screwed the cap back on and held it out.

She shook her head. "Let me see that arm."

He was about to argue but realised he didn't have the will or the energy. Instead, he let her peel off his jacket and held his arm out, wincing as she took it. His elbow looked swollen, the skin around it discoloured and angry.

She frowned. "Needs looking at."

"I'll see a doctor when we get back to civilisation. If we ever do get back."

She shook her head again. "Sooner than that."

"Brilliant." He felt a stab of anger and sat up straight, looking around. "Correct me if I'm wrong, but this place doesn't seem to me to be over-populated with medical men. Or with anyone else, come to that. So who do you suggest I call on for a quick diagnosis?"

It was clumsy and uncalled-for and immediately he felt ashamed of himself. But if it was meant to shut her up, it failed miserably. She looked at him calmly: hazel eyes, snub nose, spray of freckles, copper hair. "I was thinking of Rudd."

He blinked. "Rudd? Who is Rudd? Is he a doctor?"

"Rudd's a mountain man."

Adam stared. "I thought mountain men were just a story. Folklore. Something that never really existed."

"Oh, they existed, right enough." She looked up towards the circling peaks. "Time was, the only people up here was Indians, trappers and mountain men. But come winter, the Indians and trappers went down to the valleys. Only the mountain men was here all year 'round."

"I didn't think there was any such thing."

"There ain't, no more. Not for a hundred, two hundred years. 'Cept for Rudd. If he's still up here. If he's still alive."

"You don't know?"

She laughed. "Nobody knows. Not for sure. Because nobody knows Rudd. They just know about him. Tell stories about him. Most folks've never seen him, even."

"You have?"

She nodded. "Two times. Once, when I was a little girl, with my daddy. We was on our way to camp at the beginning of the season and I seen this man standing watching us from the trees. And I said daddy, there's a man, and daddy said I know it, that's Rudd, he ain't gonna hurt us, don't pay him no mind. So we went on and when I looked back he was still standing there, he never moved.

"Second time was about five years ago. I was with Sonny." She sat up, looking round. "We was somewhere not too far from here, I guess, and Sonny was hunting deer, which you ain't supposed to do without a licence and even then there's all kinds of restrictions but Sonny don't care about stuff like that. And Sonny suddenly says hey lookit, it's Rudd. It's gotta be. And there he was, up on a ridge, just standing there watching us, like before."

"Did you talk to him?"

"Uh-uh. Not then. He took off and Sonny said let's get after him, so we tracked him — Sonny's a great tracker — till we come to where he lived. That's when we talked with him."

"What did he say?"

"Not a whole lot. He weren't too pleased we found him, I guess. He was real quiet, you know? But Sonny was good. Sonny was mannerly, he didn't cause no trouble. I reckon that's something you don't do around a person like Rudd. Sonny talked some and Rudd listened. Like I told you, he didn't say much. And after a while, when it was time for us to go, I said Rudd, we may tell some folks we seen you, but we ain't gonna tell nobody where you live. That's a promise. And Rudd looked at me, and he looked at Sonny, and he looked at me again and he said I believe you. And we never did."

They sat in silence. "That's very interesting," Adam said. "But why should we try to…ah…contact him now?"

"So's he can take a look at your arm. Rudd has power."

He blinked. "He has what?"

"Power. Healing power."

"You believe that?"

"Sure I believe it," Winona said. "Why shouldn't I? It's true."

A long moment passed. The only sound was the horse pulling and chomping on the long grasses. Adam looked at his arm. He moved it slightly and frowned. "How long will it take us to get there?"

She puckered her mouth, considering. "Seven-eight hours, maybe. With luck we'll be there by morning."

"You mean, travelling through the night?"

"Moon's nearly full, so there'll be light enough to see. And part of the way's open ground so it'll be safer. Helicopter don't fly at night."

"And you're sure you can find the place?"

"No, I ain't sure," Winona said. "And if I do find it, Rudd may not be there. He may've moved on. Or like I say, he could be dead. But I believe it's worth a try." The hazel eyes looked at him steadily. "Up to you, though,

Adam. What do you say?"

His arm throbbed. He reached for the silver case and stood up. "Let's do it."

There were no clouds and the nearly full moon was brilliant. She was right: even in the forest they had no difficulty seeing their way. For the first few hours he was alert, observant, aware of the terrain and its sounds, hearing the sudden rustle in the bushes, the call of a night bird above the steady plod-plod of the willing horse. Later on, it was harder. Tiredness came over him in waves. He became clumsy and stumbled and would probably have agreed to get up in the saddle if she had suggested it but she didn't. She had more than enough problems of her own, he realised. Finding the way wasn't easy.

From time to time she halted, checking the horse suddenly, and he hung on the stirrup, leaning wearily against the saddle while she stood looking ahead or off to one side, muttering to herself. Once, she stopped and swore loudly, then said sorry, Adam, and turned the horse around, retracing the way they had come for a full half-hour before striking off in a different direction. Another time she said wait here and went off by herself, leaving him slumped against the warm flank, almost out on his feet by the time she came back. When they started again he was still half-asleep.

He sensed rather than saw the morning. Perhaps it was the faint breeze on his face that seemed to come out of nowhere, or the different bird calls that one-by-one were starting up. Or was it the new smell in his nostrils that he couldn't identify but had definitely not been there five minutes ago? It was all of those things, obviously. It had to be. Day was breaking. You could feel it all around you: the whole world starting up. Then the light grew and there was no question the night was truly over.

He saw the first of the sun on the mountain, saw the mist on the slopes start to wreathe and dissolve and at last, as they broke into a clearing, he heard Winona give a low, triumphant whoop.

They stopped on the edge of a little meadow, facing what looked like the base of a steep cliff, a sheer wall of solid rock. There were a few small trees and low bushes but as far as he could tell that was all. Winona walked forward and stopped a few yards from the rockface.

"Rudd? You there, Rudd?" she said.

Her voice bounced back to them off the stone sounding-board. Otherwise, there was nothing to hear and nothing moved. Winona shoved her hands into her jeans pockets.

"It's me, Rudd. I was here before. I made you a promise, remember? Come on out."

Nothing happened. This is crazy, Adam thought. And getting crazier each moment. This girl is mad.

Winona took a couple more paces forward. "We got trouble, Rudd. Someone's hurt. We surely need your help."

Again, nothing. He was about to say you got it wrong, Winona, forget it, this isn't the place, let's move on. But there was movement at the foot of the cliff and Adam saw the rock wall wasn't completely solid after all. There was some sort of construction built out from the base that he hadn't noticed because it was so well obscured – camouflaged? – by bushes and earth.

A man walked out of the cliff and stood facing them. Winona took her hands out of her pockets. "Hello, Rudd."

"God Almighty," Adam thought. *This one's King Lear.*

 **EIGHTEEN**

HE WASN'T A TALL man. Not much more than five-nine or five-ten, Adam guessed later. But that wasn't how he seemed the first time you saw him. The first time you saw him he seemed huge. His hair was pure white, a great mane that hung thick below his shoulders. His beard, just as thick and almost as white, reached his chest. His eyes were dark-hollowed, deep-set under sweeping eyebrows, his features scored as if cut from stone with a chisel. How old was he? Fourscore? He could be, easily. Because he was Lear, no question; or a William Blake Ancient of Days.

His clothes – tight leggings and shirt – were made of skins sewn together, the seams clearly marked in bold stitching. Over them he wore a sleeveless coat of dark fur – bearskin, it had to be – that bulked his shoulders, adding to the impression of size. It reached almost to his ankles. He looked ageless, like something out of pre-history, Adam thought. Apart from the rifle he held, pointing towards them.

"Do you remember me, Rudd?" Winona said. A moment passed and then the man nodded. "I surely do 'pologise. We wouldn't have come here. Only…" She jerked her head towards Adam. "He's hurt."

They waited.

The man lowered the rifle. "Bring him inside."

His voice was a surprise. Not the rattling thunder you half-expected but light, modulated; slightly hoarse-sounding (from under-use?) but musical enough. A baritone, not a bass. Who did it remind him of? There wasn't time to think and anyway, he was too tired to do anything more than follow Winona, stooping under the low rock into the half-light of the cave.

Only it wasn't a cave. Not exactly. Or rather, part of it was – the part at the back. The front part, where they entered, was man-made and built out from the cliff, and somewhere in the roof there were little slanting holes that must be deliberate because they let in enough light for you to see. And halfway along there was a fire in a fireplace that must have a chimney, because the very faint smoke it made was disappearing straight up. There was a plank table and some kind of chair with a dark fur covering – another bearskin – and some benches, and several chests along the walls, where there were shelves with things arranged on them, and he was vaguely aware of other things hanging from the roof above his head.

Rudd came in behind them, pulling a heavy curtain closed across the entrance. He pointed with the rifle. "Sit there."

Adam sat at the table. "It's his arm," Winona said.

Rudd sat across from him. "Show me."

Adam eased the titanium case from his shoulders. It seemed to have become much heavier since they started. Winona helped him take off his jacket. It was filthy, he saw, and ripped in several places. She rolled back his shirtsleeve and he laid his arm on the table.

"What kind of pain?"

"It aches," Adam said. "Throbs."

"How often? Show me."

Adam closed and opened his fingers in time with the throbbing in his arm.

"That's enough." Rudd put down the rifle, reached out and took his wrist. His hands were small, with short, blunt-ended fingers. Their touch was light, though. They moved up his arm.

"Where does it hurt most?"

"…There."

Rudd nodded and worked up above the elbow. Then he grunted and sat back.

"Is it broke?" Winona said.

"I do not think so. There is a dislocation and deep bruising but not a break." Rudd stood up and went to one of the shelves, returning with a stone jug and a small glass. He took the stopper from the jug and filled the glass. "Drink it."

Adam lifted the glass. The liquid was clear, almost colourless. He sniffed. Was there the faintest smell of woodsmoke? Or some kind of berry? He couldn't be certain.

"What is it?"

Rudd didn't answer. After a moment Adam lifted the glass and drank. It was smooth and almost tasteless. And with a kick like a dray-horse. He felt an immediate glow.

"That's a pretty…ah…powerful drink."

Rudd refilled the glass. "Again."

Adam looked at Winona. She nodded. He drank.

"Wow. Punchy stuff."

Rudd tilted the stone jug. "One more time."

He replaced the stopper, got up and went further into the cave where it was darker. Adam held up the glass and grinned at Winona. "Cheers."

Rudd came back to the table. He carried a small jar filled with what looked like yellow grease flecked with tiny spots of red, brown and green. He took Adam's arm in his hands, holding it just above the wrist. As before, his touch was gentle, delicate: soothing, Adam thought. The fingers moved slowly towards his elbow.

"That's the spot," Adam said. "That's exactly where —" then he roared in sudden agony as the fingers dug, twisted and pulled. He slumped forward, eyes swimming.

Rudd let his arm go and pushed the jar to Winona. "Rub it in. Hard."

Adam saw her take a handful of grease from the jar and felt it being rubbed on his skin.

"Harder," Rudd instructed.

He heard her grunt and felt the pressure increase. And that was all he remembered because that was when he passed out.

He was fishing with the Dean. He knew it was a dream and he was dream-
ing it, but he didn't wake up. They were at one of the Dartmoor lakes,
either Fernworthy or Kennick – although, as there were some splendid
rhododendron bushes in full purple flower on the opposite shore, it was
most likely Kennick – and they got into an argument about who could
make the longest cast. What was so infuriating was that the Dean would
only talk about it; he wouldn't actually use his rod, which was a brand-
new Sage. The Dean said it was the Ferrari of fishing rods and miles better
than Adam's old Hardy, but each time Adam cast, his line flying arrow-
straight almost to the backing, the Dean sneered and said pathetic, I can
do much better than that.

Adam felt the rage building inside him. He threw down his rod and
began to hit the Dean, punching as hard as he could. But he couldn't make
contact. The Dean's face was somehow always just out of range. The Dean
started to laugh. Adam's punches grew feeble. The harder he tried, the
weaker he became. He began to cry with frustration and suddenly his
teeth started to crumble and his mouth was full of bone. He bent over,
spitting teeth onto the grass, when Dad said come here, both of you,
there's something I want you to see.

They went into the vegetable garden and the Dean said what's so special? Look, Dad said, and pulled up a cabbage. He brushed the dirt off
the roots and held it out. It was green on top and bright purple underneath. A genuine western cut-throat cabbage, Dad said. Either that or it
has a *naevus*, in which case I pity it. The Dean's wife appeared in the doorway and said come on you lot, tea's ready.

Indoors, it wasn't the sitting room at home but his main room in college. The Dean's wife poured tea from a huge pot with daisies on it and

there were babies everywhere: on the carpet, on the window sills, on the sofa and the bashed-up chairs. Adam took his cup and was just about to sit down to drink it when the Dean's wife screamed and he saw he was going to sit on a baby. You're trying to kill it! the Dean's wife said and he was so horrified he woke up.

He lay panting, staring up at the stone ceiling. It was early evening. He could tell by the light, softer and warmer than this morning and slanting in a different direction. He was lying on some kind of bed towards the back of the cave, covered with one of the bearskin rugs. After a while his breathing eased and he turned his head towards the entrance.

Winona and Rudd were sitting at the table, framed in the angled overhead light like two actors spotlit on a stage. She was leaning forward, saying something. A tableau. What did they look like? Yes – Cordelia and Lear, in one of those Stories from Shakespeare books they used to give to children. A full-page colour illustration with a piece of text underneath: *"How does my royal lord? How fares your Majesty?" (Act IV, scene vii).*

No, it was a silly idea. He felt a sudden disgust. She wasn't Cordelia, don't be a bloody fool. So who was she, then? He couldn't think. Stop it! Pull yourself together. He pushed the rug aside, stood upright and went towards the front of the cave.

Winona looked up. "How's your arm?"

His arm. He lifted it, looked at it. "I don't feel anything," he said. "The pain's gone."

He bent his elbow a couple of times. "It's true. Nothing. I don't believe it. Look."

He bent his elbow again. "No pain. Incredible." He laughed out loud.

"I told you he had power," Winona said.

There was an empty seat next to her. "How did you do it? What was that stuff in the jar? What was in it?" he said to Lear.

The man looked at him. Adam saw the deep-set eyes under the jutting eyebrows were blue – but a blue so pale they looked almost blind, as if bleached by too much sun. Or the glare of winter snow?

"All I did was a little manipulation. The ointment was bear fat with herbs to help take down the swelling. You will probably have a slight recurrence of the pain during the next day or so, a kind of memory, but nothing to worry about. It will pass. You seem a healthy young man," Rudd said.

"He done good getting up here. Trail weren't easy," Winona said.

"I'm very grateful," Adam said. "Truly. I can't thank you enough." Who did this man remind him of? He frowned. It wouldn't come. He bent his elbow. "Incredible," he said again.

Rudd said nothing and they sat in silence for several moments. Adam coughed and looked around. "Where's…ah…where's…?"

"On the shelf behind you," Rudd said.

The titanium case had been wiped clean. It was silver again. He placed it on the table between them. "Perhaps I should explain…"

"I told Rudd about it," Winona said. "I told him it was worth a whole heap of money and somebody was trying to kill you for it."

"Yes. Well, that's more or less true." Adam looked at Rudd. "Would you like to hear the whole story?"

"If you would like to tell it."

Adam thought for a moment. "I think I would."

Winona stood up. "Gotta go see to the horse."

"You don't have to go," Adam said.

She seemed not to hear him. The heavy curtain swung closed behind her.

"That is a good kid," Rudd said.

Adam cleared his throat. "About a week ago…"

"One moment."

Rudd stood up, went further into the cave and came back with the stone jug and two glasses this time. He set them down and poured. He lifted his glass and they drank a little.

"About a week ago," Rudd said.

"It may have been more. Eight or nine days. Or ten. The truth is, I've lost count. My sense of time has gone a bit haywire. Do you know what I mean?"

Rudd said nothing. *Idiot*, Adam thought. Of course he knows. "I'm sorry, that was stupid," he said. "Anyway, this is what happened."

He told him the whole story from the beginning, including the night with Soraya, which he hadn't mentioned to Winona. Towards the end she came back inside, her face shining with sweat, and took her place at the table, sitting in silence until he had finished. Then she leaned forward.

"What do you think, Rudd?"

The bleached eyes turned from her to Adam. "I think I would like to see the manuscript."

"So would I. In fact, I'd like it more than anything in the world. But I don't know the combination, so I can't open the case," Adam said.

There was a moment of silence. "I could blow the locks for you."

"Can you guarantee the pages won't be damaged?"

"Ninety-seven percent," Rudd said.

Adam thought for a long moment. He sighed. "I'm sorry. I can't risk it. I daren't."

Rudd nodded. "That is the answer I would expect from a scholar." He stood up. "And I think you must be very hungry, so now will be a good time for us to eat."

"Ain't gonna argue with that one," Winona said. She got up and followed him deeper into the cave and soon after, Adam heard the sound of metal pots being stirred and wooden dishes being clattered.

The fire burned suddenly brighter as fuel was added and by its light he saw there were large pieces of blackened meat hanging from the ceiling and bunches of what looked like roots and herbs strung on lines above his head. The slanting light from outside had become a pale rose. It must be a lovely evening out there.

He picked up the case and turned to put it back on the shelf. There were several other things there, he noticed. Some large needles made from yellow bone, with pierced eye-holes and sharpened points; some hand-wound balls of waxed thread; a collection of stones; some more bones that looked like animals' teeth; a large, indented stone and a smaller one lying on top of it that made a natural pestle and mortar. And at the back, a photograph in a narrow black frame. He took it down.

Ten men were lined up facing the camera. Six were standing, four kneeling at the front. They wore army fatigues and carried automatic weapons. Two of the men kneeling were Asiatics; one in the row behind was black. There may have been a second black but it was hard to tell — the photograph was faded and anyway their faces were daubed in a kind of war paint he supposed was camouflage. Some were wearing helmets; two or three had head-bands, one of them with feathers stuck in it like an Indian's war bonnet. One of the kneeling Asiatics wore a cowboy hat with a tightly curled brim. A couple held up cans of beer; one was giving the camera the finger; most of them were smiling. *We happy few.*

Adam looked at the man standing on the end of the back row. He was older than the others and even though he wore no badges or insignia you could tell he was the officer, the captain or lieutenant, or at any rate the senior man. He stood slightly apart, the automatic rifle hanging loosely from his left hand, a heavy army pistol on his right hip. His eyes were dark and deep-set under heavy brows and although he was smiling, his smile wasn't like the others'. Not false or superficial, but somehow more — more what? More aware? Yes, perhaps. More informed? Adam frowned. Who did this man remind him of? He held the photograph towards the slanting light, but the glass in the frame was dusty and the angle made it almost opaque. Should he move closer to the doorway?

"Chow time," Winona said from the other end of the cave.

He put the photograph back on the shelf, returned to the table and waited for them to arrive.

The meal was a sort of casserole, pungent and gamey with two kinds of meat, a dark meat Rudd said was deer and an even darker meat he said was bear. The sauce was thick with herbs and there was a vegetable flavoured with red and green berries that was delicious. Rudd said it was bitterroot, *lewisia rediviva*, after Meriwether Lewis, who found it when he came through on the famous expedition with William Clark in 1805. They may have been the first white men to discover it, Rudd said, but the bitterroot had been known to the Indians for centuries. It was a staple of their diet and prized for its medicinal qualities.

Adam listened to the low, modulated voice (was it slightly less hoarse-sounding now?) as Rudd talked about Lewis and Clark and their men. How dauntless they were, what hardships they endured, what it must have been like to come upon this country for the first time and what discoveries they made. How they had hoped to find a river route clear through to the Pacific. Or a river flowing from Canada that would allow them to claim territory there. How, in spite of everything they achieved, Lewis counted the expedition a failure, which may have been the reason why four years later he shot himself. How Thomas Jefferson believed it would take a thousand years for the nation to expand to the West Coast, but then someone invented the railroad and they did it in eighty.

Afterwards, they each drank a glass of moonshine and when Adam said he was afraid he'd eaten too much, Winona laughed and blew her cheeks out and said same here. Then Rudd showed them where to sleep and Adam lay in the dark listening to her breathing on the other side of the cave. Sometime later there was movement near the entrance and a sudden current of air and he knew Rudd had gone outside. He didn't know how long he was out there because before Rudd came back he was asleep.

 **NINETEEN**

"YOU WILL NOT BE needing the horse," Rudd said. He picked up the rifle and worked the action. The well-oiled breech slid open and closed.

"How steep's the climb?" Winona said.

"Steep enough. The first two or three hours will not be easy. After that it is not so hard, apart from a mess of scree you will have to traverse near the top. That is the worst part. There will not be any snow to speak of and what there is will not be deep. Once you are over the peak it will be more straightforward. Do not be fooled, though. You will need to take good care until you are safely down."

"And it's gonna save us some time?"

"Four days, at least. And that is a conservative estimate." Something - something he had said? – made Rudd smile slightly. He picked up a square of worn leather and began to wipe the rifle barrel.

"Sounds good to me," Winona said. "What do you think, Adam?"

He looked at the titanium case on the shelf behind her. "I'm game if you are. Anyway, I shall do as I'm told. You're the boss."

She made a growling sound and stood up. "Gotta go get my stuff to-gether," she said to the wall and went out.

Rudd looked after her. "That is a great little girl," he said. "Special." The blind-looking eyes fixed Adam. "But you already know that."

And then it hit him, and he knew exactly who Rudd reminded him of. It was Farlow, of course! His friend and mentor at Cambridge. Why had it taken him so long to work it out? He should have seen it immediately! There was the same pitch to the voice, the same authority behind it, the same way of looking at you when he spoke – even the same kind of expression used. How many times, when they were discussing some point of interpretation, had Farlow indicated the line to take and said, "But I don't have to tell you, Adam. You know it already, don't you?" That was the essence of the man, George Farlow in a nutshell. And here he was, hearing it again. Only this time from a Vietnam veteran who lived in a cave in the Wilderness and looked like King Lear.

He stood up. "Yes, I do know. She's very unusual." He picked up his tattered corduroy jacket, shook it out and shoved an arm into one sleeve.

"Hold up a moment."

There was a narrow chest against the wall behind him – an ammunition box, Adam realised. Rudd opened it, took something out, unfolded it and held it up. "My guess is, this will serve you better."

It was made of pale leather, the skins matched and sewn with tiny stitches, with horn buttons that fastened with dark-leather loops. "It's beautiful," Adam said.

Rudd nodded. "Deerskin. Do not thank me. Put it on." He stood back and frowned. "Is it tight across the back? If it is, do not worry. Deerskin is supple. It will shape itself to you."

"It feels absolutely fine," Adam said.

"Then it is yours."

Adam picked up his old jacket and took out his wallet and passport. "I won't try and thank you. But will you accept this?"

He placed the little tool kit on the table. Rudd picked it up and opened the blades. He examined each one, folded them back carefully and nodded. "Thank you kindly," King Lear said.

They went out into the sunshine. "Wow. *Nice jacket*," Winona said.

One hour later, he shouldered the silver case and they were ready. It was still early morning and there was a whole day ahead of them before they would have to climb.

Winona picked up her rifle. "Take care of yourself, Rudd," she said.

He nodded. "I shall see the horse is returned."

"I know it." She looked at Adam. "Moving out."

She turned and set off across the meadow. The tethered horse lifted its head and whinnied softly as she passed. Adam hesitated and put out his hand. "Thank you."

There was a moment of silence and then Rudd took his hand. "It was Cambodia," he said. "The photograph."

"I didn't mean to pry."

"Of course not." The blunt-ended fingers gripped firmly; the bleached eyes held him. "Sometimes it is necessary to retain things," Rudd said. "Even the most shameful. To remind us what we were. To confirm what we have become." His grip relaxed and let go.

"Goodbye, Rudd."

"Goodbye. Travel well."

He caught up with Winona where she was waiting on the other side of the meadow. He looked back but there was no sign of Rudd or his cave; just a wall of blank stone at the foot of a cliff.

"What an amazing old man," he said. "What will become of him, do you think?"

"You mean, when it's time for him to die? Oh, he'll go off somewhere in the woods or he'll climb the mountain and it'll just happen."

"He won't stay in the cave?"

"Uh-uh. Not unless he has a stroke or breaks a leg, stuff like that. He'll just follow his instinct. He'll know." She looked around, lifting her face to the morning, spreading her nostrils slightly, as if scenting the air. "We had an old dog once. Smartest, most cleverest dog I ever knew. I really loved her, but she was old and started to get sick and one morning I whistled for her and she didn't come. And when I asked daddy why, he said it was her time and she knew it and she'd gone off to die. I was awful upset, but later I come to see it was right." She nodded slowly. "It's the nature of things and that old dog knew it. It'll be the same with Rudd."

He shook his head. "Extraordinary."

"Not really. Just the way things are. You'd understand if you'd lived here a while." She hefted the rifle. "Now let's get moving. We got a long ways to go."

Once again, there was no sign of a trail but the old man had given her clear directions so there was no way they'd go wrong, she said, and pushed on without hesitation. They were moving upwards all the time, climbing the middle slopes of the mountain, heading for its broken shoulder where Rudd had said they would find the track that would take them across. Around midday they halted for a short rest, and again towards the middle of the afternoon, when they found themselves on a slope thick with flowers and stopped, partly because it looked a good place to eat but mainly because it was so beautiful. He sat with the sun on his face, gazing out across the deep valley.

"How's the arm?" Winona said.

"It's okay. It's like Rudd said – a little ache from time to time like a memory. Otherwise it's perfectly normal."

"So you're feeling good?"

"I'm feeling fine. No! Better than fine. I feel great." He took a deep breath. "I don't think I've ever felt so good." He took another deep breath and laughed. It was true. He had never felt fitter, healthier. Was it the air? The altitude? Who cared? He felt terrific. A soft breeze blew across the slope, rippling the flowers, making them dance.

"I have to pick some!"

She jumped to her feet and ran down the slope. He lay back against the warm earth and stared at a bank of cumulus towering fantastically above the distant peaks. *Sometime we see a cloud that's dragonish.* Then, minutes later, she was back, flushed and out of breath, with a bright handful of flowers. Most of them were unfamiliar, but he thought he recognised a blue gentian, a white campion he knew from home – although the ones there were mainly red – and a clutch of yellow ones that couldn't be anything but buttercups. He sat up.

> *"O Proserpina,*
> *For the flowers now that frighted thou let'st fall*
> *From Dis's wagon!"*

"What did you say?"

He laughed. "It's Shakespeare."

"Is there more?"

He nodded.

"There is? Say it!"

He closed his eyes to help himself remember.

> *"Daffodils*
> *That come before the swallow dares, and take*
> *The winds of March with beauty; violets dim,*
> *But sweeter than the lids of Juno's eyes*
> *Or Cytherea's breath; pale primroses,*
> *That die unmarried, ere they can behold*
> *Bright Phoebus in his strength, a malady*
> *Most incident to maids."*

He opened his eyes. "Can't remember any more. Sorry."

She dropped to the grass beside him. "Say it again! The bit about the daffodils!"

> *"Daffodils*
> *That come before the swallow dares, and take*
> *The winds of March with beauty."*

"Oh, my," Winona said. "That's so pretty!"

"Yes, it is. It's the best."

"Say it one more time! All of it! Please, Adam!"

He did. When he had finished she sat back on the grass, hugging her drawn-up knees and thought for a long moment, frowning. "So is that who I am?" she said at last. "Proser-whoosis?"

"Proserpina? No, I don't think so. She was taken down to the underworld and was the reason winter came to the earth. That's not you." He reached out and took a flower, a blue gentian. "You might be the girl in the play, though. The one who gives the speech. She's called Perdita. And though she seems like a country girl she's actually a long-lost princess." He looked up at her and grinned. "Yes, now I come to think of it, that's exactly who you are. *Perdita.*"

It was late afternoon when they reached the wall. He was relieved to see it wasn't as sheer as he'd expected, although from where they stood at its base it seemed to go on forever. She pointed out the narrow goat track that led upwards, turning and doubling back on itself in places, disappearing behind outcrops and skirting the holes that pitted the rockface. He was surprised at how many there were and thought he saw movement in one of them.

Winona nodded. "Mountain sheep. There's a whole bunch of them around here. And eagles higher up." She looked at the sky. "Listen, Adam, there's at least two-three more hours daylight, so we got a choice. I guess it depends on how tired you are. Either we stay here and start on up in the morning, or we keep going and see how far we can get. What do you think?"

"You want me to decide?"

She glared. "No, I don't want you to decide. I want to know how you're feeling, dummy. Is that so hard to understand?"

"Sorry. I didn't mean to…ah…Yes. Right. Well, then. Since you ask, I feel fine. Not in the least tired. And I'd say…" He looked upwards, scanning the rock-face. "I'd say let's keep going."

Winona looked pleased. "Good choice."

The track was narrow, not more than a couple of feet wide in most places, so they had to walk single-file. But it wasn't as steep as it had looked or he had feared, following the natural gradient of the rock at an angle that, if not exactly easy, wasn't all that much tougher than some of the hill-walking he was used to at home.

Winona sniffed. "See if that's what you think an hour from now."

But he didn't get to find out, because before they had climbed another hundred feet, a rifle cracked and the first bullet hit the rock between them.

"*Sonofabitch*," Winona said.

 **TWENTY**

HE LAY FACEDOWN IN the dirt, his head level with her boots. "You hurt?" she said.

Before he could answer, the second bullet smacked the rock a foot above her head. *"Sonofabitch!"* she said again.

"I'm okay," he said. "Where is he?"

"Can't say without looking and I ain't gonna risk that. But my guess is, somewhere in the rocks near where we started up."

"So what do we do?"

"Take cover is what we do. You see that hole up ahead?"

"No."

"It's about twenty yards away. There's a standing rock then a hole. Ain't much but that's where we're going."

"How?"

"By crawling on our bellies. I figure, the angle he's shooting at we're safe so long as we stay low. I mean *low*, understand?"

"Yes."

"Okay, then. Better get rid of that case."

"No!"

"Suit yourself." She shrugged off her pack. A bullet struck the wall below them. *"Bastard,"* Winona said. "You ready?"

"Ready."

"Stay low."

She wriggled forward, pushing the rifle in front of her. A bullet struck the cliff as he followed, hauling himself on his elbows, his face turned flat to the dirt. There were six or seven more shots — maybe more but he wasn't counting — before they reached the standing rock and the hole behind it.

She was right: the shooter's angle was so steep the bullets passed over them, but only just. Splinters of rock flew as she reached the opening, turned and grabbed his hands, pulling him after her into the hole. She was right about that, too. A hole is what it was: narrow, damp, and smelling of rot and mildew. *'Tis some savage hold.* He pulled off the titanium case and squeezed himself around to lie beside her.

"You're hurt!"

"I don't think so."

"There's blood on your face." She touched his cheek and showed her fingers.

"You did that."

"I did?"

"You kicked me."

"Oh, Adam!"

"Don't worry about it. It was my fault, anyway. I got too close." He wiped his stubbled face and tried to sit up but the overhang was low and he hit his head. He flopped down again beside her. "What the hell do we do now?"

She put a hand on his shoulder. "Stay there."

She wriggled forward, hauling herself halfway out of the hole. The rifle cracked three times, the air whined and dirt sprayed from the cliff above the hole. She wriggled back.

"Sonofabitch has got us pinned real good. There's no way we're getting outta here without he shoots us. I'm sorry, Adam."

"It's not your fault."

"It is. I should've been more careful."

"You couldn't know. Neither of us could."

She shook her head. "I should've been more careful," she said again.

He touched her arm. "Listen, Winona…"

She pushed him away. "Quiet. I gotta think."

She lay on her back, staring up at the low rock. He eased away from her, felt a sharp jab in his side, reached behind him and found he was half-lying on a pile of loose sticks. There were white splashes on the stone and the ammoniac smell of bird droppings was sharp in his nostrils. An eagle has nested here, he thought. Thank God it's not here now. Several minutes passed. At one point she sighed and then swore and said something too low for him to hear. She put her hand on the rifle and drew it closer. Then she made a little grunting noise and turned on her side to face him.

"Okay, here's what we do. First off, you take that case and throw it down to him   "

"No!"

"Listen to me, Adam —"

"I'm not going to —"

"Will you shut up and *listen?* The goddamn case is what he's after. That's what he's trying to kill us for. Am I right, Adam? Answer me! *Am I right?*"

"…Yes."

"So if you throw it down he has to go for it. He has to come out from behind them rocks and show himself. And I get the chance of a shot."

He stared. "You'll shoot him?"

"That's the general idea."

He thought about it. "Suppose you miss?"

"I most prob'ly will. I ain't that good a shot. Which means he takes off and you say goodbye to the damn case. But what counts is, we're still alive. I don't know about you, but with me that's pretty important. So throw him the case, okay?"

He thought hard. "I don't like it."

"Who said anything about liking it?" She looked furious. "You got a better idea, mister, let's hear it. Because if you have, you're gonna make me real happy!" She waited.

He shook his head.

"Okay, then," Winona said. "Now listen good: when you throw it, make sure you toss it hard enough so it clears the slope below us. We don't want it to get stuck halfway or bounce around so it falls anyplace, okay?"

He nodded.

"But don't toss it too hard, or it'll land too close to them rocks and it'll be easy for him to get to it."

He nodded.

She looked at him doubtfully. "Maybe you'd like me to do it."

"No, I will." He reached for the silver case.

"Not too little, not too much."

"I'll do my best." He inched away slowly.

"And stay *low.*"

He crawled forward, his face in the dirt, dragging the titanium case behind him, easing himself from the hole. The goat track outside was narrow, not much more than a ledge. The standing rock that partly masked the entrance wasn't so much a rock, more a big stone, about three feet high, squashed like a misshapen loaf. He edged himself towards it and stopped a few inches from the edge. Should he look over? It was important to know what it looked like down there, he told himself. To get some idea of the layout before he threw the case. He inched forward and peered over.

He caught a brief glimpse of the open ground below and the scattering of rocks beyond it, before there was a near-simultaneous *crack* and *smack* and the earth near his head burst open.

"Adam!"

He pulled back from the edge. "Don't worry. I'm okay."

She was lying beside him, trembling. With anger? *"Do it!"*

He reached back, drew the case level and took hold of the leather strap. She cocked the rifle and settled herself on the other side of the standing rock. He took the weight of the case.

"Now!"

He overarmed the silver case into the air. The evening sun flashed as it turned over and was gone. A few seconds of silence – then the thump and bounce of it striking the ground below. Silence again.

"Did it work?"

"I don't know. I don't see it yet." She shifted her body in the dirt. "Now I see it." She frowned. "It's a mite close to them rocks."

"Too close? I got it wrong?"

"No, you did fine. Good enough for one shot. That's all I'll have time for, anyway."

"What about him?"

"What about him?"

"Do you see him?"

"Uh-uh. He ain't gonna show himself yet." She eased back from the edge. "Not for another couple hours, at least."

"What makes you so sure?"

"Because it's still daylight. He ain't gonna make a move till it gets dark. Would you?" She looked up at the fading sky. "Good thing for us it's a full moon."

"Let's hope there are no clouds tonight."

She shook her head. "Ain't gonna be no clouds. My guess is he'll wait till around midnight. Give himself plenty of dark to get clear once he's got hold of the case." She frowned. "Gonna be a tough shot, though. Shooting downhill at an angle this steep, you gotta aim way below your target. Sure to miss him, if you don't."

She checked the rifle and shifted forward, settling herself on the other side of the rock. A long half-hour went by. A bird screamed in the air somewhere high above them. Was it the eagle they had driven from its eyrie? The sun was much lower now, slipping closer to the range of peaks far off to their right.

"Only thing we gotta worry about is falling asleep," Winona said.

"I don't think there's much chance of that."

"Maybe not. Still and all…" She shifted in the dirt, moving her hips, snuggling down behind the rifle. "You know what, Adam? It'd be real good if there was sump'n to keep us awake. Sump'n interesting, know what I mean?"

He put on a straight face. "Something interesting? What exactly do you have in mind?"

She glared. "Quit your teasing. You know what I'm saying. Start talking."

He grinned, turned on his back and looked up at the sky where the first faint stars were already appearing. Where had he got to? What came next? He cleared his throat.

"One of the biggest mysteries, the question that probably intrigues Shakespeare scholars as much as any other, is what happened during the lost years."

"The lost years? What are they?"

"Be patient. I'm getting there. As I told you, William's first child, Susanna, was born in 1583…"

"I know it. Only six months after that bitch Anne Hathaway fooled him into marrying her."

"If you say so. Well, less than two years after that, Anne gave birth again, this time to twins, a boy and a girl called Hamnet and Judith."

"Were they his?"

"There's no reason to think otherwise."

She snorted. "I bet they weren't. I bet they were some other guy's, like the first kid was. Poor old William. Can't help feeling sorry for him, can you?" She shook her head. "So what happened after that?"

"That's what we don't know. What follows is silence. There is no record of Shakespeare after the birth of the twins until we hear of him seven years later in London, when he is beginning to be known as an actor and playwright."

"You're saying, after the kids were born he upped and lit out?"

"It looks like it."

"See? I was right!" She looked across at him triumphantly. "His shitty wife lands him with a couple more kids ain't his and the guy takes off.

Course he does. Hell, it's natural. What any self-respecting guy would do!" She wriggled lower in the dirt and gave a little chuckle. "So where did he go?"

"Again, we don't know. It's a total blank. There are various theories, of course."

"Like what?"

"Well, one is that he was a schoolmaster or private tutor somewhere."

Winona frowned. "That don't sound much fun."

"Or that he became a soldier and went to the Low Countries where he served in the wars. There's plenty of stuff in the plays – not just battles – about soldiers and soldiering that might have been learned from real experience."

"Sounds possible. I know some guys did that. Enlisted in the Marine Corps. Don't know where they are now." She shook her head. "Fighting Arabs, maybe?"

"Another theory is that a company of travelling players came to Stratford, as they regularly did, and were a man short because one of them had been killed in a quarrel, and Shakespeare stepped in and left with them."

"Sounds possible, too."

"Then, of course, there's the deer-stealing story," Adam said. "But we needn't concern ourselves with that."

"Deer-stealing? Hey, tell me about it!"

"Don't get excited, Winona. It's only a story. There is absolutely nothing to say it really happened."

"Don't matter. Tell it."

"All right. Just outside Stratford there was a grand house owned by a local bigwig called Lucy..."

"That's a girl's name!"

"Sir Thomas Lucy. He was a landowner and a magistrate, and on his estate he had a deer park. The legend is that Shakespeare poached some of his deer, but he was caught and brought before Sir Thomas who had him whipped. In revenge, Shakespeare wrote a rude poem about Lucy, stuck it up on the gateway to his house and then left town in a hurry."

"That's it! That's what happened, I know it! That's the reason Shakespeare took off!"

"Winona, it's a story. A legend. A myth. Nobody believes it anymore."

"Then they're stupid. They got no notion how things really are. Poaching deer? Getting in trouble with the law? Why, it's the exact same kind of thing Sonny'd do. It's just like him. Fact, tell you the truth, Adam…" she leaned across to him, her voice low, confidential, "more you tell me about Shakespeare – him chasing after girls, getting into fights, shooting deer – more he sounds to me like Sonny. He really does. You reckon there's any chance they could be kin?"

"I don't think it's very likely. The odds against it must be pretty steep."

"Wouldn't surprise me one bit. Okay – what happened next?"

"First, I think I should talk a little bit about the actors' companies and the London theatres. So you get an idea of the world Shakespeare was becoming part of. At that time, to be an actor was technically against the law."

"They were outlaws, too? Oh, my Lord!"

"Only technically. They were classified as rogues and vagabonds and liable to prosecution unless they had the protection of an aristocrat and could claim they were his servants, available to perform for his entertainment whenever he required."

"And is that what they did? Act plays for some old lord?"

"Occasionally, but not very often. It was a kind of trick to get around the law, because their real business was performing for the general public, which is how they made their living. But it explains why they were called the Earl of Derby's Men or the Earl of Pembroke's Men or the Admiral's Men or the Lord Chamberlain's Men, which was Shakespeare's company. Their life wasn't easy. Sometimes, when times were bad, they broke up and went out of business, or joined together for a while until things got better and they could re-form as separate companies again. Sometimes, if there was plague in London, which happened pretty often, they had to go on tour, which they don't seem to have liked very much. Rather like actors today, I'm told. Still, you can understand it. London was the capital, the third or fourth biggest city in Europe, the place to be."

"It was where the action was, right?"

"Right. It was also where the theatres were, the buildings specifically put up for the performance of plays. The first one was called, naturally enough, the Theatre. It was built by James Burbage, whose son Richard would become Shakespeare's friend and the leading actor in his company...."

More than three hours later, under a moon so refulgent it cast indigo shadows, he had reached the War of the Theatres and was deep in the question of how involved Shakespeare had been in it, and whether Ajax in *Troilus and Cressida* was a satire on Ben Jonson, when he heard her draw her breath in and saw her sit up.

"Something's moving down there," she said quietly. And a moment later, "He's coming out."

 **TWENTY-ONE**

SHE SHIFTED CLOSER TO the edge and lifted the rifle, laying her cheek against the stock. He lay very still. *"Aim low,"* she said to herself. A moment passed and he saw her finger curl round the trigger. Another moment and he saw it squeeze.

The report was loud enough to make him jump. It was the rockface, he realised, acting as a sounding board as it had done when she called out to Rudd. But this sound was bigger; it seemed to roll around the whole mountainside. Or perhaps it was his imagination or simply the ringing in his ears.

"Shit." She lowered the rifle. "Sorry, Adam. I guess I missed."

He pulled himself forward and looked over the edge. He could see nothing down there. "Maybe you wounded him."

"It's possible." She sounded doubtful. She sat back on her heels. "Guess we better go see."

Getting down was harder and took much longer than he thought it would, partly because of the narrow track but mainly because she was so cautious, leading the way on her belly, stopping every thirty seconds or so to peer down and scan the ground below in case the shooter was still there among the rocks, waiting to take them out. At one point he got impatient and tapped her ankle and said couldn't they go a bit faster? She didn't reply, but turned and looked at him stone-faced over her shoulder, her wide mouth clamped tight, staring him down until he said sorry, I'm an idiot, and they went on again in silence, inch by inch, yard by yard, until they were all the way to the bottom.

They half-rose cautiously to their feet and he followed her, crouching, across the open ground towards the scattered rocks. They were nearly halfway when she stopped and pointed to a scuffed tear in the earth.

"That's where it landed. Bounced a couple times, see? And he come out to get it from..." She looked ahead and pointed. "Over there."

She went on slowly, eyes on the ground in front of her, stopping from time to time, reaching down to touch the earth, grunting softly and shaking her head, straightening up and moving on. He followed silently until they came to the first scattering of rocks. She had started to pick her way amongst them when suddenly she stopped, was still for a moment, then knelt down quickly. He squatted beside her, staring.

The stain was purple in the moonlight. "You hit him!"

"Looks like it." She reached out to touch it.

"How badly is he hurt, do you think?"

She shook her head. "Hard to say." She looked at her fingers and then wiped them on the earth. She stood up and looked round. "Guess this'll do."

"For what?"

"For us to get some sleep."

He stared. "You're not going after him?"

"No point," Winona said. "Follow a trail like this you need daylight and that ain't for a few hours yet. So we may as well make the best of it and get some rest while we can. Could be hard going tomorrow."

"But he's getting away!"

"Adam, listen." She turned to face him. "Only a great tracker like Sonny could follow that trail by moonlight and Sonny ain't here. We try, we'll lose it inside ten minutes and spend the rest of the night driving ourselves crazy and wearing ourselves out. Which means we won't be in any kind of shape come the morning. Is that what you want?"

"No, but it seems so... I don't know... *Defeatist*. The man is hurt and we're letting him get away."

"If he's hurt bad – real bad – you don't have to worry. We'll catch up with him sure enough. If he ain't..." She shrugged. "Trust me. I know what I'm talking about."

They lay down in the lee of one of the bigger rocks. The wall rose sheer behind them. At any other time he would probably have found it beautiful. Not now.

"We'll start soon as it gets light," Winona said. "Meantime, try and get some sleep."

He didn't, of course, and neither, he thought, did she. Or at least not much. She might have dozed off for a minute or two, but from the sound of her breathing he knew she was as wide awake as he was most of the time. Still, it wasn't much more than two hours before the wall began slowly to change its texture in the pre-dawn half-light, and shortly after that it was sun-up and they were on their way.

It turned out to be easier than either of them expected. She found the first blood-stain in less than three minutes and the next one even sooner after that.

"He's heading south," she said after a while, "and pretty much in a straight line. My guess is he's using a compass."

"What does that mean?"

"Means he's someone who don't know the country too well. Or maybe he's got a meeting fixed at someplace he has to head for."

"Is he going anywhere near Rudd?"

"Uh-uh." She shook her head. "Rudd's over to the west of here. Looks to me this guy's making for the river."

Half an hour later they were in the trees again, moving down the slope through the thick stands of larch and fir. Less than a hundred yards inside the forest they came upon a strip of coloured fabric that looked as if it had been torn from a shirt or jacket and some broken sticks lying near the base of a tree. There were bloodstains on the flattened grass.

Winona squatted down and picked up a couple of the sticks.

"He's tried to make himself a tourniquet." She looked at the spattered ground. "He's hurt bad. Wouldn't surprise me if…"

She broke off abruptly and lifted her hand. From somewhere in the distance far ahead of them he heard a series of faint, percussive thuds.

"Rifle," Winona said.

"What does that mean?"

"Guess we'll know soon enough." She tossed the sticks away, checked her rifle and stood up. "Keep your eyes open and stay close. After the next couple miles he could be laying up anywhere."

They walked more slowly now and more carefully, and it was a full hour before she stopped and put her hand on his arm. They stood in un-moving silence for the next minute, staring ahead to where, a hundred yards away near a thicket of young trees, something lay on the dark ground. Winona stirred, looked around and nodded to him and they made their way forward cautiously, stopping every ten yards or so to check the forest where, as far as he could tell, nothing moved among the tall trees.

The man lay on his back on the torn, blood-spattered earth. His eyes were wide open, staring up from a face that, apart from a deep cut in the scalp, was unmarked. Lower down, his chest and belly had been torn open, ex-posing the rib cage. Snakes of blue-white entrails and gobbets of chewed flesh were mixed with the bloodied scraps of ripped clothing.

"Grizzly," Winona said.

The man's rifle lay half-covered with soil. She picked it up. Adam went to where the titanium case lay a few yards away at the foot of a young larch. He lifted it and wiped the earth away.

"How is it?"

There were some new dents in the shell where it had struck the ground after he had thrown it, but otherwise it was intact. He went back to where she stood by the body.

"It seems okay."

"Well, that's something." She looked down at the man. "Guess we oughtta bury him."

"Yes."

He's a pretty mean-looking guy."

"Yes."

"What is he – some kind of Latino? Puerto Rican? A Mex?"

"Mexican, I think." He looked down at the high cheekbones and the heavy, down-swept Zapata moustache. "His name's Enrique."

Exit pursued by a bear.

 **TWENTY-TWO**

"THEY'LL BE CALLING YOUR flight soon."

He looked through the open doors to where, on the edge of the runway, several men in fluorescent overalls — ground-crew, he supposed — were pushing a wheeled stairway into position, manoeuvering it towards the doorway near the front of the plane.

"I suppose they will."

The door opened and a middle-aged woman in airline uniform stood waiting for the head of the stairway to arrive. One of the men in overalls started to climb the steps. A set of heavy earphones — or were they sound-mufflers? —hung around his neck and he was holding a clipboard. The airline woman smiled and said something to him and they disappeared inside.

Her chin came up. She looked at him, scowling. "You want to go now?"

The departure lounge was a glass-walled room on the other side of a security barrier, where three people sat far apart from each other on steel-frame chairs with seats and backs made to look like cowhide.

"There's no hurry."

A telephone rang at one of the car rental desks behind them. No one was there to answer it and it went on ringing, shrill and insistent in the small terminal space. A man at one of the other car rental desks looked up for a moment, scratched his cheek, yawned and went back to his newspaper.

"How long's the flight?"

"I'm not sure. I have to change somewhere. Seattle, I think. But I should be in San Francisco this evening."

The car rental telephone stopped ringing. He looked back along the hall towards the far end where there was a cafeteria and bar.

"Would you like a drink?"

She made a little lifting-dropping motion with her shoulders, he picked up the silver case and they walked the length of the terminal, passing the wall-map of Montana he had looked at — how long ago? Twelve days, was it? More? It seemed like ten years. A man came out of the rest room where he had washed half an hour earlier and stared at himself for a long time in the mirror above the hand basin. It was more than stubble on his face now, well on the way to being a proper beard. Should he shave it? When? Did it matter? He'd decide later. There were other things to think about.

Four young people were sitting at a table in the cafeteria. Two boys and two girls drinking beer and giggling. About the same age as his students. One of the boys wore a scarlet bomber jacket with a big white K on it. He was a good-looking kid with broad shoulders and bright yellow hair. He looked at Winona and then at Adam and said something to the others. They looked up and he said something else which made them all laugh. What did they call kids like him? A high-school jock. Yes.

They stood at the bar. "What would you like?"

She made the up-and-down shoulder motion again. Her copper hair gleamed in the little overhead spotlights. "Coke, I guess."

"One Coca-Cola," he said to the lady behind the bar. "And one coffee, please. Regular."

He peeled back the cover of the little capsule, poured the half-and-half mix into his coffee and stirred it with a plastic spoon.

"We ought to be drinking champagne," he said.

She made a little gulping sound and lifted the bottle. Her eyes were filling. He looked away. An amplified voice came on from somewhere in the ceiling, announcing the departure of Flight 219 to Seattle and requesting all passengers to proceed to the departure gate. He put down his cup.

"Time to go." He bent to pick up the silver case.

"I got something for you." She reached into her pocket. "Didn't have time to get you a real present, so this'll have to do." She put a lump of grubby Kleenex into his hand.

He unfolded the damp tissue. It was the little butterfly from her hair-grip. "When this you see, remember me," Winona said.

He closed his fist on it and stared at her. What should he do? Shake hands? What should he say? Thanks very much? See you again sometime? And then, in a great rush, it came to him. Dickhead! It was obvious! He took her in his arms and kissed her.

"Winona," he said, "I love you."

She burst into tears and started to hit him, fists drumming his chest. "You asshole! What took you so long?"

Once he had got used to the rental car and reminded himself always to keep right, the only problem was finding the freeway. He almost took the one marked San Francisco but remembered just in time that was wrong. It was the San Bruno one he needed, otherwise he would end up downtown in the thick of bewildering rush-hour traffic and it would take him hours to find his way through the packed city grid.

There was a tricky moment when he swung hard across three lanes with car horns blaring all around him and red-faced drivers mouthing obscenities behind their windshields, but after that it was easy. He drove through the Park, then the tunnel and swung up onto the bridge. The toll-gates were open. You paid going the other way. He drove across the great rust-orange span, the lights of the city bright behind him, and entered the Marin tunnel with the hippy rainbow arching the entrance. Out the other side it grew darker and he drove more slowly, cruising the nearside lane, looking up watchfully at the green-and-white turnoff signs until he came to the one that led eventually to the Foundation.

Once past the new housing development, the minor road was almost deserted and he switched to the high beam, headlights sweeping the brown hillsides as he made the tight upward curves. He met only one other car, switching down hurriedly when it flashed him and slowing almost to a stop until it was past. Apart from that the road was empty, and he drove without stopping until he came to the great iron-barred gate.

It swung open immediately because the security men were expecting him. They waved him through the chicane and minutes later he was pulling up outside the Tudor manor house. She was waiting on the flagstones, framed in light from the entrance porch, and he was scarcely out of the car before her arms were tight around him and she was kissing him frantically.

"You're here! Adam — it's a miracle!"

Her mouth was soft and warm and he could feel her breasts against him. She took his hand.

"Come in the house!"

"Just a sec."

He reached back into the car and took out the titanium case. She stared in wild astonishment.

"You've got it! *Still!* Oh, Adam, that's *incredible!* How did it happen? I mean, where *were* you all this time? Darling — what did you *do?*"

"Let's go inside," he said.

There were lights in the entrance hall and in the long living room where the piano was. Otherwise, the house was in darkness.

"Where is everybody?"

"Marisol's in town with the others. There have been all kinds of people here — lawyers, the newspapers. It's been so awful, Adam, I can't tell you!

I've been just frantic! And when you called this morning and I heard your voice – I just couldn't believe it! I thought I was going crazy, I truly did!" She put her arms around him. "But now it *is* you, it really *is*, and everything's going to be perfect, I know it!" She held him close and kissed him. She was wearing silk, smooth and lovely under his fingers. She smelled delicious. "Let's celebrate!"

He waited in the hall, surrounded by glowing panels of carved redwood, until she returned with the bottle and glasses.

"Where shall we drink it?"

He lifted the silver case. "The library."

They walked through the living room and followed the pink carpet into the huge book-lined tithe-barn, where she paused in the doorway and dimmed the lights in the wall sconces, throwing the gallery into deep shadow, turning the stained-glass window at the far end opaque, making the wind-braced roof scarcely visible above their heads. The line of portraits glowed softly from the walls. She lit the two huge candles that stood at each end of the stone mantel with its carved motto. *Non Sans Droit*. They sank into the leather chairs by the great fireplace with the Davenant bust looking down at them.

"I should have lit a fire." She poured the wine. "I would have, if I'd thought about it."

The glasses as they touched them made a delicate ringing sound. The wine when he sipped it was nectar in his mouth. He picked up the silver case and placed it on the low table between them.

"What's the combination?"

She stared at the battered shell. "I've no idea."

"You haven't? Not at all?"

She shook her head.

"Not even the slightest notion?"

She shook her head again.

He frowned. "That's…a pity. I was rather hoping you did. In fact, I was counting on it."

He ran his finger across the eight little wheels below the broken handle. There was dried mud on some of them and he flicked it away.

"Did he have a method? A preference? With other locks, I mean? For safes or strongboxes, things like that?"

Her forehead creased.

He put his glass down and leaned forward. "Was there any kind of pattern to the numbers he usually chose? Was there a logic to them? *Think*, Soraya. Did he have a system? Most people do."

She stared at the empty fireplace. He waited through the long silence until she looked up.

"He liked dates," she said.

"Dates?"

She nodded. "1776…9/11. Things like that."

He frowned.

She leaned forward and put her hand on the titanium shell. "Why don't we just break it open?"

He sighed, looking for a moment much older than his years. "Because for one thing it's precision-made, fool-proof, and breaking it open will be so difficult we may damage the manuscript. If there *is* any manuscript left to damage. And for another thing," he rubbed his stubbled face wearily, "it deserves better than to be sledge-hammered open. I deserve better. We all do."

She drew her lips together and sat up, arching her back, pouting slightly. She looked wonderful, he thought, even more stunning than he remembered.

"That's all very well, Adam. It's a fine thing to say. And if I were in your shoes maybe I'd say the same. But what about Mr. Blankenship? Have you thought about him? How would he feel if…?"

She broke off as he sat up quickly.

He looked different suddenly. His eyes were shining. He was young again. "What is it?"

"Nothing. An idea." He reached out and pulled the case towards him.

"No, not an idea. A hunch."

"What is it?" she said again.

"It's crazy." He touched the first wheel and laughed. "A crazy hunch."

She watched as he worked along the row, rolling each little wheel up or down. Then he looked up at her and grinned.

"Fingers crossed!"

He thumbed the locks. Nothing happened.

"Blast."

His eyes dulled and he slumped back in the chair, not young anymore. "I thought – just for a moment – I thought I'd got it. When you said he liked dates, I suddenly remembered something someone said to me a few days ago. Something I thought was bloody stupid at the time."

"What was it?"

"That when they set combinations, most people use their birthdays. Yes, I know, it's ridiculous. But suddenly I thought *hold on a minute! That's it!*"

"What? What did you think it was?"

"The 23rd of April, 1564. Shakespeare's birthday." He shrugged and picked up his glass. "Eight numbers. Perfect. I put them in. 2-3-0-4-1-5-6-4. Great idea, oh yes. Only, it didn't work." He made a face and drank deeply. "That's the trouble with great ideas. They usually don't. You have to be either a genius or bloody lucky. And as far as I'm concerned, luck is something…"

He stopped. He looked at the silver case. He put his glass down. He looked at her. "What was it you said earlier? About him liking dates?"

"That's all I said."

"No. You mentioned a couple, didn't you? 1776. 9/11."

"So what? What's significant about that?"

"You're American, that's what's significant. And Americans put the month before the day. They say 9/11, not 11/9. So instead of 23rd April…"

"We say April 23rd!" She sat up straight, breathing quickly. "Adam – do you think that's it?"

"Might as well try."

He leaned forward and re-set the first four wheels. "0-4-2-3." He thumbed the locks. They snapped upwards.

"*Bingo,*" Adam said.

 **TWENTY-THREE**

THE LID CREAKED SLIGHTLY as he opened it. There was a dark stain across one corner of the lining, probably where water had got in when he fell into the river. But the central recess was just as he remembered it. *The Booke of Loues Labours Wonne.* Untouched. He lifted it out and placed it on the table.

"Safe and sound."

"Darling." She rose from the chair and came across to him. He stood up and she took his face in her hands. "You're *amazing.*"

She kissed him, pressing herself close against him. She was trembling and he could feel her heart beat.

"It isn't worth killing for," he said.

Her back went rigid under his fingers. "What do you mean?"

"What I say. It isn't worth killing for. Not Willard Blankenship. Me. Not anyone. When did you decide to do it, Soraya?"

She tried to pull away but he held onto her firmly. "I don't know what you're talking about. Let go of me."

"Was it when I told you how much it might be worth? Or was it later, in Montana, when you realised it was the perfect opportunity to get rid of him and set me up for his murder?"

"Adam, if you think —"

"Sit down."

"Listen to me —"

"Sit *down*."

She began to struggle but he held her tightly, forcing her backwards into the deep chair.

"Were you in bed with him? Or did you choose to be somewhere else when Enrique cut his throat?"

"This is crazy! Ricky is in Montana trying to find you!"

"He's in Montana but he isn't trying to find me. He's dead. A bear killed him. After he'd tried several times to kill me."

Her hand went to her mouth and she gave a little cry.

He stood over her. "You killed Willard Blankenship, Soraya. You and Enrique together. You smashed up the cabin so it would look like someone had wrecked it searching for the manuscript. Then you woke me and said you had just discovered the body. The pair of you looked so terrified, so completely helpless, that I immediately took over and started giving orders. That was clever of you, making it seem as if I was the one in charge.

"You led me into the forest, deliberately taking the wrong direction. You planned to ditch me there, so it would look as if I had killed Blankenship and tried to escape but lost my way. You even gave me the manuscript to carry, in case I had any suspicion of what was really going on. I have to congratulate you on that one, Soraya. It was inspired. Your father would have been proud of you."

"Don't you dare mention my father! You're not worth the dirt on his shoes!" She was ugly with hatred.

He shrugged. "Once you had reported the murder, Enrique was going to track me, kill me, retrieve the manuscript and get rid of my body. And that would have been the story. Professor kills to gain priceless manuscript but disappears into Wilderness. Body never found." He shook his head and sat down facing her.

"It would have worked too, if I hadn't had an accident and rolled the car. And someone hadn't happened by and pulled me clear. And that titanium case hadn't deflected the bullet when Enrique took his first shot at me. And someone hadn't wounded him when he tried to kill me again."

"You're insane. I haven't the slightest idea what you're talking about."
She smoothed her hair and sat up straight. "If Ricky did all those horrible
things you say — and personally I don't believe it — but if he did, none of
it has anything to do with me. My relationship with him was one of employer and employee, nothing more. Those terrible things, if he really did
them, were entirely his idea."

He nodded. "I suppose that will be your defence. And maybe you'll
get away with it, a beautiful woman like you."

She smiled. "I can be very convincing when I want to be."

"You don't have to tell me. I remember our evening at the opera. And
the night afterwards. I believed every word." He gave a wry smile. "As
for this…" He picked up the stack of yellowed parchment. "I'm beginning
to think there's a curse on it."

"That manuscript is the property of the Blankenship Foundation," Soraya said, "and as its current representative I demand that you hand it over
to me."

He laughed — the first proper laugh he'd had in ages, he realised. "Nice
try, my darling, but it won't work. And anyway, something tells me
Willard Blankenship wasn't even its true owner. If he was, why did he
come to me to authenticate it, when he could have gone to the Folger or
the Library of Congress or the Huntington or any number of places with
people far more qualified than I am? Because he didn't want it known, I
guess. Not till he had stopped up all the loopholes."

He rubbed the back of his neck. "I should have thought of that, shouldn't
I? But I was too flattered to be asked. Too excited at the prospect. And
too attracted by the bait. Did he tell you to seduce me? Yes, I see he did.
What a wicked old man." He grinned. "Serves me right, doesn't it? Ah,
well." He placed the manuscript carefully into its recess. He looked down
at it longingly, his fingers still touching it, reluctant to let it go.

"For all I know, this really belongs to Ch'a Min-su — or even the antique dealer in Sonoma, whoever he is. Well, I daresay the courts will

sort it out." He closed the lid and snapped the locks shut. "In the meantime…" He spun the little wheels. "It stays safe with me." He lifted the silver case and hauled himself out of the deep chair.

"Adam, where are you going?" Soraya said.

"To bed. I'm exhausted." He yawned hugely. "And in case you have any plans tonight, I'm locking my bedroom door."

Her face twisted. "Don't flatter yourself." She stood up. "Ricky was a real lover, not a sad little college jerk-off. He knew how to please a woman. He was ten times the man you are."

He nodded. "That doesn't surprise me — although I doubt if anything could at this moment." He yawned again. "Sorry — but you know, since I got here I've met the most amazing people, and the extraordinary thing is they all seemed like characters out of Shakespeare. There was Prospero, King Lear, Perdita — and now I come to think of it, Enrique would have made a pretty good Caliban. But I haven't been able to place you, Soraya. Not until this moment. And I could kick myself because it's so obvious."

"Is it? Who am I, then?"

"You're the Dark Lady."

She stared at him hatefully. "I guess you think that's clever," she said. "And it makes you the hero, right?"

"Me, the hero? Not even close." He made a wry face. "My part's much simpler and I've played it to perfection. You only have to look at me. I'm the Fool."

 **TWENTY-FOUR**

IF IT HADN'T BEEN for the hedge that ran along the front of the house he would surely have died. Burning, asphyxiation or a broken neck, it was a toss-up which would have done for him. But the little four-foot hedge saved him. He woke, choking. Smoke was pouring in around the door. By the time he had located the key and opened it, the landing outside was blazing and the stairs beyond them an inferno. The heat smacked him in the face and drove him backwards. The noise was appalling. He had no idea fire *roared* like that. He slammed the door closed, groped his way to the leaded window, forced it open and peered outside.

It wasn't much better. As far as he could tell, the whole front of the house was ablaze. He looked at the ground. It seemed a horribly long way down. He crawled back into the room with a half-formed thought about dragging sheets from the bed and knotting them together to make a rope. Wasn't that what you were supposed to do? But before he got there the bedroom door burst inwards and flames poured into the room, sucked by the draught he had created. He wriggled forward, groping for the silver case where he had left it on the little table beside the bed.

It wasn't there.

Maybe it was the other side, and he'd made a mistake out of panic or sheer confusion. He forced himself to crawl round the bed to the side nearer the door, flinching as he felt the heat scorch his face.

It wasn't there either.

There was no time to search. He staggered back to the window, hauled himself onto the sill and jumped.

A couple of feet either way and he'd have landed on the flagstones and that would have been it. *Good night, sweet Prince.* But the little hedge caught him like a mattress, inflicting no more serious injuries than a rash of scratches across his lower back and shoulders that he wasn't aware of until much later. He lay sprawled across it, winded and semi-conscious, until a couple of blazing timbers crashed down within feet of him, showering him with scraps of burning roof shingle. He rolled clear, beat the sparks out and hauled himself upright, retreating drunkenly from the inferno until headlights swung into view on the other side of the lake and wheels tore up the gravel as the security men arrived.

It took another twenty minutes for the first fire engine to show. That was pretty good apparently, seeing they had to come from the nearest little town a couple of miles away. Then two more fire engines came from somewhere else and another four from somewhere else, and soon whole squads of firemen in their great bulky overalls and huge sculpted helmets were everywhere.

To his surprise they made very little attempt to save the house itself. It was too far gone, they said; the fire had taken too strong a hold. What in hell happened to the alarm system? And the overhead sprinklers inside, why hadn't they done their job? Forget the house. The house is finished. Concentrate on containing the fire.

They doused the surrounding area, beating out the little blazes started by windblown sparks and falling debris, spraying the nearby trees until they sagged under the weight of water. The one thing they couldn't risk, they said, was for the fire to take hold of the ground and sweep over the hills into the next valley. If that happened, nothing could stop it. The brush was tinder-dry. A fire like that could rage for days and wipe out whole communities. Better lose a dozen fancy Tudor manors than risk that.

It wasn't until late afternoon that he was at last able to make his way through the buckled steel framework, stepping gingerly over the charred ends of redwood panel, through mounds of smoking ash still hot under his feet, to the approximate spot where his bedroom had been. He searched carefully, finding various lengths of twisted metal, most of it ruined plumbing or the melted remains of bathroom fittings, but nothing that resembled the titanium case.

After a while he moved to where the library had been. It looked as if the fire had been at its most intense here. All that wood! All that paper! The little strong room was only partly intact. One wall had burst inwards and all its contents had been destroyed. Lousy construction work, the firemen said. Must have been a jerry-built job.

He crossed to the gaping fireplace and the scorched chimney-stack. *Non Sans Droit*. The carved letters were still visible on the blackened stone mantel. The niche above it was empty, but there were some pottery fragments in the debris around his feet. He bent down and picked one up.

"Looking for something?" It was one of the firemen. He nodded. "Something important, huh?"

"I don't know," Adam said. "It might have been."

The little terracotta shard was still hot, much too hot to hold onto. A piece of Shakespeare's forehead. He let it drop. A breeze stirred the ashes at the far end of the great room where the stained-glass window had been. Grey powder drifted across the empty space, carried by the wind beyond the smoking framework towards the distant, rounded hills.

Adam wiped his hands on his shirt, turned and walked out of the ruined Foundation, making his way through the tangle of hoses and cables, past groups of exhausted firemen leaning against their huge trucks, drinking coffee and talking in low, weary voices, to where he had left the rental car.

"So where is she now?"

"I don't know. Nobody does. The security men say she left just after midnight. It was another couple of hours before they saw the red in the sky and realised what was happening, and that was when they called the fire department. It wasn't their fault. The alarm systems weren't working."

"She switched them off?"

"She must have. I don't know whether they'll be able to prove it, though."

"Is that what they said?"

"Who, the police? Not in so many words, although they hinted at it."

"Hinted? The cops?"

"Actually, they were rather nice. Why are you laughing?"

"Because of the things you say and the way you say them. *Rah-ah-ther nice.* I never heard anyone say that about cops."

"Well, they were. I didn't know what to expect and they surprised me. The guy in charge is called Inspector Scanlon, and he was courteous, friendly, couldn't have been nicer. He showed me around the precinct and introduced me to some of the detectives on his team. They were charming. Not a bit like they are in the movies. You're laughing again. Don't you believe me?"

"Sure I do. I believe everything you tell me."

"Now you're teasing me."

"I love you and it's the truth."

"When did you decide?"

"That I loved you? Right off, I guess. From when I pulled you out of that wreck."

"Good Lord, that was quick."

"Don't mock me. At least I wasn't an old slowpoke like you. I was so mad at you! That night at the party, remember? I sat there and sat there and you never asked me to dance. Not once. And I dressed up special for you. Then that horrible Charlene with her horrible boobs came along and you danced with her quick enough. Why did you do that?"

"Because I was stupid and insensitive and a bloody fool. Please try and forgive me."

"I did already."

She kissed him and they lay still for a while, his arm loose around her, propped on the huge downy pillows, watching the sun on the water and some heeled-over yachts.

The view from their penthouse suite was impressive, taking in the Golden Gate and the first sweep of the bay. He had insisted on inspecting it before confirming the reservation. When she saw it she gave a little scream, rushing to pull open doors, screaming a little louder at the bathroom with its walk-in shower and deep marble tub, and loudest of all at the bedroom with the emperor-sized bed where they were now and had been since they arrived.

That was yesterday afternoon, straight after he had picked her up at the airport, and their clothes were still scattered across the carpet, tangled with the bathrobe he had worn to bring in the food from room service, plus the several bottles of wine they had ordered since then.

"So where was her car when they found it?"

"In Oakland, on the other side of the bay. It looks as if she was heading for the airport there."

"Only she never made it?"

"That's right. At least, there's no record of her on any of the outbound flights. And her car was by the roadside a few miles away. It had been left on the hard shoulder, like it had been abandoned. The keys were still in it."

"Beats me why no one boosted it."

"That's what Inspector Scanlon said."

"And no sign of your silver case?"

"No."

She turned to face him. "She took it, though, didn't she?"

"Yes, I think so. In fact, I'm certain she did." He frowned. "It was my fault. I ought to have realised she'd have a key to all the rooms in the house. But I was so whacked, so exhausted, I wasn't thinking straight. All she had to do was wait till I was asleep, let herself in and walk off with the case."

"Next time make sure you leave the key in the lock."

"Are you laughing at me again?"

"Just a little." She stroked his face gently, her fingers tracing the line of his mouth. He kissed them. She sighed. "So she's got away with it, free and clear." She scowled. "Bitch."

"Not necessarily."

"What does that mean?"

"According to Inspector Scanlon there was a big dent in the front of her car. On the driver's side. And there were tyre marks on the road surface just before the place they found it. He said it looked as if…"

"I know - don't tell me! Some guys drove into her and forced her off the road!"

"Yes."

"And they grabbed her and took her! With the silver case! And left the car with the keys in it!"

"It's a possibility, he said."

"Possibility, nuts! It's what happened! What else could it be?"

"Well, she might have been waiting for them and gone along willingly. The whole thing might have been prearranged."

"So how do you account for the dent in her car?"

"It could have been an accident, something she did earlier. She was scared and driving too fast and just hit something."

"An accident? You believe that? Adam, sometimes you crack me up, you really do. A smart guy like you and you come up with something as stupid as that! Who were the guys in the other car, do you think? Was it that old Korean? I bet it was!"

"I don't know. Don't ask me."

"Why not? You're not interested?"

"Of course I'm interested. Only, I'm tired of it. No, that's not true. I'm sick of it. No, that's not true, either. Look, it's in the hands of the police and that's all that concerns me."

"You don't want to get your old papers back? You don't want to see her in jail?"

"They're not my papers. I don't know whose they are. They've been lost for over four hundred years, Winona. And listen - shall I tell you something?"

He turned to face her, propping himself on one elbow. "A few years more aren't going to make very much difference. If the manuscript still exists, someone's going to find it. And then we'll know whether it's genuine or not. For a while I thought it was going to be me – that I was going to share in the glory, become famous. I think it made me a little crazy. Well, I'm not crazy anymore."

He leaned down and kissed her. "I don't give a damn what happens to Soraya Kamali. I don't want to think about her or the manuscript. Not now. Not this minute. I just want to be here and make love with you."

"But Adam ..."

"*Sssh!*"

A little later she said, "Don't you want them to catch her?"

"Why do you ask?"

"Well... Seems to me you were kinda stuck on her."

"That's because I was stupid. And anyway, it was before I met you. And there's no need to frown like that. It's the truth."

"I know it. That ain't the reason."

"So why are you looking so miserable?"

"Because... Because this is all so... It's so *wonderful*... I don't want it to end. Not ever."

"Don't think about it." He kissed her chin. "Think about all the things we're going to do instead."

"Like what?"

"Like *everything*. All the corny tourist things, you know? Like riding the cable cars and taking the tour of Alcatraz…"

"Yes!"

"Visiting Chinatown and Golden Gate Park. Buying you lots of pretty clothes and then going to Sears to eat pancakes. Seeing the Giants play baseball…"

"*Yes!*"

"Driving to the Napa Valley to see the wine country and Sonoma. Going down the coast to Monterey and taking Highway One through Big Sur, which I've always wanted to see. Stopping off at Carmel and staying there a few days till you're ready to come back. Things like that."

"Yes, *yes,YES!*"

"Unless of course you'd rather stay here and just make love for the next couple of weeks… Winona? You're frowning again."

"It's real tempting. Oh, Adam, can't we do both?"

"My darling, we can try!"

 **TWENTY-FIVE**

MISS BROWNLOW LAUGHED. "IT was a disaster! A total disaster! We never even got to France, let alone the Loire!"

She slid the lecture list and the notes for her first assignment into a transparent folder and put it down by her feet. She was wearing brown suede ankle-boots, he saw, and black leggings, with tiny cut-off shorts and a loose, belted shirt. It seemed to be the look this term. Knicker-revealing jeans and bare midriffs had clearly had their day.

"Two of the boys pulled out at the last minute. They said they couldn't really afford it and anyway they had too much work to make up. Person-ally, I think they were lying — in fact, I know they were because a girl I know from home was in Marbella this summer and she says she saw them there. Which was crapsville of them, but who cares?

"Then one of the girls got ill — and I know that was true because she had to go to hospital and only came out a couple of weeks ago. And one of the other girls decided to go away with her parents, which I couldn't really blame her for because they were going to the Seychelles which must have been incredible. And before I knew it there was only me and one other guy who I hardly knew and certainly didn't fancy — he was *creepy*, a real perv — and I thought, what am I doing? This is insane!

"So I went to stay with my sister in Edinburgh instead, which wasn't exactly funtime because she's got this new boyfriend who's Scottish and like, *ugh*." Miss Brownlow made a horrible face and gave a stomach-heaving shudder. "Still, I was there for the first part of the Festival which was okay and the Fringe which was great. And that was my summer." She laughed again. "What about you? How was yours? Was it quiet, like you said?"

"Not exactly. Not the first part, anyway."

Through the half-open window overlooking the garden came the sound of a lawnmower. Not for much longer, surely? Summer was over. It was autumn out there. The clocks would be going back soon and the next thing you knew it would be winter. *When all aloud the wind doth blow, And coughing drowns the parson's saw.*

"Did you start your new book?"

"Not quite. I got a bit…um…a bit distracted. At least, to begin with. I made a few notes when I got home."

"You did go away, then? Anywhere special?"

"I suppose you could say so. I was in America. California and…ah…the Rockies."

"Was that where you grew the beard? It looks really cool." She picked up the folder and put it into her nylon backpack. "Oh, and congratulations on winning the Duff Cooper Prize. You must be very pleased."

"Thank you. Yes, I suppose I am."

Feet sounded on the staircase. Someone called to someone else, who replied in a high, excited voice. There was the sound of laughter, male and female. Freshmen.

Miss Brownlow fastened the flap of her backpack and stood up. "I'm really looking forward to this term."

"Good. So am I."

He smiled, got up and went to his desk. His notes for the first chapter of *Gorgeous Palaces: Shakespeare and the Masque* were arranged neatly on the left. A little plastic butterfly sat on top of them.

The mail he had picked up from the Porters' Lodge was in a pile on the right. A note from the Dean: sherry at 6:30 p.m. tomorrow. An invitation from the Union to second the motion in this term's opening debate: *That this House believes Biography to be an Expense of Spirit in a Waste of Shame.* A saucy seaside postcard from Ivor Williams showing two bulging ladies in red swimsuits dwarfing a skinny little bald-headed man. A list of Classical Society meetings with a red-inked star next to a talk Jill Hardwick was due to give. A letter from the BBC asking him if he was interested in hosting a new arts series they were proposing to do. And a thick, creamy envelope with a South Korean stamp that he hadn't opened yet.

"Doctor Searle?" Miss Brownlow was still standing by the battered armchair. "I hope you won't find this embarrassing. And please feel free to say no. I'll completely understand if you do." She made a little self-deprecating face.

He sat back in the chair, waiting.

"Only, there was a meeting of the Drama Soc last night - I'm like, Secretary this year — and it was decided — that is, after a lot of discussion they asked me if I would ask you… Look, we're going to do *Much Ado about Nothing* for the College play this term. And what we thought was, it would be great, I mean *amazing*, if you agreed to direct it for us."

He looked at her and said nothing.

"You don't have to decide now," Miss Brownlow said. "Take all the time you need to think it over. And like I said, we'll completely understand - I mean *absolutely* - if you're too busy or have much more important things to do. It's only a student production, anyway." She laughed again.

He looked at her and said nothing.

"Only we've got this *incredible* idea how we're going to do it. It's really cool! I'd love to know what you think." She took a step towards his desk.

"We're going to set it in the Wild West! Don Pedro and Don John are a couple of cattle barons who are having a range war. Benedick and Claudio are hired gunslingers. You know - cowboy hats and six-shooters! Leonato and Antonio are homesteaders, Dogberry and Verges are the sheriff and his deputy, and the Watch are the posse. And best of all, Beatrice and Hero are saloon girls in shiny dresses and fishnets and feathers!

It'll be like, *fantastic*, and we'd really love you to do it, we really would!
So is there any chance you'll say yes? Is there? What do you say, Doctor
Searle?"

A moment went by. From First Court the Chapel bell began to toll
slowly. Evensong.

"Let me think about it."

"Great!"

He picked up the creamy envelope and looked at the stamp with the
South Korean flag and its red-and-blue Taoist symbol. Yin Yang. How all
things connect.

"Doctor Searle?" Miss Brownlow had stopped in the half-open doorway. "Did you see that piece in the *Times Literary Supplement* this morning?"

His copy lay in its unopened clear wrapper with several other maga-
zines where Mrs. R had put them on the little table by the walnut book-
case. He shook his head. "Not yet."

"It's on the back page. You know, the gossipy bit. It says someone's
claiming to have discovered a new play of Shakespeare's, one nobody's
ever seen before."

How contrary forces are interdependent. Dark and light. Pain and
pleasure. Sorrow and joy.

"And what's really weird is, it's in Japan or Korea, or somewhere
crazy. Do you think there's any truth in it?"

Outside, the Chapel bell stopped tolling. The Chaplain would be en-
tering in his surplice and stole, prayer book at the ready. *Dearly beloved
Brethren, the Scripture moveth us in sundry places to acknowledge and confess our
manifold sins and wickedness...* Would there be anyone else there, or would
the Chaplain be playing to an empty house?

Miss Brownlow made a coughing sound. "Doctor Searle?"

Adam reached out and dropped the thick envelope into his wastepa-
per basket. He looked at Miss Brownlow and smiled. "Why don't we wait
and see?"

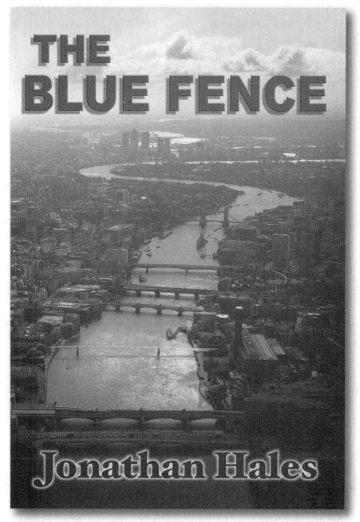

Danny Ballard was a child music prodigy. Her father was London's most notorious gangster.

Now she plays cocktail piano in a West End nightclub, where a chance encounter entangles her in a criminal conspiracy linked to London's Olympic Park and the 2012 Games. Murder, corruption, and the international drug trade all collide, forcing Danny to confront her half-buried past as well as the lethal dangers of the present.

"Great story — great writer. It's like a contemporary Hitchcock. Brilliant!"

— George Lucas

Available at <u>Amazon.com</u>